A Noble Pair of Brothers

by

Suzanne Sullivan

This is a work of fiction. Any resemblance of any of the characters
to persons living or dead is strictly coincidental.

FIRST EDITION

UNIVERSITY EDITIONS, Inc.
59 Oak Lane, Spring Valley
Huntington, West Virginia 25704

Cover by Joan Waites

For Joyce,

Best Wishes,

Suzanne Sullivan.

"Carpe hunc librum"

Dedication

In loving memory of my father Joseph H. Sullivan, and also for my mother Ann. With much love and thanks to my husband David Downes, dear friends Susan and Brian Wilson, who never ceased to believe in me; and for Louise, Janet and Maria, who are always there for me.

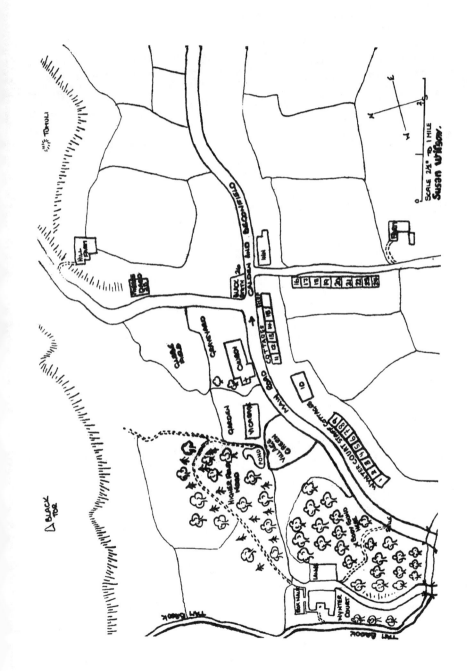

SCALE 2½" TO 1 MILE.

Seagram Village.

Bracken Tor
1820

CHAPTER ONE

("Hoc Opus, Hic Labor Est"—
This is the toil, there's the difficulty.)

"Afternoon, Mr. Underwood!"

A sudden gust of wind tugged at the Reverend Mr. Underwood's cape and he was forced to grasp the edges of it before he could frame a reply to this greeting, "Good afternoon, Tom. Rather blowy today!"

"It is indeed, Vicar. You waitin' on the carrier's cart, then?"

"Yes. Yes, I am."

"Expectin' a visitor, are you?" Pursued the old man, with more determination than tact.

Rev. Underwood kindly hid his smile, and bowed to the inevitable. He was obviously not going to be allowed away until Tom knew every detail, "My brother." He replied.

"Ah, your brother, eh?" Tom was able to add no further rejoinder, for at that moment they were approached by Miss Charlotte Wynter and her younger sister Isobel. Miss Charlotte was a vivacious young lady who seemed, this day, to be even more spirited than usual, due, no doubt, to the blustery weather, which seemed intent on tugging her bonnet from her auburn locks and thereby forcing her to hold it tight against the crown of her head. Her sandy-haired sister was hatless and had drawn up the hood of her cloak instead. This afforded her little advantage over her sister, however, as her cape was quite as uncontrollable as Charlotte's hat and she was, like the vicar, holding it against her body.

"Good day to you gentlemen!" Said Charlotte with a bright smile, "Do we interrupt?"

Neither man could resist returning her smile, though one was of a serious demeanour and the other inclined to grumpiness, and immediately they both replied in the negative.

"Vicar's just waiting for his brother to arrive on the carrier's cart, Miss Charlotte." Tom informed her helpfully. Charlotte and the vicar exchanged glances of subdued amusement, for Tom was

7

well-renowned for his incorrigible gossiping.

"Really? How very nice for you, Rev. Underwood. But I had no idea you had a brother."

The vicar smiled slightly, "Oh yes. I have a brother. I should imagine most people have siblings, Miss Wynter, if one only took the time to enquire."

She and her sister giggled appreciatively at this sally, for their own family was a large one, "I expect you are right. Is he to stay with you for very long?"

"I really have no idea. His visit is somewhat in the form of a convalescence."

"Oh dear! I trust he has suffered from nothing serious?"

"I'm afraid the affliction from which my brother suffers is totally incurable!"

Miss Wynter and her sister looked suitably sympathetic, "How terrible!"

"Not really," Replied the vicar with a comforting smile, "I merely refer to his acute hypochondria!"

The girls began to giggle again, but poor old Tom looked absolutely appalled, "Here, now! There's no call for that, young Misses! It doesn't do to mock the afflicted!" When Rev. Underwood and the girls seemed to find this even more amusing, Tom shuffled off rather disgustedly, muttering to himself about the heartlessness of the gentry.

"Oh my goodness," Said Miss Charlotte, gazing ruefully after his retreating figure, "I fear we have mortally offended poor Mr. Briggs!"

"It would seem so." Answered the vicar, "But I'm sure he will get over it. I'll explain all to him when I see him later, for bell-ringing practice."

Charlotte glanced sideways at the vicar, noticing for the first time that when he smiled, he seemed a little younger and less serious, and could be said to be quite good-looking. She wondered vaguely if his brother was the younger. This thought made her intrigued to see the expected visitor, and she now desired nothing more than to await the arrival of the carrier and see the vicar's brother for herself, but she could think of no reason to loiter which would not make her unmannerly curiosity obvious. Added to which, her younger sister was beginning to tug fretfully at her sleeve and Charlotte was well aware that this was Isobel's way of reminding Charlotte that her crippling shyness made meeting new people a torture not to be endured unless absolutely necessary.

The elder Miss Wynter had no choice but to take pity on her sibling and wish the vicar another cheery 'good afternoon.' Even as she did so the awaited vehicle swept around a curve in the road, raising a cloud of dust and a volley of ferocious barking from the Inn's guard dog. Though she hesitated momentarily, the expression of sheer panic on her sister's face forced her to speed her pace a little. Her longing backward glances afforded her no satisfaction, for by the time the solitary passenger had alighted, she was too far away to observe him clearly and she told herself wistfully that she supposed she would have ample opportunity to meet him, since his stay would appear to be protracted.

It is difficult to say whether or not Charlotte would have been disappointed by her first view of the stranger, for the figure which descended from the cart was not precisely a young girl's idea of romantic manhood. He was tall, it is true, and his hair, uncovered by a hat in spite of the current fashion, was fair, but after his arduous journey he had little else to recommend him. Even his age would not have pleased her, for he was actually the elder of the brothers. He informed the vicar that he felt "like a limp rag" and it was not an inaccurate description, for he had the sort of slim physique which does not stand up well to exhaustion. A goodnight's sleep would make all the difference to his pale-faced, heavy-eyed lethargy. He moved with a languid grace which bordered upon the foppish, but his clothes, being of a rather somber colour and cut, denied the suggestion. In fact his dress was not unlike his clerical brother's, and it is doubtful that Miss Wynter would have approved of anything about him.

The brothers greeted each other with a swift handshake, both being unwilling to make a public spectacle of their mutual affection, then the newcomer proceeded to vilify coach travel in general and his own journey in particular, "Why don't you accept a living somewhere along the coaching routes, Gil? I have rarely experienced a more appalling journey than on that rickety old cart! Could you not have come to Beconfield to meet the stage?"

"My dear fellow, you look exhausted! After such a tiring journey, I trust you have the strength to walk to the Vicarage. Since it is so near, I hardly thought it worthwhile to hire a cart from Mr. Briggs." The vicar cut across his brother's complaints with such aplomb that the latter was immediately side-tracked and began to object strongly to this new inconvenience—much to the vicar's relief, since the carrier was glowering angrily at the previous derogatory remarks regarding his own handling of horse-flesh.

"But my dear Gil! In this wind! And what about my trunk?"

"Oh," Said the vicar, rather absently, "Have you a trunk? Well, it can be left at the Inn and called for later—but I had not quite realized that you were intending to stay long enough to require a trunk!"

His brother gave his charming and disarming smile—a smile which lifted the weariness from his eyes and might have caused a mild flutter in the female breast, "How could I resist the warmth of your invitation, Gil?" he asked.

"You resisted it for almost a year!" Remarked the vicar tersely, then repented, "Of course you could not! Nor could you resist a good long separation from your dreadful boys! Come then, brother, let us be on our way. Tea awaits us and I know how you detest your crumpets cold!"

Mr. Underwood gave an eloquent shudder of distaste and closed his eyes as though against a vision too painful to be endured, "Ugh! A fate not to be bourne! Lead on."

Rev. Underwood slipped his arm through his brother's, gave his instructions to the carrier over his shoulder, then guided their steps towards the vicarage. As they walked along, blissfully unaware that their lively conversation and contrasting appearance were causing much comment behind the twitching curtains which lined their route, they fell easily back into their childhood habit of good-natured ribbing.

The vicar was well-known and liked among his flock, having achieved a happy balance of gravity and humour when the occasion warranted it. His chestnut hair and dark brown eyes made him seem both warm and trustworthy to the older members of his congregation, and his not infrequent little puns, so diffidently delivered, endeared him to the younger. He little knew how honoured he was to have been thus welcomed by the close-knit community. His year of residence made him a positive newcomer, and it was only his own warm personality which had caused him to be thus accepted, when his predecessor had earned no such concession despite a twelve year stay.

The unexpected advent of this tall, blond-haired, grey-eyed visitor, so delicate seeming and wan, provided much good-natured speculation in the village. If Mr. Underwood was surprised that the street should be so empty, he made no comment upon it.

They rapidly approached the vicarage, which was, indeed, only a few yards away from the inn, nestling in its traditional spot on the far side of the squat-towered, part Norman church.

It was, of course, far too large, cold and ancient for real comfort, but it was of picturesque appearance, being stone built, like the church, stone-lintled, diamond paned and making no harsh lines against the heather covered hills behind.

The Southern bred brothers were united in finding the Northern landscape rather harsh, but staggering in its rough beauty. The vicar had had a year in which to accustom himself to the ragged hills, rock-strewn and windswept, but his brother was still suffering from a slight sense of shock that anywhere in England could contain such an alien environment.

Even the village itself, despite the protection offered by those same hills, gave the appearance of weather-beaten hardiness. All the houses and cottages were of stone, and those with gardens were surrounded by walls, in an attempt to protect the vegetation within from the whistling Pennine winds. Trees were scarce at this level, but lower in the valley there was a large copse and it was to this that the newcomer pointed, "Trees can grow here then, Gil?" He enquired good-humouredly. The vicar glanced down towards the area indicated, "Oh yes. But mostly in the valleys. Any saplings foolhardy enough to attempt to grow on the hills turn out to be stunted excuses for trees, almost bent to the ground by the wind. That particular wood belongs to Sir Henry Wynter, a local landowner and Magistrate. His house is hidden amongst the foliage. He has six daughters and one son—born, as you can imagine, amidst great rejoicing—tempered by the fact that the mother died in childbirth."

"Great Heavens! Six girls!"

The vicar, knowing his brother's complete avoidance of the fair sex, with the exception of their mother, could not help but be amused by the emphasis placed upon these words, "Yes. Six. and every one of them a red-head, just like their late mother." Mr. Underwood closed his eyes and his expression was pained, "Red heads! Good Lord! I can only hope that you are not going to thrust me too much into their society! Women terrify me at the best of times, but add the legendary fire of the red-head and my soul quakes!"

The vicar had a brief, but graphic, vision of Sir Henry's six daughters and reflected silently, but with some amusement, that his brother had little fire to fear—except perhaps from Charlotte.

"My dear brother, you have been locked up in that University for far too long! Don't you think it is about time you gave up trying to din Greek and Latin into the heads of young men who desire nothing more than to be allowed to drink, gamble and wench away their youths?"

Mr. Underwood looked rather stunned, as if the thought had never occurred to him before, "Give up? And what pray, do you suggest I do instead?"

"You need not sound so appalled! It was merely a suggestion. You seem to detest your existence so! I simply thought it might be time to call a halt to the misery on both sides and find yourself another occupation. Perhaps a wife and children of your own would renew your faith in human nature?" Gilbert knew he was taking a risk speaking thus to his brother, but he was frustrated by years of skirting around the awkward subject and had decided to call his brother's attention to it.

His brother shuddered delicately, "Gil, I pray you, have a little compassion! Have I not suffered enough without your foisting a family upon me?"

Whilst this conversation was progressing, they had traversed the village street, passed the church and were approaching the front door of the vicarage. The vicar heaved his shoulder against the old oak door and burst rather unceremoniously into the

11

gloomy hallway, "I think you take an unnecessarily dim view of marriage." He said breathlessly, but as though nothing had occurred to interrupt the flow of conversation. Mr. Underwood raised a quizzical brow, but made no mention of this odd method of entry, and followed him into the house, "I notice that whilst you advocate the institution, you have thus far managed to avoid committing yourself!"

The vicar chose to ignore this remark and led the way into the drawing room, "Make yourself at home. I shall go and see if Mrs. Selby has managed to salvage your crumpets!"

Left alone, Mr. Underwood took a few moments to look about him. The furniture had evidently been inherited with the house, for it was dark, heavy and old-fashioned—puritanical in design, purely practical and far from comfortable. He walked past the vast fireplace and squeezing between the overcrowded chairs and tables, made his way to the window.

He immediately decided that the effort to reach this destination had not been worth the aspect afforded, for this particular room overlooked the churchyard. The wind seemed to have grown more boisterous—or did it simply blow more savagely over the open space between the walls of the church and the vicarage? A couple of saplings lashed about, almost bent double by the stronger gusts, and only the two ancient yews refused to yield to the growing gale. They deigned only to bow slightly, and rustle a little, like irritated dowagers who refuse to be drawn into an unbecoming display of temper.

Mr. Underwood seemed to sink into a reverie as he stared at the bending grasses covering the graves and the moss bedecked headstones. His face grew more drawn than mere tiredness dictated. There was sadness in his eyes which could not be explained by the depressing proximity of the graveyard. He did not hear his brother's re-entry and Gilbert was rather concerned by the picture he presented. The vicar had been convinced that his brother had succeeded in putting his past behind him, that he had recovered himself fully, but this unguarded moment made it clear that no such transformation had taken place. Mr. Underwood was as haunted now as he had been ten years before.

"Come to the fire, old fellow. There are howling draughts by the window, and Mrs. Selby is bringing the tea."

Underwood stared blankly at his brother for a moment, before he came to himself and remembered where he was. He straightened his shoulders in a visible effort to shake off his previous mood and managed a slight smile, "I hope my bedroom is at the front of the house."

Aware that he had made a serious error of judgment, the vicar answered timerously, "I thought it would be quieter for you at the back."

"Too quiet!" Retorted his brother emphatically.

12

"I'll speak to Mrs. Selby after tea."

"Thank you."

Mr. Underwood watched his brother with faint amusement as he fussily unlocked the tea caddy and carefully mixed measured spoonsful of the two different sorts. The kettle was lifted from the trivet by the fire just as the wisp of steam grew steady and the first drop was used to warm the pot, before being emptied into a small bowl provided for the purpose.

"Wouldn't it be easier for Mrs. Selby to do all that in the kitchen?" He asked, when the ritual was almost complete. it was the vicar's turn to look appalled, "Oh dear me, no! I've tried and tried to teach her the art of tea-making, but she insists upon a slapdash approach that quite ruins the flavour!"

It occurred to Mr. Underwood that he was not the only member of his family who had spent rather too many years alone. He was suddenly uncomfortably aware that many little habits acquired over the years could turn all too easily from quirks into eccentricities and doubtless caused great amusement among the irreverent young.

He said nothing more, but accepted his cup with a nod of thanks. The first sip proved to be nectar, but whether this was due to the care taken or merely the result of his tiredness and thirst was a debatable point. He rested his head against the back of the chair and closed his eyes, "Perhaps you are right, Gil, the kitchen may not be the place to make tea." Rev. Underwood took this as a compliment and smiled with gratification, "I'm glad it meets with your approval. And now you are a little refreshed, perhaps you can tell me how things are with you? Have you seen mother recently?"

Mr. Underwood jerked himself upright and opened his eyes. "God bless my soul! My cursed memory! I should have told you sooner! She sent her love and bade me tell you that she's getting married."

"Married!" The vicar leapt so swiftly to his feet that he almost overturned the table upon which stood his precious tea things. "Great Heavens! She is seventy years old! What the devil are you thinking of, letting her talk such nonsense?"

"Apparently she doesn't think it nonsense—and since she reached her majority before I was born, I could hardly raise an objection!" Mr. Underwood looked and sounded testy, and this seemed to calm his brother a little. He sank back into his chair and raised his tea cup to his lips with a slightly shaking hand, "This is something of a shock to me." He admitted apologetically. Mr. Underwood raised one eyebrow, "I was not exactly delighted myself, but since father has been dead these twenty years, and she expressed a desire for companionship to warm her declining years, I felt there was little I could say or do which would appear anything other than small-minded and

13

selfish."

The vicar was forced to acknowledge the sense of the pronouncement, but he still looked pale and shocked, "Did she give you any indication when she intended to go through with this piece of folly?"

"She did not. But she did not seem to be in any particular hurry, as she expressed a hope that either you or I might yet beat her to the altar."

The Reverend gentleman immediately took hope from this, "So that is her game!" He declared triumphantly. His brother looked blank, "You seem to read something more into this than is apparent to me, Gil. Pray enlighten me."

"Do you not see? She is simply trying to shock one or the other of us into matrimony. She is hoping this madness of hers will put the idea of marriage into our minds."

Mr. Underwood seemed unconvinced, "If that was her intention, it has sadly misfired upon me! She has merely reinforced my belief that I had better avoid women more assiduously than ever before! If they are still capable of such recklessness at her advanced age, how much more chaos could they cause a man with youth on their side?"

The vicar, completely sure that he had correctly read his mother's intention, was able to smile again, "Nonsense! A little firmness is all that is required! I shall write to her this very evening. You will soon see that she will take note of my strictures!"

His brother remained impassive, "I trust you are right, Gil, but I would not place a wager on the outcome if I were you!"

Rev. Underwood merely smiled contentedly, "We shall see, we shall see." He said.

"She wants you to perform the ceremony!" Commented Mr. Underwood, and having saved the worst until last, had the satisfaction of seeing the smile slide from his brother's face.

They drank their tea in silence for a few moments, both busy with their own thoughts, until the vicar chanced to glance towards his companion and notice that he had once more slipped into the same curious reverie he had experienced when looking out of the window onto the churchyard. It took him several seconds to decide that he must say something, for he was loathe to intrude upon his sibling's private thoughts, but obviously the air must be cleared between them if the visit was to have any hope of success.

"Tell me, why have you come here?" The question was asked softly, with no hint of accusation or reproach, but Mr. Underwood looked almost as startled as if it had great measures of both, "Great Heavens, Gil! What a thing to ask! Naturally I have come to visit my only brother in his new parish. What other reason could there be?"

14

"My dear fellow, I have been in Bracken Tor for precisely a year and have seen nothing of you in that time! Mistake me not, I say this not to offend you, nor to have you imagine I feel offended with you. We are brothers, and brothers are often apart for much longer periods with no hard feelings on either side, but ever since I received your letter, I have had the strangest sensation that something is amiss. You have never felt the need to take a sabbatical before, so why do it now? Will you not confide the reason to me?"

Mr. Underwood hesitated for a long time before he raised his eyes to meet his brother's and commented, "You know me too well, Gil. I should have known I could keep nothing from you."

"Sometimes I feel I do not know you at all!" Replied the vicar with a smile, but he was quietly relieved that his meddling had been taken so well—not that Underwood would have been anything but remorselessly polite, that was really the trouble. When he chose to, Underwood could transform civility into a refined torture for those who were fond of him.

"Did you know that Elinor's house has at last been sold?" This apparently innocuous and unconnected snippet of news had an altogether unexpected effect on the vicar. He seemed to grow a little paler and to eye his brother anxiously from behind the rim of his tea cup.

"I had no idea. I knew it had been let several times in the past."

"No, this time it was sold and not let." Asserted Mr. Underwood, placing his now empty cup and saucer carefully on a convenient table.

"How came you to know of it?"

"It was a very curious circumstance. Almost unbelievable, in fact. It seems there was considerable repair work needed to the structure of the house."

"Having stood for the most part unoccupied for so many years, that is scarcely surprising." Temporized the vicar reasonably.

"Quite." Agreed Mr. Underwood, "Some of the renovation work involved replacing rotted floorboards and when they were lifted a small box was found, containing quite a bundle of letters.

"Letters?" Repeated the vicar, but in a tone which suggested that he might know what direction the conversation was going to take.

"Yes. And they were all addressed to me."

"Oh."

Mr. Underwood glanced at his brother, then resumed, "The workman who found them handed them to the new owner, who, it seems, is a man of high morals. The sort of man who would never read letters which were not addressed to him. He wrote me a charming little missive, explaining the circumstances of their discovery, and forwarding them belatedly to the addressee."

"Dear God!'" The vicar could not be accused of using blasphemy, for the tone in which he spoke these words transformed them into a prayer, "Do not tell me they were from Elinor?"

Mr. Underwood merely nodded his head, "Intercepted by her Uncle and, for God knows what reason, hidden by him and not destroyed. They were delivered to me ten years too late."

"Did you read them?"

Mr. Underwood shrugged, "No, I could not bear to do so."

"It must have been incredibly painful for you."

His brother did not attempt to deny the suggestion. He gave a humourless little laugh, "Incredibly!" He agreed, "I cannot begin to describe the jolt it gave me when I recognized the handwriting, as clear and neat as though it had only been written yesterday. The paper had not yellowed, nor the ink faded."

The vicar could think of nothing to say. He could well imagine his brother's distress and sympathize silently with him. He could not picture a more macabre situation than to receive letters from a loved one who had lain ten years in the grave, and he could easily believe his brother's nerves had taken a shock from which they would take time to recover. Small wonder Underwood had needed to get swiftly away. He thought, with a pang of guilt, of the jocular reference he had made to hypochondria when discussing his brother with Charlotte Wynter. In the light of what he had just heard, that seemed now to have been horribly unkind as well as unjust. He felt he must voice his regret, even though his brother had no idea that he had been the butt of a joke. "I'm terribly sorry—and I apologize if I seemed unsympathetic when you first arrived. Naturally you are welcome to stay here for as long as you wish."

Underwood smiled, "Good God, Gil, you sound as though the world were about to come to an end! I've had time aplenty to grow accustomed to Elinor's loss, so pray don't imagine I have been devastated by this. I took a facer, then pulled myself up again! Pray think no more about it. I don't intend to!"

The vicar did not reply. He knew when his brother was putting a brave face on things and he strongly suspected that this was one such occasion. Without saying as much, he resolved to keep a very careful watch upon his brother's well-being. Underwood's state of health was always precarious, but never more so than when his nerves were shattered. He could feign utter contentment if he liked, but Gilbert knew better.

CHAPTER TWO

**("Medio Tutissimus Ibis"—
You will find the middle course safest.)**

The wind increased in intensity during the evening, buffeting the old vicarage and sending draughts whistling through the windows and along passage ways. Curtains bellied like ships' sails, falling back against the window panes with a crack as sharp as a whip.

Smoke from the fireplace billowed back into the room where the brothers sat, and since the howling of the wind in the chimney made conversation almost impossible, they decided to retire early.

Neither managed to actually sleep until the gale began to die away towards dawn, and so it was two weary eyed gentlemen who met for a rather belated breakfast and lethargically discussed their plans for the day ahead.

"I'm afraid I really can't spare any time today to show you around the village." The vicar was apologetic, but firm. He was determined to remind his brother that only one of the parties concerned was actually on holiday. His strong sense of duty would not allow him to neglect any of his commitments, however minor.

His brother sketched a gesture of denial in mid air, "My dear Gil, put me completely from your mind! I'm perfectly capable of finding my own way about and I desire to be as little trouble as possible."

In the vicar's opinion this was a politely empty statement which would have very little bearing on the future. His brother was the only man he knew who could protest that he wanted to cause not a ripple on the pond of life, proceed to stir up a positive maelstrom, then walk calmly away with not a hair out of place. It did not appear to be purposeful trouble-causing, merely something in his make-up which sought out strife, and having sought it, proceeded to find a solution, usually one which would have been better left undiscovered.

"You are quite sure?" He asked doubtfully.

"Quite!" Mr. Underwood assured him emphatically, "Just point me in the general direction of a pleasant walk and I shall endeavour to blow away the cobwebs until lunch time."

Quite unreassured, but having little choice in the matter, the vicar accompanied his brother to the front gate where he gave him very careful directions, "You won't get into any difficulties, will you?" He concluded, rather nervously.

"Difficulties? I? My dear brother you behave as though I were about five years old! What sort of difficulties do you suppose I could get into out here?"

"I've no idea. I only know that if 'difficulties' should arise, you'll be the man who falls into them."

Mr. Underwood patted his brother's arm affectionately and shook his head, "Dear old Gil. You worry too much."

They parted company, the vicar heading for the village, his brother taking the path indicated to him.

After the wind of the day before there was considerable damage to the countryside, grasses lay flat to the ground and here and there the trees showed the raw, white wounds of lost branches. Other than these stark reminders, however, the gale was a thing of the past and almost forgotten, for the sun shone from a brilliant blue sky and the birds were singing.

For the first time in many months Mr. Underwood felt himself relaxing. The slight stoop left his shoulders, and he filled his lungs with the pure air. He even allowed a small smile to play about his lips as he contemplated his surroundings.

So engrossed was he in his enjoyment of his peregrination that he ceased to take note of his way and before long he found himself at a point where the path suddenly diverged and he could not recall which branch his brother had bid him take. A glance about him gave him no indications so after a momentary hesitation he took the path which appeared to incline slightly, since his walk was intended to take him upwards to the moor.

It was not very long before he realised his error. The path sloped upwards for only a matter of yards, then it dropped steeply and seemed to be heading toward the copse which the vicar had indicated the day before as belonging to the magistrate of the district.

Mr. Underwood decided to continue on his way despite the mistake, for he felt it could not be long before he met some other wayfarer who could put him back upon the right track.

He met no one. Very soon he came to a high stone wall alongside which the path wound. It was marked now with horses' hoof-prints and was apparently frequented, though over-grown on either side with a tangled mesh of brambles and nettles. When he came to an open doorway set deep in the wall, he decided to walk through it and try to find his way up to the house. After his disturbed night he was growing weary and had taken so little heed of his way that he now doubted his ability to find his way back. Neighbourliness surely dictated that Sir Henry or some member of his family would see him back to the vicarage—preferably in some kind of vehicle.

On the other side of the gateway he was plunged into the sudden gloom of too-closely packed trees and uncared for undergrowth. He fought his way through for what seemed like hours, until, more by accident than design, he stumbled into a clearing and confronted a very irate gentleman, who was holding a long-barrelled gun to his shoulder.

A crashing in the undergrowth away to the right of where they stood indicated that whatever quarry had been within the man's sights had now made good its escape.

"What the devil!" As he spoke the man turned and Mr. Underwood found himself staring down the barrel of the gun, "Who the hell are you? What the devil are you playing at, you blithering idiot!"

Mr. Underwood remained quite calm, undoubtedly aware that one false move could result, literally, in the loss of his head, "Good morning. The name is Underwood."

"Damn your hide! I don't care what your name is! Do you realise that you're trespassing on private property?"

"Do you mind turning that gun away from me?"

The older man reluctantly lowered the gun, "Underwood? I suppose you are some relation to the vicar?"

"His brother."

"Well, he should have more sense than to let you wander about alone! Don't you realise that these woods are littered with traps!"

Mr. Underwood appeared to be unimpressed, "Animal or man?" He asked coolly.

The man shifted uneasily, "As far as I'm concerned Poachers are animals!" He answered testily, "What are you doing in here? The usual method of approach is through the lodge."

"Yes, I realise that, but I've rather lost my way and I was hoping for a little help."

"Oh. Well, you have a cursed strange way of seeking aid, I must say! Follow me. I think my daughter Charlotte is riding in the paddock. She can set you on your way."

From this Underwood assumed that he was speaking to none other than Sir Henry Wynter himself, but he made no comment upon it, for the irascible old gentleman was looking increasingly bad-tempered. Evidently he did not care for trespassers, poachers or having his sport interrupted by clumsy interlopers.

A further ten minutes walk lay ahead of Mr. Underwood, but he bore it with fortitude. His companion made no attempt at conversation, so Mr. Underwood likewise remained silent. He was

19

not much taken with Sir Henry and had no wish to further the acquaintance. He did, however, take the opportunity to examine the man more closely. Mr. Underwood had an abiding interest in his fellow man and despite his aversion to this particular specimen, he could not completely ignore his existence.

Sir Henry strode on, seemingly unaware that he was being scrutinised. Underwood was given the distinct impression that Sir Henry thought that no one would be impertinent enough to do any such thing.

Underwood could, in fact, be quite forgiven for his original assessment that Sir Henry was one of his own game-keepers, for his black coat was so old and worn that it appeared dark green, his breeches were soiled at the knees and stretched tight over his bulging stomach. His face was the unhealthy broken-veined red of the habitual drinker. His hair was extremely thin on top, but far too long and untidy at the back and sides. Mr. Underwood, whose personal appearance was of the utmost importance to him, was not impressed and could only hope that Sir Henry tidied himself a little for his sessions on the Bench. He estimated his age to be somewhere around mid-to-late fifties, but he could quite easily have been younger, for his face bore all the hallmarks of a full and debauched life. Presently the trees thinned out a little, then quite unexpectedly they stepped out of the shelter of the wood and into bright sunlight. Mr. Underwood blinked in the glare and as his sight cleared he saw that they were standing at the edge of well-trimmed paddock, around which was trotting a chestnut stallion of impressive proportions and upon whose back reposed a young lady, sitting side-saddle, and whose hair was exactly the same shade as her mount.

To say that Underwood was startled would be an understatement. The animal, the ease and grace with which his rider sat him and the spectacular matching of colour were all magnificent.

Sir Henry noticed his companion's amazement and grinned unkindly, "Way above your touch, Underwood." He said. Mr. Underwood, amazed that a father could speak so coarsely about his own daughter, and appalled that he should have so misinterpreted the younger man's admiration, could not prevent an expression of disgust passing briefly across his face.

Sir Henry merely laughed and called to his daughter, "Charlotte, get down off that nag and come here. I have a caller who is very eager to meet you."

Mr. Underwood could gladly have melted back into the shade of the trees. The last thing he desired at this moment in time was to be introduced to this dashing young woman, who had obediently slid from her horse's back and was even now leading her mount towards him. God alone knew what other coarse remarks Sir Henry was about to make. And judging from the father, what manner of woman was she?

He prepared himself for excruciating embarrassment and was very pleasantly surprised when she drew off her glove and extended a long, white hand towards him, "How do you do?" Her voice was pleasant, neither too loud nor too quiet, not cultured, nor yet as vulgar as her father's.

"Do I mistake the matter, or are you Rev. Underwood's brother?"

He took her hand and bowed over it, "You are entirely correct, madam, I have the honour to claim Rev. Underwood as my kin. I understand I have the added honour of addressing Miss Wynter?"

"Indeed you do, Sir," Interrupted the father, apparently unable to bear being excluded from the conversation for too long, "Charlotte, you will oblige me by showing Mr. Underwood off the premises. He apparently finds it impossible to follow even the simplest of directions and has already managed to lose himself once." With that, and without even a cursory farewell, Sir Henry disappeared back into the woods, leaving Mr. Underwood suffering the unaccustomed sensation of blushing violently.

By now his humiliation was complete and it occurred to him that he would far rather stare down the barrel of Sir Henry's loaded gun than now meet the gently laughing eyes of Miss Charlotte Wynter.

"Before you leave, Mr. Underwood, can I offer you some refreshment?"

"Please don't put yourself to any inconvenience on my account. Your father has somewhat mistaken the matter and I am not quite the imbecile he takes me for. Simple directions to the vicarage will suffice, and you need not put yourself to the trouble of accompanying me." He knew he sounded stiff and unfriendly, very possibly even pompous, but he felt he could not escape from her company soon enough.

"Please forgive my father, Mr. Underwood. He does not mean to be quite so offensive as he sounds." She smiled gently and he found himself smiling back, albeit somewhat ruefully, "I think he does!" She laughed gaily, "Very well," She agreed, "He does!" She looped the dangling rein more firmly about her hand, "Come up to the house while I stable Merryman, then we can have a drink before seeing you back to the vicarage."

He allowed himself to be persuaded and fell into step beside her as she led the stallion across the paddock, through the gate, past long lawns which ran down from the wide terraces of the house—a fairly new facade tacked onto an older building, but imposing in its way.

They skirted around the house and entered the stable yard, which was empty but for one grubby old dog scratching its ear with a hind foot and groaning with pleasure. Charlotte called for the groom who came rushing from a tack room, hastily shrugging himself into his waistcoat, "Beg pardon Miss Charlotte, I was just having my dinner. I wasn't expecting you back from exercising Merryman just yet."

"That's all right Abney. I'm sorry to have disturbed your lunch. Can you take care of Merryman for me. I'm going to walk Mr. Underwood back to the vicarage."

"Mr. Underwood? Would you be the vicar's brother, Sir?" Abney spoke directly to Charlotte's companion, taking him rather by surprise.

"Yes. How do you do?" Mr. Underwood extended his hand and Abney shook it warmly, after wiping his own hand on his breeches, "Fair to middling Sir, thank-you. I'm very pleased to meet you. We are all very taken with your brother, Sir. He's a very pleasant man, Sir. Very pleasant."

"One of the best." Agreed Mr. Underwood, with a warm smile. Abney delayed them no longer, with a cheery "Good day" he took Merryman's bridle from his mistress and led the horse into the dark interior of one of the stables.

Charlotte turned to her reluctant companion, "Will you come indoors for some refreshment?"

"A glass of water would be welcome." He admitted, "But I'll drink it here before going on my way."

"Very well. I shall change my boots too, if I may, they were not meant for walking!" She crossed the courtyard and approached what appeared to be the kitchen door. She disappeared inside and left him to look about. The sun's rays seemed drawn into the walled-in square, making it unbearably hot and almost blindingly bright. Mr. Underwood felt he could gladly drink a gallon of water, not merely the glass for which he had asked. Swallows flew above his head and the tantalising scents of cooking food began to drift across the courtyard to him.

Charlotte returned bearing two overfull glasses, which slopped over as she walked, "When we've drunk our water, I'll show you the short cut to the vicarage. Along the drive and back to the main road is such a dull walk. It's much prettier going through the woods. There may still be a few bluebells."

"The woods?" Mr. Underwood was immediately on the defensive, lowering his glass from his lips and almost choking on the water, "I hate to sound rude, but I have no wish to run into your father again."

Charlotte laughed, "Don't worry. You won't. He's up at Higher Fold. We are going by the lower path, through Shady Copse and over the stile."

With that Mr. Underwood had to be satisfied. He handed her his empty glass and she placed both side by side on a convenient window ledge.

It was with great relief that he realised that they were indeed entering the wood at a very different spot than that where they had had the last sighting of Sir Henry and he began to feel rather less tense.

"Abney was quite right when he spoke so well of your brother, Mr. Underwood. We have all grown very fond of him." Charlotte spoke so warmly that it occurred to Mr. Underwood that his brother might have an admirer. He glanced keenly at his young companion, wondering how old she was and if she were quite vicar's wife material. He noted that she was quite tall for a woman, coming above his own shoulder, and very elegant in her movements. He could not quite see her in the setting of the draughty old parsonage, contending with the uncomfortable furniture and his brother's curious preoccupation with properly brewed tea.

"I'm glad he has drawn so favourable a picture, Miss Wynter. He is, as I said, the best of men."

"Are you the older, or is he?" She asked ingenuously, displaying not only her curiosity, but also her youth. A woman of the world would never have couched the question in such bald terms. Mr. Underwood smiled, "I, but only by a bare three years. Are you the oldest in your family—which I understand is quite a sizable one?"

"Oh no, I fall in the middle. I have four older sisters, one younger and youngest of all is my brother, named Henry, after my father."

"Are there many years between you all?"

"No. We arrived with monotonous regularity, one a year."

"Your older sisters, are any of them married?"

"Maria, the eldest, she was twenty-one in the spring, and was married last year. My second sister Jane is engaged."

Having thus learned her age without her knowledge, Mr. Underwood had cause to smile again. Seventeen. Gad! it seemed a very long time ago when he had been seventeen. But old enough to be married—and Gil was three years younger than himself.

"Oh look, there are still some bluebells. How pretty they are. I do love bluebells." Without any further preamble Charlotte stepped from the path and picked her way past the tearing brambles, the unfurling ferns and the deep scattering of last year's leaves.

Before Underwood could see what was happening there was a loud report and Charlotte was falling to the ground. For one horrified moment he thought she had been shot and he hurried to her side.

Even as he reached her she was endeavouring to raise herself from the ground and he was flooded with relief, "What happened? Are you hurt?"

23

She looked stunned, "I don't know, something caught my skirt and dragged me down. I've hurt my ankle."

Mr. Underwood shifted aside the long train of her velvet riding habit and discovered the cause of the noise and her fall.

"Good God, a man trap!" She had been lucky. The weight of her gown had tripped the mechanism and as it had snapped shut on the material it had merely grazed her ankle, tearing the knitted silk stocking and closing upon the edge of her shoe. Even as he watched blood began to seep into the livid gouges left by the teeth of the trap in her white skin.

"A trap?" he barely heard her, so low was her voice, "Good God, I'm not caught in it, am I?" he glanced up at her face and saw that she was terribly pale. He smiled reassuringly, "No, no. Only your dress. Your ankle is a little cut, but nothing serious. I'm afraid I'm going to have to cut your gown to get you out."

She swallowed deeply and closed her eyes, "Do it then, and be quick. I want to go home." It wrung his heart to see her looking so young and frightened. He took her hand in his and squeezed it comfortingly, "Don't worry. I won't hurt you."

He searched his pockets, hoping that he had his pen knife with him, velvet would be the very devil to try and tear. Luckily he had it and he lost no time in slashing away the piece of material held in the cruel grip of the trap. The vicious teeth sent a shiver down his spine. Had she actually fallen into the trap, her leg would probably have been completely severed. Her father must be the most inhuman creature to have set these things about his grounds. Perhaps his daughter's lucky escape would serve as a warning to him.

"I'm going to have to remove your shoe." She merely nodded, then winced as his fingers quested for the fastenings. Moments later she was free and he was able to wrap her injured ankle in his handkerchief.

"Will you wait here while I run back to the house for help?" He was stunned by the reaction provoked by this simple question. She shot upright from her reclining position and gripped his arm in a positive panic, "Don't dare to leave me here alone!"

"Why on earth not? I won't be long and you are still on your father's land. What could possibly happen to you?"

She seemed reluctant to speak and when she did it was in a shamed undertone, "I'm afraid of being here alone. There was a murder here."

He grinned, though not unkindly, "Afraid of ghosts? There's more to fear from that monster you were riding earlier, than long dead victims of ancient crimes."

"I'm not afraid of ghosts!" She retorted testily, "And it wasn't an ancient crime! It only happened last year and they never found the culprit!"

Mr. Underwood was rather taken aback, but decided that

this was neither the time nor the place to pursue the matter. "Very well, put your arm around my neck."

"Why?" She asked suspiciously, "What are you going to do?"

"I'm going to carry you."

She managed a little laugh despite the feeling of shock she still sustained, "You couldn't."

Without further ado, and without the aid of her arm about him, he swept her up into his arms, and was pleased to note that a blush crept over her cheeks. Embarrassment was not going to be entirely confined to him this day, then!

CHAPTER THREE

("Necessitas Non Habet Legem"—Necessity knows no law.)

For all his bravado, Mr. Underwood was staggering slightly by the time they came within sight of the house, and his breathing was rather heavier than it had been before. Miss Wynter was no light weight, and was apparently too shy to even put her arm about his neck and thus give him some slight aid in supporting her.

Charlotte had used the intervening time to covertly peruse his face, and was not displeased by what she saw. He was rather older than she had at first imagined—being rather nearer to forty than thirty, but his blond hair was undimmed by silver, and the creases in the skin around his eyes and brow gave him a worried air that quite enchanted her. She found herself wondering what troubles life had served him, to give him that air of quiet sadness.

She told herself that such thoughts were a distraction, taking her mind away from the throbbing pain in her leg and the utter mortification of finding herself clasped close against the chest of a comparatively unknown male.

Mr. Underwood was aware, even if she was not, that reaching the house had become of prime importance. He could see that beneath the ragged hem of her torn dress, the once white handkerchief was now completely red and they were leaving a clearly discernible trail of blood behind them as they travelled. Apparently the wound was a great deal deeper than he had at first thought.

Their arrival must have been observed from one of the windows, for as they crossed the lawns, a host of people swept down the terrace steps to meet them.

Questions and answers flew, amidst cries of dismay and anxious comments, but nothing very constructive was done until Isobel quietly remarked, "Charlotte is bleeding all over the steps!" Whereupon the cries turned into full-blooded shrieks and

26

Mr. Underwood was rushed up the steps and into the house, where at last he was able to lay his burden upon a waiting sofa and ask quietly how she did.

"I'm happy to be home. Thank you Mr. Underwood."

"The pleasure was entirely mine, I assure you. I'm only sorry a very pleasant outing had to end so uncomfortably." She noticed that when he smiled he suddenly looked very young—almost boyish in fact—and that his teeth were very white and straight except for one engagingly crooked eye-tooth.

"You've been very kind."

As he brought himself upright, he was approached by a dark-haired young woman, considerbly smaller than Charlotte in height, though apparently slightly older in years, dressed in unrelieved black but for a white lace collar at her throat. "If you would like to follow me, Sir, I'll have some refreshment brought to you."

"Our governess, Miss Chapell, Mr. Underwood." Said Charlotte. Miss Chapell was charmed to be offered his hand and shook it with a tiny smile. So many people considered governesses to be little more than glorified servants and treated them as such. It made a very pleasant change to be greeted as an equal.

Mr. Underwood bade farewell to his erstwhile guide and voiced a wish that her recovery would be speedy and complete, then he turned and accompanied Miss Chapell from the room. His departure unremarked by all but Charlotte, who was already growing weary of the fuss her siblings were making, and longed for the doctor to come so that she could be rid of them all.

Miss Chapell showed Mr. Underwood to a small, but richly decorated withdrawing room, where he found a tray already laid upon the table.

"Can I pour some tea for you, Sir?"

"Please. Perhaps you will join me?" Miss Chapell smiled again, "I should be delighted, thank you."

As she poured the tea with one hand, she lifted a silver dish cover with the other and offered him the sandwiches which lay beneath. By this time poor Mr. Underwood was ravenous and had no compunction at all in accepting the hospitality of the absent Sir Henry.

"Is what I hear true, that you are the vicar's brother?" She asked, as she handed him his cup and saucer.

"Is there anyone in this village who has not heard that I am the vicar's brother?" There was the slightest edge to his voice which did not go unnoticed by Miss Chapell.

The giggle she gave did not quite match the severe aspect that her plain dress tried to portray, "I'm so sorry. We must seem unforgivably impertinent, but you should understand that we are so cut off here, very little happens and any visitor is of excessive

27

interest to us all. I'm afraid your arrival was all around the village within hours."

"The hope of maintaining a low profile is rather remote then?"

"I should say so."

"Since you know so much about me, may I be allowed to know a little of you? We should be kindred spirits, since I too earn my living by driving a little learning into reluctant youth."

"I hardly think we can compare your career at Cambridge with mine, here, but it was kind of you to put it that way."

"Nonsense! It is simply a question of degree! I'm driven to despair more frequently and completely than you because I have more and older charges! Essentially, it is the same!"

"You are a very unusual man, Mr. Underwood."

"I?" He stopped his cup midway to his lips as though stunned, "Not at all. The most extraordinary thing about me is my complete and utter ordinariness. You've simply had the misfortune to meet me on a very unusual day!"

The door opened and a white-capped head appeared around it. "The carriage is here for Mr. Underwood, Miss Chapell."

"Thank you Sally."

With the utmost alacrity and efficiency, Mr. Underwood found himself being ushered out of the house and into the waiting vehicle. He barely had time to shake Miss Chapell's hand and express a hope that they meet again, before being bowled off down the drive at a spanking trot. In fact he was given the distinct impression that he was wanted off the premises with all possible dispatch.

His anxious brother, who had been sent a garbled message via a very young and breathless groom to explain the whereabouts of his missing sibling, was hovering worriedly at the gate of the parsonage, not quite sure what injuries to expect when his brother descended from the carriage.

He was caught between extremes of emotion when Mr. Underwood finally made his appearance, for it was obvious he was unharmed, but then he was travelling in Sir Henry's carriage—and he was not a man given to generous gestures, as Rev. Underwood was only too aware. Relief therefore fought with irritation and curiosity and Rev. Underwood was rendered speechless being unable to decide which emotion should be given free rein first.

The voluble Abney took care of any awkward silence which might have ensued, "Good afternoon Reverend. Here he is, safe and sound! I hope you've not had too worrying a time?"

Rev. Underwood smiled weakly, "Not at all Abney."

"Good. There's not the least little thing to concern you. Miss Charlotte will be as right as rain in no time."

"Miss Charlotte?" There was the distinct hint of annoyance

in the vicar's voice which his brother recognized, even if Abney did not, "What has happened to Miss Wynter?"

Mr. Underwood hastily intervened, "Come indoors Gil and I shall tell you the whole story."

Bidding the grinning Abney farewell, Mr. Underwood slipped his hand under his brother's elbow and quietly led him through the old oak door.

They had barely entered the parlour before the vicar found himself exclaiming, "What on earth have you been doing now?"

"Now?" Mr. Underwood had had an extremely trying day. He was hot, tired and still hungry. The implied criticism in his brother's tone was rather more than he could take, "What do you mean 'now'? You make it sound as though I do little else but fall into scrape after scrape . . ."

The vicar was rather on edge himself. He had been told a confused and confusing story which somehow involved his brother and a sprung trap. He was not inclined to take care with his words when he answered, "Is that not precisely what you do? You seem to be entirely incapable of minding your own business!"

"And what exactly did you expect me to do with the wretched girl? Leave her lying among the bluebells?"

"Bluebells . . ." His mouth dropped open and the word was a strangled gasp, "Lying? Dear God! What have you been doing?"

Mr. Underwood gave his brother a very severe look, "Evidently not what you are imagining. Pull yourself together Gil! What do you take me for? Kindly remember I was brought home in her father's carriage."

The vicar drew his handkerchief from his pocket and mopped his brow as he sank into the nearest chair, "perhaps you should just tell me everything—from the beginning."

"A very sound idea."

***

Since the afternoon was still not very far advanced and the vicar felt a curious need to keep his brother firmly under his eye, he suggested that perhaps a tour of the church would be of interest?

Though Mr. Underwood did not share his brother's deep devotion to religion, he was nevertheless immensely intrigued by the thought of the older sections of the little church and he readily agreed to this plan—or at least he raised no objection, which amounted to the same thing in his opinion. He was unaware that he had rather hurt his brother's feelings by his seemingly lukewarm attitude.

Somewhat heartlessly, he noticed nothing amiss and if he thought the vicar was a little quiet, he thought it merely a remnant of the morning's mood of worry.

Rev. Underwood was very proud of his church and his brother's enthusiasm for the architecture, the stained glass, the rood screen and the enclosed pews, eventually worked upon his injured vanity and very soon there might never have been any awkwardness between them. Parts of the church were indeed very old, and Mr. Underwood's interest was genuine. It was a minor miracle that many of its beauties had survived the turbulent years of England's history and it was only the remoteness of the village which had saved it. Being completely cut off from the outside world every winter was a fact of life which was stoically accepted by all who lived there. It was by no means unusual to have snow as early as October or as late as May. Having been told these things, Mr. Underwood could only shudder delicately and express a hope that the weather would not suddenly turn inclement during his stay. He was reassured by the vicar's affirmation that he had heard that there had never been a warmer May than the one they were now experiencing.

Returning to the vicarage across the churchyard well over an hour later, Mr. Underwood's attention was drawn to a small, unkempt grave, almost hidden beneath the shadow of the drystone wall. That he noticed it at all was something of a miracle itself, for his brother was hurrying him past the graves, under the mistaken impression that the very sight of these stark reminders of death would plunge his brother into renewed depression. Mr. Underwood was unaware that he had planted this notion in his sibling's mind with his strongly spoken wish not to have a room overlooking the graveyard the previous evening. He had simply not wanted his last view at night and his first in the morning to be the windswept desolation of a country churchyard. There was nothing more sinister to it than that, but the vicar was ever aware of a painful past which had devastated his brother.

He therefore tried to rush his brother on when he hesitated for a moment over the lonely little grave with it poignant, one word epitaph, almost obliterated by long grasses and tussocky weeds.

His eye had been drawn to it as they passed simply because it was so uncared for and overgrown. In such a small community, family graves were used over and over again, and there were very few residents who did not have at least one remembered relative whose remains lay within the grey walls. It seemed to Mr. Underwood that almost every other grave was cared for but this one.

The Reverend, who had not noticed that this brother had paused to gaze upon the insignificant stone and had hastened on, was called back by the quietly spoken remark, "Surely this is very unusual, Gil?"

As he turned, he saw, with a sinking heart, exactly where his brother was stood. It was a grave that he tended himself when he had the time, and one which engendered a certain sadness in himself, so Heaven knew what effect it would have upon his brother's sensibilities.

Without seeming unutterably callous, he could not ignore the situation so he was forced to retrace his steps and take his place at his brother's side.

The stone bore the simplest yet the most complex epitaph ever carved in stone. "Unknown". No other information was included—none was available. It was several seconds before Mr. Underwood spoke again, "How is it possible that there should be someone 'unknown' in this tiny, out of the way place? Surely everyone who lives or dies here must be known to all?"

"Well, even the smallest of places have the occasional vagrant passing through!" Pointed out the vicar reasonably, rather inclined to take offence yet again at his brother's dismissive attitude. 'Tiny, out of the way place' indeed. Did he have to make it sound as though the parish of Bracken Tor was next door to nowhere and that her vicar had been sent there to rot? "But as it happens, there appears to be a rather tragic element to this story. I'm afraid the poor girl was killed here. Just over a year ago. Before my time."

"Killed? You mean in an accident of some sort?" His brother's interest made the vicar err on the side of wariness. "No, not an accident." Obviously the vicar did not wish to expound further, but his brother would not allow himself to be put off.

"If it was not an accident, then what was it? I can think of only one other alternative."

"She was murdered." Curt and to the point, thought Mr. Underwood, but why was he so reluctant to talk about it? There was obviously a great deal more to the tragedy than the vicar was admitting.

"In the wood on Sir Henry Wynter's land?" Guessed Mr. Underwood, suddenly recalling the conversation he had had with Miss Wynter.

Rev. Underwood looked faintly surprised, "That is where she was found, yes. But how did you know?"

"Something that someone said." Answered Mr. Underwood tersely, "So no one was able to identify her?"

The vicar became more and more reluctant to speak on the subject, "It is over and done with. Discussing the matter now will not bring the poor girl back."

"No, but it might bring the swine who killed her to justice—and prevent him ever laying another young girl beneath the soil before her time!" There was a harshness in his voice and

31

a violence in his eyes that the vicar had never witnessed before. Perhaps it was this which caused the vicar to regard this remark as somewhat ominous, and his face reflected the fact as he asked, rather diffidently. "You are not intending to involve yourself in this, are you?"

"I have not been unsuccessful in the past, have I?" The vicar, recalling only too clearly what the consequences of that past had been, was unreassured, "Chuffy . . ." He said, pleadingly. The use of a childhood pet name may have been unconscious, but it was not lost on Mr. Underwood. Since he absolutely refused to use his two Christian names, which only his family knew, his brother generally managed without calling him anything at all, or resorting to the use of his initials, C.H. To his students he was Mr. Underwood—or Snuff behind his back, due to his habit of occasionally imbibing the same—to his colleagues he was simply Underwood. It had never occurred to him to worry what a woman would call him, should he ever allow one to become that closely involved.

To hear his brother call him Chuffy was a momentary return to their youth. An eloquent appeal for him to behave himself. Though it did give him cause to hesitate, it was an appeal he fully intended to ignore.

"Gil, if you won't tell me what I need to know, I shall simply ask elsewhere. For, understand this, never shall anyone lie beneath the soil unavenged whilst I have breath in my body!"

The vicar spread his hands in a gesture of mute despair, "but your health . . . I beg you, don't do this. You are not strong enough . . ."

Mr. Underwood knew full well that his brother was under no illusions about his legendary ill-health. He had, it was true, suffered a great deal of physical and mental anguish a few years before. Since then he had utilised his frailties entirely to his own ends. His many and varied minor afflictions were simply a pastime, and a very successful way of avoiding unwanted tasks. He gave his sibling a look which is commonly known as 'old fashioned'.

"Come now, Gil! There is a reason why you do not wish me to investigate this matter, but I know it is not concern for my health!"

For the first time the vicar raised his eyes and looked directly into his brother's. He looked very worried, "Chuffy, the girl who lies in that grave is unknown because no one ever saw her face. Her head had been hacked from her body—and it was never found. I'm afraid you would be dealing with a madman."

***

32

Sir Henry Wynter returned from his shooting expedition some hours after Charlotte had been carried up to the house by Mr. Underwood. He was tired, dirty and had been unsuccessful in bagging even a pheasant, something for which he was inclined to blame the unfortunate Underwood. Upon being told that Charlotte had sustained a nasty injury from one of his traps, his fury exploded in a way which always terrified his daughters.

"God damn you, Lottie! why the devil did you wander off the path? You should know better!"

Usually Charlotte was the most spirited of the girls, and could charm her papa out of the sullens, but this evening she was feeling tired, shocked, pained and weepy. At the first sign of trouble she burst into loud sobs, and Sir Henry was forced to leave her alone. It was not, however, the end of the matter for him. He railed all through dinner, until his family were heartily sick of the name Underwood, and hoped fervently that the vicar's brother would keep well away from their father for the rest of his stay.

CHAPTER FOUR

("Veni, Vidi, Vici."—I came, I saw, I conquered.)

"I assume you are going to see Miss Wynter today?" Gil ventured rather tentatively, well knowing that his brother was quite likely to do the exact opposite to any suggestion made to him, should the mood so take him.

C.H. Underwood was not an aggressive man, he did not appear to be stubborn, overbearing or even particularly decisive, but he never actually did anything he did not wish to do. He made no fuss, he didn't argue, he did not even point out that he was his own man. He simply did not do anything at all and should the neglect of his duties cause him to fall foul of anyone, he merely apologised sweetly for his awful memory. In fact he apologised so adroitly, it was rarely noticed that the expressions of regret did not, at any time, ever include the promise to atone. If Mr. Underwood decided not to do something, then it would certainly never be done by him.

The vicar would not, for the world, have admitted it, but his interest in Miss Wynter's welfare was not entirely personal, because during a long and, for the most part, sleepless night it had occurred to him that Miss Charlotte Wynter would be an admirable choice of wife for his rather fusty brother. A woman of spirit was just what C.H. needed to liven him and sweep away any of those grim cobwebs which might still be lurking in the dark reaches of his mind.

These thoughts were far from matching Mr. Underwood's own. His intention had been to spend his day beginning his investigations and he had, in fact, almost forgotten the events of the day before except in the light of what Charlotte had told him of the scene of the crime.

"Most certainly not." He answered promptly, "Miss Wynter would appear to know very little about the incident, but for the fact that it happened on her father's land. The gory details have, quite properly, been kept from her. There are several others I should like to interview before I turn my attention to her."

The vicar kept very calm—admirably so under the circumstances. He was not entirely sure that his brother was not being deliberately obtuse, "I was referring to a social call, to enquire after her health. She was, after all, in your company when she came by her injury—trying to do you a service, if my recollection of the matter is not at fault! I should have thought a polite enquiry was the very least she could expect from you!"

"Ah!" Mr. Underwood was unable to deny that this was indeed a valid point, but he made one last effort to escape the meshes of duty which his brother had cast about him, "Perhaps a visit from you would be more welcome to her, Gil. I rather gathered that she likes you. She was at pains to tell me how very popular you are."

Gil straightened himself in his chair and managed to muster a great deal of dignity as he replied, "Naturally I fully intend to accompany you. I, at least, need no reminders of my duty!"

Mr. Underwood had no choice but to consider himself duly chastised and set about finishing his disturbed meal with no further quibbling.

He very nearly balked again when he was handed a bunch of flowers from the vicarage garden, and told severely that they were to be given to the invalid, "Good God, Gil! I haven't presented a posy to a woman for nigh on twenty years!"

"Then the time is long overdue for you to do it again!"

The vicar barely restrained himself from laughing out loud at the sight of his brother carrying a bunch of flowers from which he was trying strenuously to disassociate himself. The gift was dangling from his fingers, heads down, and almost dragging in the dust. Mr. Underwood was trying to look utterly at his ease, but was making a poor job of it. He was, in fact, hideously embarrassed, and could only be grateful that his irreverent students were not about to witness his discomfiture.

He was normally a man who was totally in control of his life, amiable and orderly, but the one thing which could be relied upon to discompose him were women. He saw few members of the fairer sex in his cloistered University life, and simply through lack of practice he had forgotten how to treat them. It was the lack of familiarity which had engendered the entire race with a cloak of fearsome mystery. In short Mr. Underwood thought of women as a strange breed of exotic animal, altogether fascinating and dangerous—and to be avoided at all costs.

His brother had rather a different attitude. He too found women fascinating and dangerous, but for entirely opposing reasons. In his capacity as a clergyman he had seen many aspects of life which his sibling would have found unutterably distasteful. This was his first country parish, and his town sojourns had brought him into contact with poor women and rich, clean women and dirty. He had met prostitutes who sold their bodies to eat, and wealthy women who gave their bodies to any who asked. For his brother it was ignorance of women and their ways that prompted him to view them with aversion. For the vicar it was the knowledge of the darker side of both men and women that kept him content to be alone and rely on no one but himself. He was more than willing to give freely of himself to aid his fellow man, but he drew a firm line when it came to personal attachments.

Both men were lost in their own thoughts as they wended their way to the abode of Sir Henry and his family. Little conversation was exchanged except for occasional remarks from the vicar, pointing out a thing of interest to his brother.

Mr. Underwood answered politely whenever he was spoken to, but it was obvious that his mind was on entirely another matter. In fact he was thinking about the poor murdered girl and who on earth she could be. He found it very hard to believe that a properly organised investigation would not turn up some clue to her name. It was rare indeed that anyone should be so completely alone in the world that some one, be it parent, spouse or friend, should not try to seek the missing person. Having discovered her identity, it surely followed that the culprit and reason for her death might also become clear. Some instinct told him that his brother was wrong; this was not the work of a madman who simply killed from an uncontrollable bloodlust. Had that been the case, there would have been other victims—and as far as he was aware, there had been no others in the recent past. Mr. Underwood might choose to live his life in the quiet of a University, but that did not mean he had entirely renounced the world. He was an avid reader of newspapers, and for someone who insisted that he could scarcely recall his own name, he had a remarkably retentive memory—at least of things which he wished to remember! There had been no outbreak of killings which followed the pattern of this one—and a year was a long time to deny oneself, if one had discovered the desire and need to kill.

Almost before he knew what he was about, Mr. Underwood found himself standing on the front step of Wynter Court, being told that yes, Miss Charlotte was at home, and quite well enough to receive visitors.

She lay on the same sofa upon which he had set her the afternoon before, looking very pale and tired, with her bandaged foot resting on a silken cushion and covered by a large, fringed shawl.

For the first time the brothers actually shared a thought—and that was one of extreme relief that she was actually dressed and up—they had both rather feared that the interview might have taken place in her bedroom, with her lying abed, and attired in her night-clothes.

Mr. Underwood, nudged gently by the vicar, produced the flowers, now dusty and limp, from behind his back, "My brother gathered you some flowers, Miss Wynter." The bright smile, directed towards the vicar, which this remark produced, convinced Mr. Underwood that he had been correct in his assumption that Miss Wynter was drawn to his brother. It was without the merest hint of conscience, therefore, that he put the flowers into her hands and added, "I really must find Miss . . . er . . . your governess, and thank her for her hospitality of yesterday."

"Miss Chapell?" That Charlotte was stunned by this was fairly obvious; what was not obvious was that she was also rather upset by his apparent desire to leave her company and gain that of the governess. Charlotte had spent a very pleasant evening in a laudanum induced drowsiness, with the memory of Mr. Underwood bearing her manfully through the woods causing her a very warm glow. To find that their little adventure had meant little or nothing to him, was a rebuff the like of which she had never received before. Charlotte had had a number of admirers since she left the school-room just a year ago and despite the ferocious guard her father stood over her, they had been only too willing to risk all for the tremendous honour of talking to her, walking with her, riding with her, or, on the very infrequent occasions she and her sisters were allowed to accept invitations, to dance with her. She was decidedly piqued to discover that there was at least one man who did not hold it a high honour to have been of service to her.

To avenge herself upon him, she turned an especially dazzling smile upon the vicar, and said airily, "I expect she is in the garden somewhere. She expressed a desire for some air about twenty minutes ago. I'm sure you'll find her if you look."

She was disturbed to see that this rather rude dismissal had absolutely no effect whatsoever. On the contrary, Mr. Underwood appeared to think she was being helpful and smiled slightly as he bade her farewell.

As he disappeared through the open door which led onto the terrace, Charlotte turned tragic eyes upon the vicar, "He did not even ask how I did." Her youth betrayed her as her lower lip trembled slightly. Rev. Underwood was torn between exasperation at his brother and pity for her, though he knew her to be somewhat spoiled, and was sure that for once not getting her own way could have nothing but a beneficial effect upon her.

"I must apologise for my brother, Miss Wynter. He meets so few young ladies, I fear he has forgotten his manners. I can assure you that he was most concerned about your welfare, and it was at his insistence that we called today." May the good Lord forgive me, he added silently. Despite the fact that the vicar was not a good liar, Charlotte brightened visibly, "Was he really concerned about me?"

"Very. I understand you had a very lucky escape. Does your ankle hurt very much?" Charlotte was never reluctant to talk about herself, and having successfully diverted her attention, the vicar needed only to sit back in his seat and leave her to prattle happily, wondering all the while where his brother was, and what exactly he thought he was doing!

Mr. Underwood spent an extremely pleasant ten minutes wandering around the grounds of Wynter Court, with the sun upon his face and the rich, warm scents of early summer in his nostrils. He had no particular desire to find Miss Chapell, since his only object in mentioning her name had been to escape from the house in order to leave his brother alone with Miss Wynter. This having been admirably achieved, he need now only make sure they remained alone together for long enough to discover each other's charms. Once this happened Nature, he presumed, would take its course and an Autumn Wedding would be duly announced.

As it happened he found Miss Chapell quite by chance, for having grown weary of the lawns and formal flower beds, he ventured around the side of the house which, until this moment, had been a mystery to him, and found himself in an avenue of box, high, but beautifully trimmed, with, at pleasantly placed intervals, arched niches set with stone benches. Miss Chapell was hiding in one of these niches, an open book in her hands and seemingly engrossed.

She glanced up as his shadow fell across her, starting slightly at his unexpected presence. His approach had been singularly silent, since he had chosen to walk upon the grass and not on the gravelled path.

"Mr. Underwood!" her hand flew to her heart, "I had no idea you were here."

"May I join you, Miss Chapell?"

"But of course." She shifted along the bench, tucking her skirts out of the way at the same time. "Is Miss Charlotte not receiving visitors?" She asked presently, when he was settled on the seat beside her. She could not help wondering why he was in the garden and not in the house talking to the invalid.

"Oh yes. I left her talking to my brother."

Miss Chapell was an astute young woman, and though inclined to say very little, there was nothing which escaped her notice. She had seen Charlotte's behaviour the evening before and was under no illusions as to that young lady's readiness to fall in love with her rescuer—albeit he was somewhat older than the other young bucks who were currently wooing her. The governess could only be amazed that he had managed to effect an escape from her headstrong charge, leaving her alone with the vicar, instead of being alone with her himself and the vicar wandering in the gardens with Miss Chapell!

It would have been too impolite to frame the question which sprang to her mind, "How did you manage it?" so she was forced to change the subject completely, "Isn't it a glorious day?"

Mr. Underwood was not about to be drawn on the weather so he answered, "Quite delightful." In a rather cursory manner before adding, "Tell me about yourself, Miss Chapell. Have you been in Sir Henry's employ for long?"

She gave him a mildly flirtatious glance from beneath lowered lids, "Do I look as old as all that?"

Mr. Underwood looked confused, as he always did when women tried to flirt with him. He was never quite sure whether the truth was required at this juncture, or if he was supposed to be heroically witty and send the lady off into paroxysms of laughter, "I have no idea." He eventually replied . . . apparently this remark was heroically witty, for Miss Chapell did indeed laugh very heartily, and it was quite some minutes before she was able to recover herself and wipe her eyes, "I do apologise, Mr. Underwood, that was unforgivable!"

Mr. Underwood had been watching her amusement in bemused silence, but was prompted to sketch a gesture of denial with a long-fingered hand, "Not at all, not at all! Think nothing of it. I don't think I have ever caused such merriment before—except on the occasion I mistook the Dean for the college scout and berated him soundly before half my students."

"Oh dear!" Miss Chapell was well aware how serious such an error could be and was immediately solemn, "What happened?"

"I am a very fortunate man, Miss Chapell. The Dean is rather deaf and had also forgotten who I was. He simply thought I was a raving madman and ordered my immediate removal from the premises. I grew a moustache until I felt he had forgotten the incident."

Miss Chapell went off again whoops of laughter, but this time Mr. Underwood joined her.

Isobel, passing the end of the avenue at that moment, was surprised to see her governess and the vicar's brother enjoying each other's company so much. She hoped Charlotte would not come to know of it.

Oblivious, Mr. Underwood and Miss Chapell were just recovering themselves, "I told you yesterday that you were an extraordinary man, Mr. Underwood!"

"Too kind," He murmured, rather embarrassed by such candour, "Now, you were about to tell me about yourself."

Miss Chapell bent to retrieve her book, which had fallen from her lap, "I'm afraid it's a very dull story. My father was a clergyman, who died ten months ago. My mother has been dead since I was quite small, so about eight months ago I had to find some sort of employment. Only Sir Henry was prepared to take on someone so relatively young and inexperienced, so here I came."

Mr. Underwood did not voice the thought, but he was prepared to wager that her salary was far lower than it ought to be. He did not think Sir Henry had a magnaminous bone in his entire body!

"I'm so sorry." He said, "It is particularly hard to lose someone, when losing them also means the loss of your home and livelihood. You must have had a very hard time adjusting to life as an employee."

For some reason she felt she could not meet his eyes and continued to stare steadfastly at the book in her hands, "I was very miserable when I first came here, but I have grown used to things now."

In a swift and fluid movement he patted her hand comfortingly, then reached into his pocket and drew forth his snuff box, "I assume you do not imbibe?" He asked, proffering the box, which he had already flicked open with a casual thumbnail.

"No, thank-you."

"I trust you have no objection to my doing so?" She shook her head, fascinated by the swift and expert way he handled the container. It was the action of a dandy, yet there was nothing else dandified about him. She was glad, for she despised dandyism, feeling it to be an indulgence of the thoughtless rich which mocked the misery of the poor. It was nothing less than scandalous that young men could pay fortunes to their tailors and boot-makers, whilst children starved on the streets and men and women sank to the depths of degradation through poverty and ignorance.

Naturally she said nothing of this to him. Such thoughts could only be regarded as subversive and hostile, and she had no idea how her companion might feel about it. Since her father's death, her own politics had inclined towards the Radical movement, especially after the massacre of the innocents the year before in St. Peter's Fields, Manchester. She had been appalled that the wealthy and powerful men of that City had had felt no compunction at turning the military loose with sabres upon the poor protesters, including women and children. Not that she had ever mentioned her feelings upon the subject—she might not particularly enjoy her work, but unfortunately it was necessary to her, and she knew that Sir Henry would bear no Radical to reside beneath his roof. She simply watched Underwood as he took his snuff, snapped shut the box—a very plain one—and returned it to his pocket. Very cleanly done, she thought admiringly, for, though he automatically dusted his front, there was not a speck to be seen.

"You do that beautifully." She heard herself saying, then blushed painfully as she realised she had spoken out loud.

He smiled, a slow, warm smile which made his eyes glitter teasingly, and showed his crooked tooth to advantage, "Thank you." He did not tell her that his snuff box was merely a device—one which he used often—and for a number of different reasons. It was a useful diverter of attention, mainly from emotions which he did not wish to display, it also served to distract other parties from their own feelings. Quite often by the time he had taken his snuff and returned the box to his waistcoat, the dangerous moment was passed. As was the case on this particular occasion. Miss Chapell had quite forgotten that she had been speaking of unpleasant things and Mr. Underwood's equanimity was completely restored.

Miss Chapell was quite ovewhelmed by the power of his smile and for the first time she understood why Charlotte had been so dreamily preoccupied the evening before.

"Do you . . ." Her voice caught in her throat on a curious high note and she had to swallow deeply before she could try again, "Do you ride at all, Mr. Underwood?" She couldn't imagine why she asked the question, except that riding was the main occupation of everyone in the Wynter household. She herself had, in the past, enjoyed riding, being lent a mount by a kind-hearted parishioner of her father's, but she had not ridden since her arrival at Wynter Court, simply because she had never been asked.

She had to admit that she was treated really rather well by the family—certainly much better than she had been led to believe was the usual lot of governesses. To the older girls she was viewed more as a friend than a paid companion, and her only real charge was Isobel, who utterly adored her. Had she spoken of her desire to ride, she would have been immediately gratified, if not with prime horseflesh, then with a passable nag, but her pride refused to allow her to ask for favours, so she waited in vain for an invitation.

"I have not ridden for many years—I have neither the time nor the mount—but I used to be very fond of a sedate trot around the London parks."

She laughed, "I fear you should not get a 'sedate trot' here, Mr. Underwood. The Wynters are all neck or nothing riders!"

"It's the red hair." he replied, quite seriously, and she laughed again.

CHAPTER FIVE

("Fiat Justitia Ruat Caelum!"—
Let Justice be done though the Heavens fall!)

Luncheon was rather a strained affair, with the vicar still seething at this brother's cavalier attitude towards Miss Wynter, and Mr. Underwood refusing to be in the least concerned.

In fact he was deeply immersed in the problem he had chosen to solve, and was scarcely aware that his sibling was annoyed—a fact which served to irritate the vicar even further.

Faced with the almost monosyllabic conversation, Mrs. Selby beat a hasty retreat and left the brothers to serve themselves.

Towards the end of the meal, Mr. Underwood seemed to stir himself out of his reverie and looked directly at his brother for the first time, "Where does the nearest doctor live, Gil?"

"Calden." Answered the vicar tersely. Mr. Underwood seemed to find nothing amiss in this reply, "Oh, so you don't have a doctor actually living in the village then?"

"Somewhere as remote as this is lucky to have a doctor as near as Calden!"

"And how far away is Calden?"

"About four miles."

"Rather a long walk. Is there any vehicle available to take me there?"

The vicar began to frown, "Why do you want to go to Calden?" Mr. Underwood seemed surprised that he should feel the need to ask, "To interview the doctor of course! I assume it was he who was called to examine the body?"

A sudden, and most uncharacteristic, loss of temper seemed to assail the vicar. He rose so swiftly to his feet that his chair was thrown backwards and landed with a clatter on the wooden floor, his napkin was slammed fiercely onto the table, "Good God! You are not still intent on that madness, are you!"

Mr. Underwood raised a quizzical eyebrow, "My dear Gil, you seem upset. Is something amiss?"

"Yes, Chuffy! Something is amiss!"

"My dear fellow. Why didn't you say so! What is it?" The voice of compassion, full of gentle concern, almost sent the vicar into a frenzy. He found it very difficult to believe that his own brother could infuriate him so much. None of his parishioners would recognise their calm and collected vicar at this moment. Taking a deep breath he attempted to elucidate.

"You simply cannot come here, a complete stranger, and begin to stir up the past! Many people were exceedingly distressed that such a thing could happen here. You will cause considerable unhappiness if you remind people of the incident."

Mr. Underwood slowly shook his head "Gil, I must say I am intensely disappointed in you! Would you rather that poor girl lay unavenged in her grave, than people were disturbed by a few simple questions?"

Feeling that he was being manipulated, but unable to frame a reasonable reply to this, Rev. Underwood was forced to capitulate.

"Very well, you have my blessing. But, please, I beg you, do not go about this thing in an insensitive fashion!"

"Insensitive? I?" Mr. Underwood seemed appalled at the very suggestion, "Gil, I am the soul of sensitivity and discretion! Half the people I question will not even realise that they have given me information."

"I hope you are right!"

Nothing further was said and the two gentlemen left the dining room of one accord. As they entered the hall the front door bell jangled and before either could approach it, Mrs. Selby, with uncharacteristic alacrity, dashed by and flung it dramatically open, "Why it's Miss Chapell. Do come in Miss Chapell." The lack of surprise in her voice led them correctly to assume that she had observed the young lady's approach from the parlour window, where she was supposed to be dusting, which overlooked the village street.

Miss Chapell entered the hallway, drawing off her gloves as she did so, "Good afternoon Mrs. Selby. How are you?" She smiled at the vicar's housekeeper, then seemed to notice the two brothers standing in the dimness of the hall, "Good afternoon gentlemen." She added, including them in her smile.

"Good afternoon, Miss Chapell." Answered the brothers in unison, then glanced in irritation at each other, aware that they had sounded like a couple of school boys.

"Can I help you, Miss Chapell?" Asked the vicar politely, gesturing that she should enter the parlour before him.

"You must forgive my coming unannounced." She said, as she obeyed the invitation and walked past him and into the room, "but I am the bearer of a message from Sir Henry."

"Oh dear, nothing wrong I hope?" As he spoke, he was forced to reach out and grasp his brother firmly by the coat tails

43

to stop him from wandering out of the front door, "In here!" He hissed.

"Did you say something?" Asked Miss Chapell, turning toward him.

"No." Answered the vicar, releasing his brother hastily and smiling brightly, "Not a thing. Now, the message . . . ?" Mr. Underwood stood awkwardly in the doorway and the Reverend was forced to push him into the room and enter behind him.

"Merely an invitation to dinner tomorrow evening." Said Miss Chapell gazing at the pair curiously, and wondering what on earth was going on. There seemed to be a lot of undignified pushing and pulling.

"From Sir Henry?" The vicar's voice was sharp with disbelief, so sharp that Mr. Underwood glanced at him in surprise, and Miss Chapell was forced to hide a smile, "Well, the actual order came from Miss Jane," She did not add that it had also been at Charlotte's insistence, since the rest of the family had deemed it politic to keep the vicar's brother and the squire well apart! "Oh." Reverend seemed suddenly to remember his manners, "I do beg your pardon, Miss Chapell. Won't you be seated. Perhaps I could offer you some refreshment?"

"Thank-you, no. I have only just finished luncheon and as it is my free afternoon, I am rather eager to be on my way."

"Then let us detain you no longer. Thank-you for delivering the invitation."

"I trust I am not included in it." Said Mr. Underwood suddenly. Miss Chapell had been endeavouring to keep her eyes upon the vicar whilst she conversed with him, but now her glance flew to his brother's face, "Oh dear . . ." She faltered, "Do you have some other engagement? I was asked most particularly . . ."

"No, no, Miss Chapell." Interrupted the vicar hastily, "No other engagement. My brother and I will be delighted to accept Sir Henry's kind invitation."

She looked very relieved and began to draw her gloves on again, "I must go. Poor old Noble hates to be left standing, especially when he's drawing the gig. I think he feels it is beneath his dignity!"

Mr. Underwood became very interested when he heard the word gig, "You are in possession of a vehicle, Miss Chapell?"

"Yes."

"Would it be very much out of your way to give me a lift to Calden?"

"We must not encroach upon Miss Chapell's free time." Intercepted the vicar, and Miss Chapell thought she heard a note of warning in his voice.

"As a matter of fact, I was planning to drive through Calden. About a mile outside the village there is a very pretty waterfall. I thought I might go there and do a little sketching."

"Then would you be kind enough to give me a ride as far as Calden?"

"Most certainly, Mr. Underwood."

"Thank you." Without further ado, he offered her his arm and led her from the house, "Goodbye Gil. Don't wait dinner for me. I may be a little late."

Miss Chapell managed to restrain her curiosity until they had mounted the rather rickety vehicle and were bowling along at a sedate trot, leaving Bracken Tor far behind them. Since it would have been unforgivably rude to ask her companion outright what his plans were, she was forced to employ considerable cunning and tact.

"I hadn't realised that you were acquainted with anyone living in Calden?"

"I'm not."

She could see that he was not being deliberately obstructive, it simply never occurred to him that anyone should be in the slightest degree interested in his actions, and so he made no attempt whatsoever to explain or justify them.

She gave a laugh which sounded, even to her own ears, rather false, "Then I can't imagine what takes you there! It's not a very interesting place—very similar to Braken Tor, in fact, but without the benefit of the church. I don't think it is the sort of place to attract visitors!"

"Oh, I'm not interested in the place myself. I simply want to see the Doctor."

She knew a moment of intense disappointment. Charlotte had gigglingly told of his supposed hypochondria, and since meeting him, she had hoped it was not true. Such a glaring defect of character was not particularly attractive in a man.

"Are you not feeling well?" She asked tentatively, glancing sideways at him.

"Never better." He asserted heartily, "Why do you ask?"

Miss Chapell began to feel that they were not communicating on quite the same level, "But . . ." She foundered in a morass of confusion, "The Doctor . . . you said . . ."

Mr. Underwood laughed, his head thrown back, his golden hair glistening in the sunlight, for he invariably went hatless despite the prevailing fashion. The truth was he constantly lost them, leaving them in shops, circulating libraries and anywhere else he happened to visit. To simplify his existence, he had abandoned to use of anything not directly attached to his person, therefore he never wore a hat, or carried a stick. "I said I was going to see the Doctor, not to consult him!"

"You also denied knowing anyone in Calden." She countered, mildly irritated that she should be laughed at, when it was he who had caused the confusion, "Why visit a man you don't

45

know?"

His abrupt change of expression made Miss Chapell feel suddenly cold and shut out, "I don't think I ought to tell you that. I'm sorry."

"Oh." She was hurt, and sounded it. Mr. Underwood felt most acutely that he had disappointed her. It was not a feeling he liked, it had been a great many years since he had allowed himself to be swayed by the guilt others thrust upon him.

"Miss Chapell . . ." He began, but she cut viciously across his attempt at reconciliation, "Please don't say any more. I quite understand that you think I am not to be trusted!"

Dammit! Why must women always bring every issue to the personal!

"It is not a question of trust, my dear child! I have been asked to keep this thing quiet, therefore my first action cannot be to tell you all about it."

"I may not have attained your great age, but I am not 'your dear child'." She said swiftly, "And I wouldn't dream of asking you to break a confidence—in fact, I insist that you do not!"

"By all that's Holy! Give me a woman for contrariness!" Miss Chapell did not realise it, but she was witnessing a most unusual circumstance—Mr. C.H. Underwood in a state of extreme irritation.

As he grew more ruffled, she simply became more serene, "There is no need to insult my gender, Mr. Underwood. I quite understand the male code of honour. You cannot tell me your silly little secret—let that be an end to it!"

"Silly little secret!" He was painfully aware that he was beginning to sound very pompous, "My good girl . . ."

"Woman," She corrected calmly, quite unsettling him and causing him to forget the gem of a rebuff he had been about to employ.

They subsided into silence, which was maintained until Calden was reached, and Miss Chapell drew her stallion to a standstill outside the gate of a large stone built house, the walls of which were festooned with rather unkempt ivy.

"Doctor Herbert's residence." She announced formally, waiting for him to vacate the seat beside her. He did so, but instead of walking away from her, as she had expected, he went to the horse's head and grasping the bridle, he began to lead the creature in through the gate.

"What are you doing, Mr. Underwood?" She asked sweetly, determined not to become rattled by his odd behaviour. Her only answer was the pleasant scrunch of the gravel beneath feet, hooves and wheels.

At the door of the doctor's house, he released the horse and approached the vehicle, "Get down." He said curtly.

"No."

46

He took hold of her hand, and jerked her unceremoniously into his arms.

"Put me down . . ." Even as she spoke, he dropped her to her feet, then taking her hand once more he began to drag her towards the door.

"Stop it, Mr. Underwood. This foolishness has gone far enough! What will Dr. Herbert think if he sees us."

"I don't give a damn!"

Miss Chapell was profoundly shocked, "Mr. Underwood!"

"I do beg you pardon, Miss Chapell. I quite forgot myself. What I meant to say was that if you don't wish Dr. Herbert to think ill of either of us, then stop struggling, and do as I tell you!" She knew he was being sarcastic, and wasn't in the least sorry that he had sworn at her, but she suddenly found herself not really minding very much.

With great dignity, she withdrew her hand from his grasp, tugged her pelisse straight, adjusted her bonnet and said, "Very well."

The elderly maid who admitted them showed no surprise at all to see a rather pink-cheeked Miss Chapell, alone and unchaperoned, in the company of a tall, blond gentleman, who was also looking far from calm. Over the years Gertrude had seen far stranger sights on the doctor's doorstep.

"What name shall I give the doctor, sir?"

"Underwood." Was the rather brusque reply.

"Oh, then you'll be the Reverend's brother?" With that she walked away, leaving them in a barely furnished little room, off the hall.

"Is there anyone in these parts who doesn't know I'm the Vicar's brother?" He asked, with justifiable irritation. Miss Chapell laughed, rather unkindly, "Why should you mind?"

"I've no idea—but I know I do mind, very much!" Actually, he knew exactly why it annoyed him so much, but at that particular moment, he was not about to confide in his companion. For the most part, his life was one of quiet and pleasant anonymity, the only fame he ever attained was within the precincts of his college, where he knew he was talked of with a mixture of affection and fury, depending upon the point of view of the speaker. He did not like having that anonymity so crudely stripped from him, and he detested the idea of being known only as an appendage of someone else's life, and not as a person in his own right. Minor matters, of course, but his very trying morning had suddenly endowed minor matters with a whole new importance.

The entry of the Doctor prevented further cogitation, and Mr. Underwood happily put his feeling of discontent aside and began to concentrate upon the task in hand.

Introductions made—unnecessary in Miss Chapell's case, since she was already known to Dr. Herbert—Mr. Underwood lost no time in pursuing his line of enquiry.

"I understand from my brother that there was an unsolved murder committed in Bracken Tor approximately a year ago, and that you performed the post mortem examination. I have set myself the task of solving the case and I would be grateful for your co-operation." If the doctor was shocked by this forthright opening, it was nothing to Miss Chapell's astonishment, but she had the supreme intelligence to remain silent.

Dr. Herbert took a moment to recover himself, then spoke, carefully avoiding eye contact with Miss Chapell, "I should be very glad to see the murder solved, Mr. Underwood. But do you think this is the sort of conversation which should be carried out in the presence of Miss Chapell?"

Mr. Underwood glanced briefly at his companion then returned his gaze to the man before him, "Miss Chapell has committed herself to helping me in this endeavour. She is quite prepared for anything shocking you might have to say."

The doctor raised his brows in a quizzical fashion in Miss Chapell's direction, "You are quite sure, Miss Chapell?"

Looking a little pale, but with a determined expression, Miss Chapell nodded firmly, "Quite!"

"Very well. Shall we go into my study? I have the notes there."

Silently the two followed him, but as they reached the door, Mr. Underwood held her back and whispered, "That was unforgivable. I had no right to thrust this upon you. Do you wish to leave now?"

She looked up at him, searching his face, "Do you really want my help?"

"Not unless you truly wish to offer it."

"I do."

With that they entered the room together and Mr. Underwood closed the door behind them.

The thirty minutes which followed were amongst the most difficult Miss Verity Chapell had ever known. She learned details of a death which were rarely discussed before a woman of her class and generation. Protected all her life from such sordid and unpleasant events, she was profoundly shocked, and almost uncontrollably nauseated, but she survived, her dignity intact, and her admiration for her two companions increased a thousandfold. The professional coolness with which they discussed their subject amazed her.

Mr. Underwood, armed with his own travelling ink-well and pen even made notes upon a sheet of paper borrowed from the doctor.

The doctor himself, for the most part, simply read his notes made at the time aloud, or answered Mr. Underwood's questions from memory. In a very short time they almost completely forgot Miss Chapell's presence and became necessarily graphic.

"The body was discovered at approximately 5:30 on the morning of 25th April, by Toby Hallam, Gamekeeper to Sir Henry Wynter. He, very sensibly, touched nothing, but ran immediately to Wynter Court. The order came from Sir Henry to fetch me. I arrived at 6:30."

"A whole hour elapsed? Isn't that rather a long delay. Surely a fast horse could have covered the distance in a matter of minutes?"

"I must admit a similar thought occurred to me at the time, but I suppose one must make allowances for the early hour, for panic and misunderstood instructions."

"I suppose so. Pray continue."

"The corpse, as I assume you already know, was headless, but judging from other indications, I would estimate the height of the victim to have been about five feet, and her age to have been between thirteen and twenty years."

"You can be no more specific than that?"

"Young girls have a tendency to reach maturity at vastly differing ages, so without the teeth as a guideline, no I cannot."

"Quite." Mr. Underwood made his note and the Doctor waited for the scratching of his nib to cease before continuing, "Judging from the amount of blood—or rather the lack of it, I should say that she was already dead when the decapitation was carried out, and that it was clumsily done, with a none-too sharp instrument. The victim was probably face down when the mutilation was inflicted, and it took several blows to attain complete severance. There were several gashes in the region of the shoulders, presumably caused by misaimed blows. I would say that the assailant was either not particularly strong, or entirely panic-stricken."

"Probably the latter, given the circumstances." Remarked Mr. Underwood.

The Doctor neither agreed nor disagreed, but continued his narrative, "In my opinion—and it is only an opinion—death occurred elsewhere, but the mutilation was carried out on a spot near where the body was found. A few feet away there is a flat rock which bore traces of blood, bone, flesh, cloth and was chipped as though struck with some sort of hatchet or hand axe. If that was the case, it probably accounted for the haste and carelessness of the deed. The murderer would have been terrified of being caught in the act. He would not be particularly blood-stained, because, as I've already said, the girl was dead, so blood-loss would be minimal. Rigor Mortis had already set in, and the heart had long-since ceased to beat."

"Have you any idea how she was actually killed—since the decapitation was obviously not the cause of death."

"There were no marks upon the body, so my own guess would be a blow to the head—but it could equally well have been a gun shot, or strangulation."

"Could you make a guess as to her social status?" Asked Mr. Underwood, much to Miss Chapell's relief. She had heard enough of the bloodier side of the case.

"Well, the next part of my task was to have the body brought here, where I performed a more thorough examination. The clothes she wore were of a good quality, but fairly worn. What was interesting was that they were obviously second-hand."

Mr. Underwood shot the doctor a shrewd look from beneath half-closed lids, "What led you to that assumption?"

"The normal areas of wear on the garments did not match the girl's own dimensions. The elbows of the dress, for example. There was a patch where the continued bending of the joint had caused the material to become considerably thinned, but that patch did not lie on the girl's elbow, but further down her arm, yet the cuffs were neat and unfrayed, leading me to suppose they were newly turned. From little things like that I deduced that the garment had once belonged to someone larger, who had worn it well before discarding it to be altered for a different—and smaller—wearer."

Mr. Underwood smiled for the first time since the interview began, "You have my unstinting admiration, Dr. Herbert. I only wish everyone had your capacity for observation."

"Thank-you—but I rather wish everyone had your capacity for realising that such details can be of importance. When I made these observations to Sir Henry Wynter, he was extremely scathing. Demanded to know what the devil use such information was. Who cared whether the girl was dressed in borrowed clothes or not—it did not help to catch her murderer in his opinion!"

"I beg your pardon, gentlemen, but I feel the need to ask the same question." Intercepted Miss Chapell diffidently. "Why does it matter what clothes she wore?"

"It gives us some indication of her possible back-ground. In order to find he murderer, we really need to know who the girl was. It could be that this was a random killing by a madman—but I suspect it was not.

"Also," Added the doctor, "It reinforces what we already imagined. That is, that the girl was poor. It is highly unlikely that a rich young woman could disappear without provoking some kind of outcry, but poor girls disappear every day of the week, without producing even a flicker of interest. I fear that the moral of this story is that had this girl been well-to-do, there would have been a greater determination to find her killer."

"Do you really believe that, Dr. Herbert?" That Miss Chapell was distressed by this assertion was obvious, but in all honesty the doctor would not now deny what he had said, "Yes, I'm

50

afraid that is precisely what I believe, which is why I welcomed Mr. Underwood's self-inflicted task. No person's life should be held less precious because of their station in life."

"My sentiments exactly." Said Mr. Underwood quietly.

"I agree, of course, but why should you think that it was not the work of a frenzied maniac? That is how it seems to me! Surely no sane person could inflict such wounds upon a corpse?"

"It is precisely because of what was done that we believe it was a sane person who killed her. Someone was very eager that her identity was never discovered."

"How do you know?"

Mr. Underwood's reply was very quiet, but his words seemed to hang on the air, striking a chill into Miss Chapell which she had never before experienced, "Because he took the head away with him."

CHAPTER SIX

("Carpe Diem, Quam Minimum Credula Postero."—
Enjoy today, trusting little in tomorrow.)

There was a moment of silence before Miss Chapell protested, "But the girl was unknown in Bracken Tor! No one recognized the body or the clothes; no one was reported missing."

The information he had given her seemed threatening. It was suddenly necessary to her peace of mind that she find some reason to deny his suggestion.

The thought that some madman had once passed through the village, leaving one sad, unknown victim in his wake was terrifying enough; but to be forced to acknowledge that the assailant could be someone she knew, someone to whom she spoke, perhaps every day, someone who was capable of committing a foul, cruel murder, who would then stop at nothing to hide that crime—Miss Chapell gave an involuntary shudder, "I can't believe what you are suggesting. The village I know is a peaceful place, the people in it are friendly and caring! I refuse to suspect anyone! It would be simply impossible for such a small community to keep such a dreadful secret!"

"We are not suggesting anything of the kind!" Intercepted Dr. Herbert, slightly impatiently, with a glance towards Mr. Underwood which clearly said, "Why did you invite a woman into this?"

Mr. Underwood, aware that the woman in question had not particularly wanted to be invited, was forced to speak in her defence.

"Miss Chapell misunderstood us, Dr. Herbert. We have not, perhaps, explained that we are simply putting forward a theory, and have no proof."

"Naturally we have no proof! If we had, we should hardly be sitting here theorising! It is a reasonable assumption that there was something recognisable about the victim—perhaps a facial scar—and because she is not known now, it does not follow that she was not known in the past! People leave villages all the time—to seek work, or to be married perhaps. If she arrived back unexpectedly, bringing with her the secret shame of someone's past, then naturally her body and clothes would stir no memory."

"It would be a great mistake not to explore every possibility." Added Mr. Underwood gently.

"Is one of those possibilities that the killer could be a woman?" Asked Miss Chapell, her equanimity almost restored by Mr. Underwood's kind tone.

"No one can be discounted at the moment—except yourself, myself and my brother—since none of us were in the vicinity at the time."

The doctor laughed, "Thank-you for your confidence in me!" His visitor smiled in return, "I'm prepared to give you the benefit of the doubt, Dr. Herbert. I feel sure a man of your skill would have made a rather neater job of the decapitation; and would be considerably less inclined to answer questions so frankly."

"Can I take it that I am off the list of suspects, then?"

"Not entirely—I am a very suspicious man, and your apparent helpfulness could be a very clever cover for a heinous crime!"

Miss Chapell was shocked at her companion's lack of respect for a man she considered to be above reproach, "Mr. Underwood! Dr. Herbert is a gentleman!"

Mr. Underwood refused to be even slightly impressed by this character reference, "I hate to have to disillusion you, Miss Chapell, but I could give you a very long list of 'gentlemen' who have stretched a hang-man's noose!"

"Nonsense!" She said dismissively, but Mr. Underwood pursued his point, "Are you a married man, Dr. Herbert?"

"I am, Sir." His friendly grin showed that he was not in the least put out by his guest's impertinence, on the contrary, he seemed intrigued to know exactly where the line of questioning would end.

"Good. Now imagine your reaction if one dark night a knock upon your door was answered and you found yourself facing a child—looking remarkably like you—who declared herself to be the product of a long forgotten love affair, and demanding to be invited into your home and treated as your offspring. No-one knows she is there and a simple way of ending the matter once and for all is a headless corpse in a wood."

"Well, I'd like you to believe that I would not succumb to temptation and murder said child—but I concede your point! No one is beyond reproach, Miss Chapell, and Mr. Underwood is wise to recognize the fact. Shall we continue?" The doctor shuffled his notes, "Where were we? Ah, yes, the post mortem examination. Are you sure you wish to stay, Miss Chapell?"

"Yes."

"Then pray forgive my candour. The girl was not a virgin, no children had been born to her and she was not pregnant."

"That removes one possible motive—had she been raped?" Mr. Underwood had apparently forgotten Miss Chapell's presence, for his shoulders stiffened slightly when he heard her shocked intake of breath. Both men seemed to think it politic to continue, completely ignoring the need for embarrassing explanations and apologies.

"No."

"Then that removes another."

"The contents of her stomach showed nothing unusual. There was not, for example, any evidence of poison."

His narrative ended, the doctor raised his head, "That is as much as I can tell you, I'm afraid. In the absence of any indication of who she was, I released the body to the authorities. A description of her clothing was circulated to the newspapers, but no information was forthcoming. Sir Henry Wynter, as local magistrate, gave permission for the body to be buried, which in due course it was. The villagers of Bracken Tor and Calden all subscribed to a fund to purchase a headstone. The vicar of the time, your brother's predecessor, caused uproar by refusing to allow anything but the word 'unknown' to be included upon the stone. The general feeling was that given the violence of her death, something of her tale should be etched there, as an expression of regret, I suppose. Rev. Boscombe was appalled by the very idea, threatening to refuse permission for the girl to lie in his graveyard if the epitaph contained a description of her death. He was backed by Sir Henry who pointed out that such a move would be an eternal reminder of an incident which was perhaps best forgotten."

"It was that quarrel, more than anything else, which convinced Rev. Boscombe of his own unpopularity. He resigned, and your brother, Mr. Underwood, was the happy choice of man to replace him." Miss Chapell finished the story, with a smile.

Dr. Herbert agreed, "Most certainly. Now, if there is nothing more you wish to know, perhaps I can offer some refreshment?"

Both were delighted to accept this offer and presently found themselves seated in the parlour at the back of the house, looking out onto a profusion of flowers, and being served tea by Dr. Herbert's wife Helen.

She was younger than her husband by several years, very vivacious, but at the same time kindly and sympathetic. Miss Chapell knew her quite well and was immediately at her ease, only noticing her companion's discomfiture after several minutes of animated chatter. She was amazed at the change in Mr. Underwood, not realizing that attractive and flirtatious women terrified him. He had lost all his ease of manner and had chosen to seat himself in a winged chair as far from his hostess as possible. The very thought that he might actually have to converse with her sent him into a state of mild panic. Miss Chapell found it hard to believe that it was the same man who only moments before had been discussing murder with obvious sang froid.

It occurred to her to wonder why her own presence did not seem to have a similar effect upon him and would have been immensely offended had she realised that it was her own unspectacular looks and manner which had quickly caused him to think of her as an 'honorary' male.

Helen Herbert, with customary understanding, swiftly realised the problem, and immediately altered her personality to suit the circumstances. Her voice became quieter, her smile less broad. The girlish chatter she had exchanged with Miss Chapell ceased and she became altogether a different creature, serious minded, very much the doctor's wife. Dr. Herbert noticed it and smiled gentle encouragement to her.

"Milk and sugar in your tea, Mr. Underwood?" She asked.

"Thank you." Was the ambiguous reply. She took it to mean yes and presently handed the cup and saucer to her husband, to be passed on, along with a plate containing home-made fruit cake. Mr. Underwood, too shy to ask for help, juggled valiantly to hold everything, until the doctor noticed his dilemma and silently presented him with a small occasional table. With much relief, Mr. Underwood laid his burdens upon it, leaving everything untasted.

"I understand you teach, Mr. Underwood?"

"Yes."

"At Oxford or Cambridge, isn't it?"

"Cambridge."

Many women would have given up at this point, but Helen was made of sterner stuff, "A lovely part of the country, Cambridge. I once spent a holiday there, with my Aunt Agatha."

If his wife had an Aunt Agatha, it was the first the doctor had ever heard of it, but he said nothing.

"Yes. It was an inspired spot to build a University." Mr. Underwood had relaxed sufficiently to manage a sip of tea, "I often think it is a pity my boys do not appreciate their surrounding more. Of course young men would always rather carouse than study the beauties of nature."

"I can't imagine that you preferred carousing in your youth, Mr. Underwood." Helen allowed herself a small smile and was delighted when it was returned, "As I recall, I did have my moments, Mrs. Herbert."

"Oh, call me Helen, please. I find formality rather tedious, don't you?"

"I had never really thought about it." Admitted Mr. Underwood, breaking off a minute crumb of cake.

"My name is Verity." Volunteered Miss Chapell helpfully.

"And mine is Francis." Said the doctor.

In the ensuing silence Mr. Underwood became aware that everyone was looking at him, obviously awaiting the pronounciation of his own Christian name. A momentary hesitation on his part was followed by the decisive comment, "I never use my Christian names."

He was surprised that they all seemed quite shocked.

"Never?" Asked Helen, rather breathlessly, "You can't possibly go through life not using your name."

"I do."

"But what do people call you?"

"They use my surname."

"Even your brother?" Asked Verity, wondering anew what manner of man she had met.

"No, my brother uses my initials—or occasionally a silly pet-name he had for me when we were boys."

Helen and Verity could not help but be amused by the distinct blush which coloured his normally pale face.

"What is it?" Persued Helen, refusing absolutely to be deterred, despite her husband's strenuous facial contortions, which were supposed to discourage her impertinence.

"Chuffy." This was greeted with another silence, then Miss Chapell made a sound which bore a remarkable resemblance to a snort.

With great difficulty Helen controlled her terrible desire to laugh, "Oh. It doesn't really suit you, does it?"

"Perhaps it did when I was six years old." Replied Mr. Underwood severely, which had the unfortunate effect of making Miss Chapell choke on her tea.

There followed several minutes of near pandemonium during which Miss Chapell gasped for breath and grew very red in the face, Dr. Herbert slapped her heartily between the shoulder blades and Helen flew to fetch a glass of water. Mr. Underwood simply watched, displaying considerable interest in the proceedings but declining, probably wisely, to do anything at all.

When she had recovered sufficiently to wipe the tears from her eyes, Miss Chapell managed to gasp, "I don't think I could bring myself to call you Chuffy, Mr. Underwood."

"Good Lord! I should hope not! If you really insist upon dropping my surname I suggest you use my initials—C.H."

"That seems very unfriendly, Mr. Underwood. Can't you possibly tell us your real name?" Helen spoke in her most wheedling tone, but it had no effect upon the determined Mr. Underwood.

"No. If my boys were ever to discover my guilty secret, I should never have their respect again!"

"Good Heavens, what can it be, to make you detest it so!"

"I should leave things well alone, if I were you, Helen. I think Mr. Underwood has borne your meddling for quite long enough." Intercepted the doctor cheerfully, "Now, Miss Chapell's horse will be growing very restive."

Miss Chapell leapt to her feet, smitten with remorse, "Poor old Noble, I had quite forgotten him."

Since, at the beginning of the conversation, Verity had told Helen the purpose of her journey, the doctor's wife now thought she ought to ensure that her two visitors stayed in each other's company for at least the rest of the afternoon.

With this in mind, she brightly suggested that she accompany them to the Tambrook Falls, filling the position of chaperone, and having a breath of fresh air all in the same happy notion.

Mr. Underwood allowed himself to be persuaded simply because he had nothing better to do, and lacked the necessary energy to think of a good reason for not going. He was inclined to hope that the two ladies, who appeared to be quite well-acquainted, would content themselves with their own company and leave him to indulge in a quiet nap. It also occurred to him that fitting three adults into the two seats of the gig was going to be rather a crushing experience, but since neither lady seemed to find it a problem, he kindly refrained from mentioning it. In this hope he was destined to be disappointed. Helen Herbert thought she scented an air of romance and was determined to leave the pair alone together once the Falls were reached.

Fortunately Mr. Underwood was neither a mind-reader, nor a particularly astute judge of the female character, or he would have been seriously concerned by the affectionate glances Helen occasionally bestowed upon her companions.

Romance was ever far from his thoughts, having, many years before, bestowed his affections upon a very special young woman, who had died, tragically young. The hurt he had endured then made the thought of ever suffering so again quite out of the question. He had submerged himself in a world where women rarely entered, and he intended to remain thus until the day he died. The truth of the matter was that had he realised Helen intended to thrust him into Verity Chapell's company, he would have immediately set out on the four mile walk back to Bracken Tor, with never a backward glance.

Since he was ignorant of her intentions, however, he quite happily hoisted himself back into the vehicle and prepared to enjoy some glorious views.

In this he was not disappointed. Craggy, heather strewn hills gave way to rocky expanses of moorland, with icy mountain streams tumbling musically over rock-lined courses. The falls themselves were surprisingly high, and surrounded by a rainbow dancing haze. Mr. Underwood was enchanted by the variety and richness of the region. He had thought the rolling hills of his own native County were quite lovely, but nothing he had read or heard had prepared him for the simple magnificence he found in this little known spot.

Helen, as she had already planned, lost no time in making her excuses and left the two seated comfortably upon a flat rock, Miss Chapell with her drawing equipment perched upon her knee and Mr. Underwood contentedly watching her.

When she had disappeared from view behind a rocky outcrop, Mr. Underwood was smitten with slight remorse, "Do you think I should have offered to go for a walk with her?"

Miss Chapell had already begun to concentrate on her task and answered him almost absent-mindedly, "She seemed quite happy to be alone, but by all means go after her, if you feel you want to walk."

"No. I'm more than content to sit here."

Nothing more was said for quite some time, then Miss Chapell finished her initial sketch and turned her attention to her companion. He had leaned back against a convenient bank, his eyes firmly closed and was giving every appearance of being sound asleep.

"Are you asleep, Mr. Underwood?" She asked quietly.

"Not any more." Was the reply, and she laughed rather unkindly.

"I'm so sorry." She said, but she did not sound very sincere.

He roused himself, sat up straight and looked at her, "What was it you wanted?"

"Just to show you my sketch." He took the proffered book from her hands and studied it. He was impressed by what he saw. With a few simple lines she had managed to capture the essence of the view. Even the trees seemed to stir in the breeze.

"That's remarkably good." He said, after a moment, "Do you think I might have it?"

"Of course. But I have other drawings which are much better. The one I did of Bracken Tor church I thought really quite good."

"No, I should like this one. But do you not wish you could earn your living doing this, rather than teaching? It seems a great pity that such a talent should be relegated to a mere hobby."

She blushed deeply at his praise, "How very kind you are, Mr. Underwood."

"Not at all. I hope I could never be accused of being insincere!"

"I did not mean to suggest such a thing! But I rarely show my work to people and I'm not a good judge of my own skill."

"Well, I'm certainly not an expert, but I know what I like."

"Thank-you." By now she was desperately embarrassed and longed only for a change of topic to take the conversation away from her and gave her an opportunity to recover her calm, "Tell me, Mr. Underwood, how do you intend to go about finding the identity of that poor girl."

He had never actually been asleep, but had been contemplating this very problem, so it was not difficult to sidetrack him into discussing it, "I think the first step must be to discover how she travelled to Bracken Tor. If she came on the Stage, for example, it might be possible to trace through their records and find out from whence she travelled. That would be extremely helpful."

"And what if she came another way?"

"That makes things a little more difficult. But I must own I'm almost sure she travelled by the Stage."

"Why?"

"Because she obviously came a long way. I cannot believe that local gossip would not have filtered through to someone who knew her. But had she been planning to travel some distance and had told people who knew her that that was her intention, then they would never have had reason to be concerned about her disappearance. It would account for the fact that no-one has ever come forward to report her missing."

"Yes. That makes sense. Do you think you'll ever find out who she was?"

"I have the greatest confidence I shall. And the greatest determination to bring her murderer to justice."

"If it is not an impertinent question, may I ask why?"

"Why what?"

"Why do you feel so strongly about the matter? After all the girl is gone and nothing is going to bring her back. Why do you feel the need to find her killer?"

"I don't really know. There was something so terribly sad about that bare little grave. It reminded me of something which happened—something I've been trying to forget for a long time. I failed then. I don't intend to fail now."

She wanted to ask him to explain more fully, to tell her how he felt he had failed, but his expression was suddenly cold and closed and she felt that she was encroaching upon his privacy. It was with immense relief she saw Helen approaching. It was easy enough now to end the conversation, and she did so, but with a slight feeling of disappointment, "Here is Helen. I think it is time we found our way home."

Mr. Underwood rose to his feet, "I'd rather we never mentioned again what has just been said. I should not have . . . No matter! Please just forget it."

She made no reply, simply smiling her agreement at him, then turning her attention to the Doctor's wife, "Did you enjoy your walk, Helen? You should have lazed with us. It has been a glorious afternoon."

Helen was optimistic enough to take this to mean that her

plans for a romance were well on their way, and her smile was benign.

CHAPTER SEVEN

("Dulce Domum."—Home Sweet Home.)

The welcoming aspect offered by the lighted windows of Wynter Court was greatly at variance with the attitude of its owner. Sir Henry was anything but welcoming—in fact it was some time before he even made his appearance, and the Underwoods found themselves being entertained by several young women who were obviously not used to male visitors, and by the only son, an arrogant young buck who gave the distinct impression he had several other things he would much rather be doing. Mr. Underwood barely restrained himself from imposing a punishment of translating several hundred lines of Latin Grammar, fortunately recalling just in time that he was not dealing with one of his more wayward students.

It was an uncomfortable beginning to the evening.

Mr. Underwood had always felt himself to be incredibly gauche when thrust into the company of flirtatious and self-assured young women and could not have believed it would be possible for him to feel more ill-at-ease, but this family of timid, unaccomplished, and, for the most part, unattractive girls, caused him to reassess the situation. They possessed no conversation, no poise and seemingly no talents. Other than Charlotte, they somehow managed to miss all the loveliness which can belong to the red-haired woman and had gathered together all the negative aspects of the colouring. Charlotte's hair was a rich auburn, but her sisters covered the whole range from strawberry blond to bright red—and none had managed to inherit the particular shade which would have suited her skin and eye colour. Their fashionably pale flesh seemed only to emphasize the freckles which adorned them in abundance, the red of their hair made their high foreheads appear to shine with a slightly greenish tinge. Compared to the bright joyfulness of Charlotte, they all gave the impression of being cowed and spiritless. Mr. Underwood, who had expressed such fears of being exposed to

61

the fire of the red-head, had nothing to fear from these—except perhaps the distinct possibility of being bored to death!—he felt sure they did not have a temper between them.

To make matters infinitely worse, they all looked to their brother with complete adoration, never realizing that his manners were coarse, his wit lewd and his interest in anything other than himself and hunting was non-existent. Only Charlotte treated him with the healthy, affectionate contempt of an older sister for a younger brother.

The newcomer despaired of ever remembering which sister belonged to which name, so insipid were their expressions and so blank their eyes. His memory was not reliable, being more inclined to retain strange facts, and Latin quotations, than important details, and this procession of limpid creatures, with no spark of fire to make them even slightly memorable, was going to be a nightmare.

Maria he could identify simply because she was the only one who wore a wedding ring. Fortunately for him, her surname remained Wynter, for she had been paired with their Father's cousin Edwin, the man who would inherit the Wynter Estate under the entail, should Harry fail to reach his majority. All this had been hastily explained to him by the vicar on the journey to the Court, and Mr. Underwood had astounded himself by actually remembering it. He could only assume that it had made so deep an impression on him because of the thought which had passed through his mind at the time, and that had been Sir Henry's peculiar determination that, one way or another, only his direct descendants should ever live in his home. To Mr. Underwood it was indicative of the ego of the man, and gave him cause for thought.

Maria's husband was a weak-chinned weasel of a man, considerably older than his bride, and rather inclined to treat her with amused contempt. His attempt at bonhomie included a very disparaging remark about his wife which Mr. Underwood certainly found offensive, and which one glance at his brother confirmed that he viewed the comment in the same poor light. It did not augur well for the future.

The second daughter Jane had taken over her older sister's position as hostess, but she filled it badly. She had little control over the household staff, the younger members being sulky and reluctant, the older completely disillusioned. Mr. Underwood had never expected to see a home so badly run.

Emma and Eliza were both struck dumb by the arrival of the two gentlemen and could barely manage to wish them "Good evening." Before blushing vividly and relapsing into embarrassed silence. The youngest, Isobel, hid behind Charlotte and peered at the brothers with large, frightened eyes.

The family was gathered in the music room when the

Underwoods were shown in by a pert little maid, who grinned wickedly at Mr. Underwood and caused him almost to bolt before they had even entered the house.

When introductions were completed, the silence which fell was so strained that Mr. Underwood could barely stand it. He was desperate for something to do, so he wandered across the room to admire the pianoforte—an obviously superior instrument, which looked as though no-one ever touched it, not even to dust it, he noticed with irritation. Being a music lover, he hated to see fine instruments misused.

In the normal course of events he would not have dreamt of drawing attention to his interest, knowing that his brother would be at pains to point out how well he played, but on this occasion it seemed preferable to the stilted conversation which he was being forced to endure.

"I see you are admiring the piano, Underwood. I always think it rather a pity to waste so superior an instrument on a household who cannot be bothered to learn how to play! Charlotte has the best voice, but unfortunately only has Miss Chapell to accompany her." Edwin Wynter spoke as though having a mere governess as accompanist was an insuperable obstacle and Mr. Underwood found himself experiencing the most uncommon—for him—sensation of bridling. He could feel his hackles rising, not only for the dismissive attitude towards Miss Chapell, but for the uninvited liberty Mr. Wynter had taken in dropping the prefix of 'Mr.'

"As a matter of fact," He heard himself saying testily, "I play a little myself, if Miss Wynter wishes to entertain us." By the time the full horror of this pronouncement was bourne upon him, it was too late to retract.

Charlotte was on her feet and limping towards him, her eyes shining, her voice slightly breathy with subdued excitement. The guests could not avoid being enraptured by her singing. What better way could there be to draw their attention to her charms?

"That would be delightful, Mr. Underwood!" She began to riffle the music sheets to find a suitable song and Mr. Underwood realized with sinking heart that he was entirely trapped.

The experience was not, however, quite the torment he had envisioned. The recital he and Charlotte gave was short and she did actually sing very prettily indeed. His only regret was the glance he gave his brother showed the vicar was viewing them both with a smile of indulgent pleasure, which clearly stated that he thought they made a charming couple. Mr. Underwood could feel himself being mentally sized for Wedding clothes. He rather wished his mother had not put the thought of wedlock into his brother's mind.

In fact, though he did not know it, they did make rather a

stunning picture, her fire, his ice. She so bright and vivacious, he so serious and cool. For such an ill-assorted pair, they went rather well together.

They performed two songs, both of which he knew quite well, then accepted the enthusiastic applause with becoming modesty, leaving the floor for others to take. Not to be outdone Edwin offered to play whilst his wife sang, but his frequent wrong notes rather marred the effect, especially since he continually berated his wife for the tuneless efforts, declaring her to be tone deaf.

Charlotte took the opportunity to draw Mr. Underwood across the room to a couple of straight backed chairs which stood in a recess by the window, sufficiently far away from the group by the piano for them to have private words.

"You play beautifully, Mr. Underwood." She told him, her eyes shyly lowered.

"No, I'm merely competent. It is simply a matter of practice. Something which I'm sadly lacking at the moment. If I have any talent at all, it is due to a music teacher I had as a boy. She rapped my knuckles with a cane every time I made a wrong note. You would be amazed how well it concentrates the mind of a twelve year old! Though, of course, I played the harpsichord in those far off days!"

Edwin made another glaring mistake at that moment and Mr. Underwood winced, "Would that she were here right now!"

Charlotte giggled nervously, not at all sure whether he was joking or serious, "I think you are teasing me, Mr. Underwood."

He looked quite staggered at the very suggestion, "I? Believe me, Miss Wynter, you entirely mistake the matter. I wouldn't have the faintest idea how to tease a young woman. I don't think it is a thing I have ever attempted. It has always seemed to me to be a rather perilous undertaking!" He sounded almost severe and she could barely repress a shout of real laughter escaping her. Only the knowledge that it would draw attention to their tete-a-tete made her control herself. A hasty change of subject seemed politic.

"Did you enjoy your visit to the Falls?"

"Falls?" He seemed at a loss for a few seconds, then the puzzled expression cleared from his features, "Of course! I had forgotten. Yes, indeed. A lovely place—which reminds me, are we to be joined by Miss Chapell?"

"No. She never dines with us when we have guests."

"Her choice, or yours?" He could not keep a note of cynicism from his tone, but she made no comment upon it.

"Her choice, of course." She said emphatically, then added ingenuously, "If the truth were told, it is because she does not care very much for Edwin. He has the heartiest dislike of servants presuming to rise above their station, and thinks we have made a grave error in allowing her to become so familiar. Whenever he sees her, he is always rather unkind."

"Unkind? In what way?" Was it her imagination, or did he sound annoyed? She eyed him curiously, but he remained impassive.

"Oh, he does all sorts of things. Usually he asks her a question which he knows she could not possibly answer, then makes a great issue of how very ignorant she is, and how unfitted for her position as our governess. Of course he does it so innocently, one would never guess he was being vicious, and she is made to look a perfect fool. Father always laughs and declares she isn't worth her hire, and Verity has to leave the room—she never cries before them, but I know she does when she is alone." She hesitated, then added in a whisper, "I think he's a beast! I can't imagine what Papa was about, making Maria marry him. I think she hates him too!"

Mr. Underwood did not find this at all difficult to believe, but it was not his habit to become emotionally involved in the problems of those he could not help; it simply led to frustration and a feeling of inadequacy, neither of which could be said to be conducive to the peace of mind of any man. So instead of asking the questions which beset him, he changed the subject, "Does your father intend to join us at all?" he asked, wondering if she detected his eagerness to hear a negative reply to his query.

"Oh yes. He will be down presently—he never comes in here—he says he can't stand the family 'en masse' unless his glass and his stomach are full—or about to be filled!"

A glance about the room, reminding himself of the unprepossessing gathering, served only to cause Mr. Underwood to concur heartily with his absent host.

In an effort not to give Charlotte any indication of his unChristian and uncharitable thoughts, he searched for another topic and happily remembered her injury, which he had so far failed to enquire after.

"I see you are on your feet again, I trust that means you are fully recovered?"

"Well, not quite. I'm disobeying Doctor's orders in walking on it, but I was so bored! I'd rather bear a little pain than be trapped in the house and completely at the mercy of my fussing sisters!"

"In that case, ought I not insist that you go and lie on the chaise longue with your feet up?"

"Yes—but then I shouldn't be able to talk to you alone." Charlotte made this declaration in a shy undertone, as though she were revealing a daring and long-held secret, but Mr. Underwood's reaction was not quite what she had expected or desired.

"Great Heavens!" He expostulated, so loudly that Charlotte

gave a nervous glance towards her family, who fortunately remained oblivious, "Where is the attraction in that? A fusty old Academian! I should have thought you would have wanted to find someone more interesting with whom to spend your time!"

She smiled up at him, "Do you have any suggestions?"

"My brother." He relied promptly.

"A fusty old cleric?" She raised her brows quizzically and for the first time managed to make him smile, "Poor Gil! Is that really how you view him?"

"No more than I view you as a fusty Academian!"

At that moment the double doors opened, "Dinner is served." Intoned Brownsword the butler, and the now chattering group rose of one accord and began to make preparations to pair off for the walk to the dining room.

"Jane had planned that you should take her into dinner, Mr. Underwood, but if I take your arm and limp horribly, she can hardly take you from me, can she?" Charlotte confided in her companion. Since it was quite immaterial to him which of the sisters clung to his arm for the short walk to the dining room, Mr. Underwood was quite content to do as she suggested and promptly offered his arm to her. Charlotte was young enough to take this gesture to mean something quite different, and classed it as a veritable victory. Her face was adorned with a triumphant smile as she passed her sisters on the arm of her chosen escort.

She was so flushed with the success of this manoeuvre that upon reaching the dining room she ignored her customary seat at the lower end of the table, and allowed Mr. Underwood to hold Jane's chair for her, so that she might be next to him. He was completely unaware of this faux pas, and oblivious of the ensuing confused shuffling of seating amongst the rest of the family.

Apart from the lack of congenial company, Mr. Underwood was also far from impressed by the food he was served. The meal began with leek and potato soup—the most bland and tasteless of all concoctions, in his opinion, and this was a particularly watery effort. His heart sank further when the next course was brought and laid before the master of the house to carve. A delicate digestion was an affliction which he actually did possess, unlike his many imaginary problems, and the very thought of roast mutton was enough to stem his rising appetite.

"Only a very little for me, Sir Henry." He protested, as great, greasy slabs of meat were thrust haphazardly onto the plate destined for him.

"Little! Nonsense man! You've spent too long crouching over your books! You need a few good meals inside you!" Since he was convinced that a 'good meal' was precisely what he was not going to get, Mr. Underwood had to restrain himself from delivering a testy response.

Sir Henry laughed coarsely and piled yet another slice of meat onto the platter. His guest wondered vaguely where he was supposed to fit the vegetables, but he said nothing, for fear of being plied with more.

At last the plate stood before him and he saw to his horror that streaks of solid, creamy coloured fat lined the meat, and the blood still ran from it. His stomach lurched in protest and it was as much as he could do to prevent himself from rising and leaving there and then.

Charlotte noticed his appalled expression and took pity upon him. Under cover of the others' conversations she managed to whisper, "Papa allows his two dogs to sit under the table at his feet. Providing you are discreet, Father will never know you have not cleared your plate."

His gratitude for this piece of information knew no bounds and was reflected in his eyes as they met hers. Colour rushed into her face, and she dropped her gaze. Mr. Underwood was baffled that a smile should provoke so extreme a reaction and the faintest crease of puzzlement appeared between his brows as he looked at her. Why the devil was the girl acting so oddly? He shrugged slightly as though to cast off the problem and began to serve himself with vegetables from the proffered dish.

Sir Henry appeared to be in an expansive mood, and it was his voice which dominated the dinner table. Unfortunately his idea of amusing conversation was to heap insults upon his family and guests.

Mr. Underwood was irritated, but by no means surprised to be chosen as the first victim.

"I see the meat is not to your taste Underwood." Sir Henry's voice cut across the general chatter, the chink of glasses and the clatter of silver on china. Though Mr. Underwood heard the words quite clearly, he quickly decided that to give an acceptable answer would be impossible, so he simply met his host's eye and waited for him to expound further.

Being the man he was, it was not long before he did so, "Well, you have no one but yourself to blame! If you hadn't blundered upon me the other day, we should be enjoying venison now!"

"In that case, the entire company has my most profound apologies!" It had been his intention to completely silence Sir Henry with this deliberate insult upon the meat being served, but his host astounded him by treating the snub as a witticism and laughing heartily at it.

"Gad! You're a man after my own heart, Underwood! Tell me, do you hunt?"

"Only when I lose something." Replied Mr. Underwood, in his most absent tone of voice, seemingly engrossed in the delicate task of trimming the worst of the fat from his mutton. This sally was greeted with general amusement, but Harry scowled. He, like his father, could conceive of nothing even remotely funny about hunting and he did not welcome it being treated in so light a manner. "My father means do you go hunting!" He spoke in a loud, clear voice, as though he were dealing with a particularly obtuse peasant. Mr. Underwood raised his head, his expression showing his complete bewilderment, "I do beg your pardon, have I somehow missed the point?"

Harry was growing more angry with every passing second, "We simply wish to know if you go hunting!" He was almost shouting, but Mr. Underwood remained quite calm, "Hunting for what?" He asked blandly. The family wondered if Harry would be able to keep his clenched fists to himself.

"Animals, of course!" He blustered, quite sure he was being made a fool of, but scarcely able to believe the man who faced him had the courage to provoke him thus.

"Oh, animals? No I can't say I do. The only animals with whom I come into regular contact tend to wear cravats and do not take too kindly to getting their hessians muddy."

"This, of course, is not ideal fox-hunting terrain." Intercepted the vicar tactfully, well aware that his brother was treading on dangerous ground, and considering it safest to turn the conversation to other matters, "But Sir Henry and Harry seem to find plenty of other sport."

"Yes. I had noticed that, Gil." Replied Mr. Underwood, before any one else could join the conversation, "Sir Henry seems to have no shortage of quarry—be it animal or human!"

"Human?" Sir Henry snapped out the word with all the deadliness of his gun, "What the devil do you mean by that?"

"You seem upset, Sir Henry. Have I said something I ought not? I would have thought it was common knowledge you have man-traps on your land—it ought to be, in order to give your prey a sporting chance! Surely a man deserves to know he risks a limb if he poaches on your land!"

"Oh, man-traps!" Sir Henry waved a dismissive hand, as though the matter were of small importance, "Of course, they all know! They tell each other. No one ever gets caught in them! You make too much of a trifle, my friend!"

"A trifle?" Mr. Underwood savoured the word thoughtfully, "A trifle which nearly caused your own daughter serious injury!"

"Charlotte should know better than to wander off the footpaths!"

Now it was to be Charlotte's turn, thought Mr. Underwood, and was immediately determined not to allow it. "Charlotte cannot be expected to know where every trap you have laid is to be found. I thought the general idea was to avert crime not to cause injury!"

Sir Henry was obviously not pleased at this criticism, but he managed to smile condescendingly at his guests, "You are a town dweller, Underwood, and cannot be expected to understand the complexity of living in the country. Life is rather harsh here, I'm afraid—or must seem so to one as cloistered as you." Mr. Underwood prepared a devastating put down, but feeling Charlotte's hand upon his arm brought him to his senses, "No doubt." He replied, effectively ending the argument.

Greatly to his relief, the plates were taken away and the next course embarked upon, and by the time this transformation had taken place, the moment of awkwardness was past and the buzz of conversation had risen again to such an extent that Charlotte was able to whisper to him unheard by their companions, "You must forgive my father. He does not mean to be rude—he just isn't used to being contradicted."

"If he intends to invite me again, he had better grow used to it," He murmured in reply and she smiled at him, "I shall make him invite you again."

"Thank-you."

For Charlotte's sake, Mr. Underwood had promised himself that nothing Sir Henry could say or do would make him lose his temper again that evening, but he had rather over-estimated his own powers of self-control. Sir Henry was a man with a talent. The talent to perceive the weakness of others and heartlessly expose and ridicule that weakness. Mr. Underwood found it more and more difficult, as the evening wore on, to keep silent in the face of Sir Henry's increasingly drunken and cruel comments to his daughters and son-in-law. Only his son seemed to escape unscathed, and the girls were left in no doubt that he considered every one of them worse than useless and counted every day that he had waited for his son a waste of his life. All the girls were pale and silent when he heaped scorn upon their dead mother and Maria tried to quiet him and begged her husband to take away the bottle of claret at his elbow—his second full bottle, to Mr. Underwood's reckoning.

Edwin Wynter, rather sensibly, refused to do any such thing and told his wife to hold her tongue. Soon after that the ladies rose and prepared to leave the gentlemen to their port. Mr. Underwood was just wondering how it would look if he made clear his intention of retiring to the music room with the ladies, when Sir Henry turned a bleary eye upon his brother and laughed coarsely, "I say, Underwood, Charlotte confides in me that she has taken a strong fancy to your brother! What say you we make a match of it?"

He completely ignored his daughter's anguished gasp of, "Papa! Please!" and continued, "Damned if I know what she sees to recommend him—I've always been more than a little suspicious of men who earn their living by electing to be locked up month after month with a crowd of boys!"

The vicar cast a worried glance in his brother's direction, being only too aware how Mr. Underwood hated anyone to suggest that his chosen profession was anything less than a vocation, but Mr. Underwood's face remained a mask of indifference. Not so Charlotte, first her cheeks had turned painfully red, then all the blood drained from her face and with tears in her eyes she darted from the room.

All who witnessed her discomfiture could feel nothing but the profoundest pity. Even Edwin admitted to himself that Sir Henry had gone too far this time. It was obvious the girl was smitten and to have her finer feelings paraded before the man in so tawdry a fashion was quite unforgivable.

Mr. Underwood himself was debating whether to break the rule of a lifetime and knock a drunken man off his feet. He not only felt sorry for Charlotte, but was excruciatingly embarrassed on his own account. Obtuse he may have been, but it had not occurred to him for a moment that his brother was correct and that Charlotte was nursing a 'tendre' for him. When he thought of her at all, it was as a child, and talk of marriage, in any case, was unutterably tasteless.

He found Maria by his side and had to lower his head slightly when she spoke in a whisper to him, "Charlotte is terribly distressed, Mr. Underwood. Could I presume to beg you to go and speak to her? If you do not, she will never be able to face you again!"

Looking down into her pale grey-green eyes, so full of suffering and patience, he could not find it is his heart to refuse, though in truth he desired nothing more at that moment than to leave the house, the village, the district, and never to return!

"Where will she be?"

"The nursery, I think. That is where she usually hides, it is so rarely used now. Go to the top of the stairs, turn left and to the end of the corridor. It is the last door before the turning to the attic stairs."

Before leaving the room, Mr. Underwood permitted himself one last contemptuous glance towards his host, but it did him no good, for Sir Henry's head had fallen forward onto the table and he appeared to be quite insensible.

CHAPTER EIGHT

("Hinc Illae Lacrimae."—Hence those tears.)

Despite his concern that his departure would be remarked upon by all, Mr. Underwood was actually only noticed leaving the room by his own brother. All the others seemed intent upon removing Sir Henry from the dining room, and more importantly, the vicinity of the port decanter.

His son and son-in-law each took an arm and with small ceremony, hoisted him to his feet—no mean achievement, for in spite of his lack of height, Sir Henry was, nevertheless, portly and completely incapable of supporting his own weight.

Rev. Underwood watched the proceedings with interest, but without making any attempt to offer his aid. Let the Wynter men grunt and sweat together in trying to get Sir Henry on his feet, but the very thought of even setting his hand upon the now snivelling, dribbling magistrate was thoroughly repulsive to the vicar. His family seemed quite unmoved by the maudlin apologies and expressions of regret and affection, apparently being quite used to such violent swings of mood in their parent.

As the only non-relation, Gilbert Underwood found the whole scene nauseating and found his heart going out in complete sympathy for the daughters of this pathetic piece of human wreckage.

He had, in the past, witnessed Sir Henry slightly inebriated and had found him merely coarse and offensive. This display he found appalling and he was honest enough to admit that he now regretted not taking his brother's advice and refusing the invitation.

This thought reminded him of his sibling's unenviable task in coping with the tearful Charlotte. He experienced a pang of guilt when he recalled how very reticent his brother was, and his avid avoidance of the opposite sex. He could imagine no more exquisite a torture for him than to have to dry a woman's tears and listen to her admissions of love.

71

How he would survive the embarrassment, the Rev. Underwood had no idea.

***

The situation upstairs was not quite as grim as the vicar was imagining. The one fact he had overlooked was that his brother was accustomed to dealing with the problems of the young—and to him that was all Charlotte was, simply young. Nature being what it is, more often than not those problems involved love—both requited and unrequited, so he was quite used to hearing impassioned outpourings of longing for entirely unsuitable idols, and upon two very memorable occasions had been appalled, though unsurprised (being quite used to the Public School system!) to find himself the object of desire.

He was not quite as new to the predicament, nor as ill-equipped to deal with it, as his brother naively supposed.

He found the room to which he had been directed with very little trouble, and upon tapping on the door, he entered immediately without waiting for an invitation to do so. Experience had taught him that a knock usually elicited the response "Go away!" and there then followed a tedious process of cajolery and assurances of good-will in order to get across the threshold.

Having successfully gained entry, he closed the door behind him and stood leaning against it.

Charlotte sat on the far side of the room on the cushioned window seat and had evidently been looking out onto the moonlit garden. She turned her head swiftly when she heard his entry, and having, apparently been expecting one of her sisters, gave a horrified gasp. Despite being illuminated only by a crescent moon and a single candle, which guttered on a table beside her, Mr. Underwood could see her face quite plainly, and was sorry to see the evidence of very great distress etched upon her features.

"Do I intrude Miss Wynter?" he asked, with infinite kindness. She responded by turning her face away and murmuring in strangled tones, "Oh, please go away!"

Mr. Underwood was rather stumped. Usually, having gained entry, the other party desired nothing more than to pour forth their troubles into his ears. He had never been ordered away before.

He hesitated momentarily, then turned and reached for the door handle—there seemed nothing else to do.

"Mr. Underwood!"

He turned back to her, "Yes?"

"I'm so sorry! That was unforgivable. Please come in."
He crossed the room and stood before her, "Do you mind if I sit here with you for a few moments?"

She shook her head, frantically searching her person, and at the same time assiduously avoiding meeting his eye. Correctly assuming that she sought a handkerchief, he gallantly presented her with his own before taking his place beside her.

"It's terribly cold in here." He observed, with the object of giving her a little time to regain her poise, "Is the fire laid?"

"No. This room isn't used any more. It's the nursery."

Mr. Underwood already knew this, since Maria had told him so downstairs, and his swift glance about the gloomy room confirmed it. He could barely discern vague items of nursery furniture which loomed in the semi-darkness; a dolls house, a rocking horse, tiny tables and chairs.

"Then you had better take my coat." He did not wait for the standard refusal, but accordingly removed it, leaving himself in shirt sleeves and waistcoat, and draped it around her shoulders. So swift was the movement, she did not have time to protest, and if the truth were known, did not really have the desire to do so. She was clad in a short-sleeved, low-cut evening dress of white sprigged muslin, as befitted her unmarried status, and she was only too glad to nestle into his still-warm garment, imagining his arms about her instead of merely his coat.

"You are very kind, Mr. Underwood." Her voice was still dangerously quavering and he thought it imperative to ensure that no further tears were shed—at least not in his presence.

"Kind? I hardly think so! I appear to have caused a furore at the dinner table—for which I must apologise most sincerely. It was unforgivable to have aroused your father's wrath."

"No!" She said bitterly, "It was his behaviour which was unforgivable! How could he humiliate me! And before you—of all people! I shall never, ever forgive him! Everything I told him was in the strictest confidence!"

Mr. Underwood could not help reflecting, rather cynically, that she had chosen a poor receptacle for her heart's deepest secrets, but his reply was couched in much more diplomatic terms, "Do not judge him too harshly, my child! He probably thought he was acting in your best interests. Secrets will get out—and when they do they have an awkward habit of becoming the object of gossip, conjecture and unkind laughter—after all 'Amor et tussis non celantur.'" The Latin quotation, as he had intended, had the effect of making her forget her tears in the intrigue of wondering what it meant. She was still child enough to be easily distracted.

Raising her damp-lashed, green eyes to his face, she said, "I know you will think me very stupid, but I'm afraid I have no Latin—I assume that is Latin?"

"Indeed it is—and I certainly do not think you stupid! On the contrary, I usually find it unmannerly in the extreme to use a language which one knows ones listener does not speak, but on this one occasion, I shall allow myself the liberty, since that particular quotation expresses my feelings on the subject perfectly."

She managed to smile, "And what does it mean?"

"Literally translated—'Love and a Cough cannot be hidden.' A truth which I think you will agree is entirely indisputable."

Her eyes never left his, "Are you trying to tell me that you already knew of my feelings for you?"

"Well, I am not intimating that I thought you had caught a chill!"

She began to laugh, "I never knew that such things could be said in Latin. I always imagined it to be a very staid language!"

"Even the Romans caught colds, Miss Wynter—especially after they invaded England!"

The laughter died from her eyes and her gaze dropped, "I must have been very obvious—was everybody very amused by my silliness?"

Mr. Underwood felt the earth shift under his feet when faced with this question. Her sensibilities had already been seared by her father's faux pas, so he could not now admit that almost everyone, with the exception of himself, had been privy to her secret. He was experienced enough to know that first love could be a strong and painful emotion, not to be treated lightly, or to be despised, however unlikely or ineligible the subject.

"I must say, I take great exception to the word 'silliness'—it rather suggests that any woman would have to be an inmate of Bedlam to give me a second glance!"

She blushed and whispered breathlessly, "Oh no! I didn't mean any such thing!" He heaved a mental sigh of relief at having successfully satisfied her without actually answering her directly. The strain of reassuring her, but keeping her at a distance was beginning to tell upon him.

He watched her as she toyed with the handkerchief, noted how long and slim were her fingers, and how the candlelight sent sparks of fire from her hair. He had not noticed before how lovely she was, how smooth and pale her skin, how bright her hair, the length of her dark lashes against the curve of her cheek, the perfection of the shape of her mouth.

The tiniest of frowns creased his brow.

"And you, Mr. Underwood, what are your feelings in all this?" Her voice was barely discernible, and for the first time, he found himself without an answer.

He had come to seek her merely because he had been asked to do so, and because he did not like to think of any creature wallowing in misery. He had thought of her as a confused child and he had fully intended to put down her pretensions with kindness but firmly. To him she was simply one of his younger students, albeit of a different gender, a youth in need of sound advice and firm handling. It unnerved him to be suddenly confronted by a lovely young woman.

He shook his head, as though to dislodge such irrelevant thoughts from his mind, and rising to his feet, he began to pace the room, rubbing his hands together in an effort to warm them. He had not realised how cold was the room, "I? I am not on the marriage market, Miss Wynter!" He assured her, rather brutally, then regretted his harshness and added, "I'm too old to think of romance. My life is half over, yours is only just beginning."

"If you cared for me, that wouldn't matter to you." She said softly.

"I scarcely know you—and you know me not at all! You have no idea what you are asking!" He drew in a deep breath and attempted to change the subject, "Miss Wynter, I think you need, very badly, to get out of this house. Is there nowhere you could go? Some other relative perhaps? Is there no-one in your mother's family who could take you in?"

She shook her head swiftly, "My only escape from this house is through marriage."

He laid his hand on the cold, stone mantle and rested his head against it, "You don't understand, Charlotte. It isn't as simple as you seem to think. When I say my life is over, I mean it quite literally. Something happened to me which I cannot forget. I can't lay the burden of my dark moods on any woman—and certainly not one as young and pretty as you."

"I don't understand you. Tell me." The anguish in her voice made him lift his head and look towards her. In the darkness he looked pale and ghostly, his blond hair barely catching the light of the candle, his eyes lost in the shadows of his face. He looked suddenly old and she was frightened, "Don't stand there. I can't see you properly. I'm afraid!"

He straightened himself and came back to her, "I'm sorry." She did not know what he was apologizing for, and he made no attempt to enlighten her.

"Don't ask me to alter things, child. My life is settled, my future decided. There is no place for change now." He stopped, suddenly aware that he sounded as though he were trying to convince himself and not her at all. His frown deepened and he closed his eyes, as though in pain, "I have work to do."

"I would not stop you." She said, "I would be there to help you."

He opened his eyes, "On the contrary, my dear. I should have to resign, women are not made welcome in the male-orientated world of the University, and I have no other way of earning my living."

"Is that really the truth?"

"It is."

"I see." She rose to her feet, "Then we may as well say goodbye now." She was very close to him, her eyes looking deep into his. He could feel the warmth of her body, smell the sweet, clean fragrance of her hair. It had been many years since he had been in such close proximity to a young woman and he told himself that it was scarcely surprising that he found he was not entirely impervious to her charms. He was a man, after all, and not exactly in his dotage.

"Charlotte . . ." He suddenly realised that he wanted to kiss her, but he could not. Something about her stopped him. Her youth called out to him, but he knew he could not take advantage, to do so would be the behaviour of a cad. But for all that, he knew that he did not want to entirely lose her.

"Not goodbye." He said quietly, "Would you thrust me completely from your society simply because I ask you to take a little time to think things over? You are too young to make decisions which are going to affect the rest of your life."

She seemed to read much more into his words than he had intended for her eyes glowed with happiness and he found he could no longer bear to look at her. Closing his eyes, he raised one of her hands to his lips and kissed it with all the fervour he longed to expend upon her mouth. He felt her free hand touch his hair, shyly, hesitantly, and he knew he had been right not to overwhelm her with the force of his suddenly discovered feelings. She had obviously never been so close to a man before.

"Will you ride with me tomorrow?" She asked, and unknowingly broke the enchantment she had weaved about him. Her words reminded him of the task he had set himself.

"Not tomorrow." He released her hand and drew himself gently away from her, "I have to go away for two or three days, but I shall call upon you the moment I return."

"Oh!" the disappointment in her voice was plain and he smiled slightly to himself, thinking how different she was from older women, who played games with a man, teasing and confusing him with swift changes of mood, "Must you go?"

"Yes." His reply was firm and she sighed, "I'll bid you farewell then." She slipped his coat from her shoulders and handed it back to him, "Thank you Mr. Underwood."

"The pleasure has been entirely mine, Miss Wynter."

"You called me Charlotte a moment ago."

He shrugged himself into his coat, "You must forgive the familiarity, Miss Wynter."

"Oh, I don't mind." She replied ingenuously, "But I should like to know your name."

"That, my dear, is something which I refuse to disclose, even to you. If you really feel you should like to call me something

76

other than Underwood, I suggest you find a name which you think suits me and use that!"

She gave a rather shocked laugh, "What on earth do you mean? You must have a Christian name."

"As a matter of fact, I have two, but I have never used them and I don't intend to start now. Farewell, Miss Wynter, until we meet again." With that he was gone, and a much happier Charlotte hugged herself gleefully, and wondered what the next few weeks would bring.

***

In the darkness of the carriage, Rev. Underwood tried hard to see his brother's face and read the expression upon it, but it was an impossible task and he could only assume that his silence betokened a meeting which had been even more traumatic than he had at first supposed.

"Charlotte took it badly then?" He asked diffidently, unable to bear the suspense any longer. C.H. appeared to be at his most absent-minded, for he murmured, "Took what badly?"

"Your rejection of her!" Answered the vicar, a trifle testily—he had endured an extremely trying evening and was in no mood for his sibling's vagaries.

"Who said I rejected her?" Responded Mr. Underwood, and had the supreme satisfaction of finding his clerical companion for once entirely lost for words.

CHAPTER NINE

("Atra Cura."—Black care—melancholy.)

So much occurred during Mr. Underwood's week's absence that he was barely missed—except of course by his two most avid admirers, Charlotte Wynter and Verity Chapell. They both pined for him, Charlotte, with loud sighs and dramatic posturings, Verity, quietly, but with much deeper misery, since she now knew of his interest in Charlotte and her own hopeless adoration.

Fortunately for Verity's pride, the arrival of Rev. Underwood's new curate quite overshadowed everything, and the whole village was far too interested in him to notice her melancholy.

A personable young man, with a decidedly frivolous attitude towards the ministry, Mr. Septimus Pollock rather took Bracken Tor by storm. The villagers' past experience of clergymen had altogether failed to prepare them for the advent of this whirlwind of a man, who, it seemed, could not enter a room without bursting through the door as though swept along in the wake of some unseen tidal wave, who could not talk quietly, who laughed boisterously and enthused about everything. Half an hour in his company left one staggering beneath the impact of his personality, and usually with a banging headache.

He arrived in a private carriage, monogrammed tastefully upon the door, and it became increasingly obvious that he was a member of an extremely wealthy family—in fact he made no secret of it. Being the seventh child (Hence the name Septimus) of a titled gentleman, he had been persuaded to follow family tradition in joining the church, since his two older brothers were heir to the family estates and in the army respectively. His sisters were, not surprisingly, well-married and, as he blissfully informed the shocked Misses Dadd, continually making him an uncle yet again!

Rev. Underwood tried to bear the invasion of his home with fortitude, but he could not help wondering how long it would be before his brother, unable to endure the disturbance, packed his bags and took himself off back to the comparative peace of Cambridge.

His other, rather more pressing, concern was shared by a few of the more devout members of his congregation—how on earth was Septimus going to conduct himself within the portals of the church? Rev. Underwood closed his eyes in the most exquisite of agonies at the thought of the ancient rafters ringing with the booming tones of his curate.

The first of his difficulties was postponed for an unspecified period, for when Mr. Underwood returned from his travels on the Friday evening, he took himself straight to his room without seeing anyone but his brother, and informed him that he was unwell and would he please acquaint Miss Wynter of the fact.

Knowing his brother as he did, the Reverend gentleman was aware that far from being unwell, C.H. was actually in the throes of one of his periodic fits of gloom, and it was probably his discoveries which had sent him there.

There was little anyone could do at these times, so the vicar simply provided his brother with food and drink, which he knew would not be consumed, and went to the study to write a note to Miss Wynter.

The following morning when a whirlwind swept through the house, it did not, for once, betoken the arrival of the curate.

Upon answering the jangling summons of the door bell, Rev. Underwood found himself thrust aside by the pink-cheeked and much agitated Miss Wynter, "Where is Mr. Underwood?" She demanded, dramatically tossing the long train of her riding habit over her arm, "Is his illness serious?"

Unwisely Rev. Underwood actually attempted to answer her questions, "Naturally he is in his room, but I can assure you . . ."

"Which is his room?"

"The one directly above us, but . . ."

Before he could say any more, she was running up the stairs and he heard the clatter of her boots across the landing. Without so much as a knock, his brother's bedroom door crashed open, bouncing violently against the chest of drawers which happened to stand to the left of it.

He was well aware that he ought not leave his brother to the mercy of an hysterical female, nor should he leave that same young lady in a gentleman's room unchaperoned, he nevertheless raised his eyes heavenward in a mute appeal for understanding, then quietly went into his study and closed the door behind him.

Mr. Underwood meanwhile had been rudely awoken from his slumbers by the crashing of wood against wood, and sat bolt upright with a very unromantic greeting, "Good God, woman! What the devil is amiss!" Blearily realizing that his visitor was not, as he had supposed, the housekeeper with his early morning tea, but an extremely breathless Charlotte, he hastily pulled the covers up to his chin and demanded, "Great Heavens Charlotte! Is the house afire or something!"

"The Reverend sent me word that you were ill, and I knew you would not break your promise to me unless it was serious, so I have sent for Dr. Herbert!"

His shocked expression swiftly changed to one of extreme irritation, "Dr. Herbert!" the quite justified castigation which sprang to his lips was quelled by the tragic expression on her face. It was rather pleasant, he discovered, to have concern for his health engender such panic. He found himself smiling, "Well, as it happens, I did have something to discuss with the good Doctor. Now, perhaps you would like to go downstairs. I'm sure my brother would be delighted to make you some tea, and I shall join you presently."

"Are . . . are you not really ill, then?" She asked, with a decided tremble to her lower lip.

"Not precisely ill. Merely very tired and brought rather low by my sojourn in the Capital, that is all. There was really no need for you to fret yourself. I only asked Gil to tell you of my return so that you should not think I had broken my word to you."

She drew herself up to her full height, "Oh!" She exclaimed crossly, "How provoking it is that I constantly make a fool of myself where you are concerned!"

He kindly tried to hide his amusement, avoiding her eye by running his fingers through his already disordered hair, "Do not be so harsh upon yourself!"

"No! Perhaps I should be a little harsher with you! All this is your fault! If you would stop treating me like a child, and take me into your confidence, perhaps I should not be thrown into turmoil every time something happens."

He looked at her across the room. She wore a wine-coloured velvet habit, beautifully fitted to her figure, and her breast still rose and fell deeply with indignation and breathlessness. She made a quite charming picture and he suddenly wondered how a creature so lovely could show such a deep interest in himself. He knew he was far from being any woman's ideal. His youth had long gone, and with it any pretensions of furthering his career, or expanding his bank balance. He had nothing to offer a young woman of such warmth, vivacity and charm. It was because these thoughts came into his mind that, instead of doing as she begged and confiding in her, he found himself coldly withdrawing from her, "Please go downstairs."

The expression on her face left him in no doubt that he had hurt her. She turned on her heel without another word, slamming the door behind her. He was left staring at the much abused panels, and listening to the clatter of her boots across the oak boards growing gradually fainter.

When he entered the drawing room some time later, he found Dr. Herbert waiting for him, as well as Charlotte, his brother and the curate. Before any introductions could be attempted, however, Mr. Pollock was crossing the room, his hand outstretched, and his great voice booming, "By Jupiter! Snuff Underwood as I live and breathe!"

It took Mr. Underwood a few seconds to place his erstwhile student, but when he did, his dismay was comic to behold. Politeness dictated that he try to disguise it, but his acting was not of the highest standard, "Mr. Pollock! What, pray tell, brings you here?" The hope in his tone did not escape anyone as he added, "A short visit, I presume?" His hand was grasped in a bone-grinding act of fervour and he could not restrain the wince which momentarily marred his features.

"Good Grief, no! I'm the new curate. I'm here indefinitely! And having met the lovely Miss Wynter, I can't say I'm sorry!"

"Curate?" Mr. Underwood managed to smile, albeit rather bleakly, "How . . . er . . . charming for us all!" He threw a glance at his brother which clearly said, "How could you do this to me?" And all Gil could do in return was shrug his shoulders in mute apology.

Dr. Herbert had also risen and now came to his prospective patient's aid.

"I believe you are not feeling quite the thing, Underwood. By the look of you, you should have remained in bed. Shall we retire to the study and see what can be done for you?"

"Yes. Thank you, Dr. Herbert. I must own I was feeling a little better, until I rose. I think I may be suffering a relapse! You will all forgive me, I trust?" He added, speaking to the room in general, then he caught Charlotte's eye. "I did not think you would wait, Miss Wynter. I do apologize. Perhaps I might be permitted to call upon you tomorrow?"

"Tomorrow is Sunday." The vicar gently reminded him. It occurred to Mr. Underwood to point out to his brother that he was on holiday and that the constraints religion placed upon him in University life should not necessarily be repeated here, but he was generally a kind hearted man and he could not bring himself to thus embarrass the man who was, after all, the priest of the parish.

"I do beg your pardon, Gil. My jauntings had quite put that out of my head. Monday, then, Miss Wynter?"

"As you wish, Mr. Underwood. Good day." She swept past him, studiously avoiding his glance, but ensuring that her train brushed against his legs and that the faintest whiff of her perfume assailed his nostrils. A close observer might have noticed that a muscle in his cheek twitched as his teeth were clenched.

He gave no other indication of his intense desire to follow her.

In the study, Dr. Herbert was the first to break the silence, "You seem preoccupied, Underwood—or should I call you 'Snuff'?" He grinned playfully, but his companion was not amused, "Damn the boy! How dare he use that ludicrous sobriquet! And what the devil is Gil about, bringing him here! Does he not think I see enough of my boys without inviting them to haunt me in my free time?"

"Calm down, my friend! You know Gilbert did not invite him! Now, put Pollock from your mind and tell me what has occurred to send you into such a pucker! I know it takes more than a highly unsuitable clergyman to disturb your equanimity!"

Mr. Underwood could have mentioned several things which had made his legendary calm boil into raging turmoil, but he confined himself to his trip to London.

"Straight to the point, as always, dear fellow!" The tension suddenly left his slim frame and he sank wearily into a chair, "Well, as I had suspected, the girl arrived by stage, but she did not take the Carrier's cart from Calden to here. She either walked or was collected by someone with their own vehicle. Since I knew that taking on board any passenger who had not previously booked a ticket is frowned upon by the coaching companies, it was obvious that my first step must be to try and find their records of a year ago. It was a quest which proved to be surprisingly simple. I had the good fortune to be dealing with a man who took his duties most seriously and was meticulous in his bookkeeping. Such a fellow would normally have driven me to the borders of frenzy with his nit-picking and preoccupation with trivialities, but on this occasion I could have kissed his prissy face!"

In spite of his vague disapproval of the task Underwood had set himself, the doctor found his interest was engaged, "You mean you found a name?"

Underwood nodded, "Naturally, I at first found dozens of possibilities, but with the help of my little friend, I gradually whittled down the list. Some had travelled again at later dates, so I was able to dismiss them. Finally we brought the list down to only five, since Calden is not one of the more popular destinations, being nothing more really than a place to stop briefly and change horses. Only one of those was a female."

"And her name?"

"Unfortunately both that and her address were false—and very unimaginative. The victim called herself Mary Smith."

"What makes you so sure it was an assumed name?"

"I hardly think she would go to the trouble to providing a false address, then use her true name!"

"You are positive the address was false."

"Oh yes. I went there. It was a mansion belonging to a rather

82

beefy gentleman and his pale wife. They had never heard of Mary Smith, had no knowledge of any servant who had left their employ in the past four years and certainly resented the vague connection with a murder, however far away it might be. Mary Smith was nothing to do with them, I am certain."

"Presumably that was as much as you could achieve?"

"Not at all. Our clerk was so highly organized he was able to furnish me with the names of the coach men who had been on that particular run. I was fortunate enough to track them to a seedy little tavern which is a regular haunt for their brotherhood."

"Good God, is it possible that they were able to furnish you with a description?"

"Not a good one—after all, over a year has passed! He could not, for example, remember the colour of her hair, since it was mostly covered by her bonnet. Her eyes he thought were brown—dark anyway. But the girl was remembered for one very good, but rather tawdry reason. It would appear that, young as she undoubtedly was, she was a prostitute—and rather a hardened one, at that!"

The doctor was unsurprised by this disclosure, but noted that it had disheartened his companion more than he was admitting.

"I did warn you that she was not entirely innocent, Underwood." he said softly.

"Yes. I know. It was foolish of me to suppose otherwise, but the truth was a little disconcerting, to say the least. The driver pointed out to me that it was not every day that a girl so young, and dressed as soberly as a governess, should attempt to solicit him for the price of a meal."

"Was that why he remembered her?"

"It was. He told me that he not only gave her the money, but a friendly warning of the trouble she was courting. He stated that he took nothing in return for the florin."

"Did you believe him?"

"Strangely enough I did. He told me he had daughters of his own and he had found her predicament distressing. I would like to think that the penultimate contact she had with another human being was that last act of kindness. She was shown little enough mercy thereafter."

"And her character in life has not deterred you from discovering her killer? You do not now feel that she might have courted death by her behaviour?"

Mr. Underwood leapt to his feet, suddenly filled with the energy of indignation, "I hope you ask that question in order to fill the position of advocatus Diaboli! If I thought you really felt that way . . . !"

The doctor smiled and held up his hand as though to ward off a physical assault, "Calm yourself, Underwood. The Devil's

Advocate indeed I am! I simply wanted to know whether you intend to go on. I am a doctor—one life is as precious as another to me!"

Rather deflated, Underwood sank back into his seat, "I'm sorry. I do not travel well. And I detest London!"

"Think nothing of it. Tell me, what is your next step?"

"Well, with the, admittedly vague, description, I was able to take out an advertisement in the London papers. Since I am now convinced that her back-ground was an extremely lowly one, I have stated that anyone with information will learn something to their advantage. That usually brings all manner of nastiness from under stones! In the meantime, I intend to quietly pursue my enquiries here and in Calden. I find it very difficult to believe that the girl was in Bracken Tor for upwards of twenty-four hours and was seen by no-one."

"Good luck, my friend, but I fear you will find our murder a closed book here! It is not something that anyone who lives here is proud to admit to! Your brother's predecessor stirred up a mess of pottage with the same subject and he hasn't been forgiven yet!"

"I'm prepared to risk it." Said Mr. Underwood, with a smile.

"You may be—but is your brother?"

"I rather wish you had not said that." Answered Mr. Underwood, displaying, for the first time, a trace of rueful consideration for his sibling's feelings.

Dr. Herbert looked thoughtful, "I think you should be careful, Underwood, and not just for your brother's sake!"

CHAPTER TEN

("Non Tali Auxilio!"—Not with such aid!)

Sunday dawned bright and clear and Mr. Underwood found himself rather wishing his brother had chosen another vocation in life. He was not in a Sunday mood and there was nothing to be done about it. He had a feverish desire to get on with things, feeling that far too much time had already been wasted, but he could not hurt Gil's feelings, nor his reputation, so he rose early and dressed himself in his customary dark garb.

The tolling of a single bell was already drawing the devout towards the church porch, and he was able to distinguish the Wynter clan amongst them. By craning his neck as he struggled to tie his cravat, he was able to peer out of his bedroom window and watch their progress almost to the actual door of the church. He did not bother to ask himself why he should be prepared to risk his appearance by indulging in such contortions, merely observing that Charlotte was indeed present and that she was looking rather more demure than usual in her Sunday cape and bonnet.

He entered the church some minutes after everyone else had settled and tried to slip unobtrusively into a pew located at the back. He was unsuccessful. Mr. Bellew, the verger, was hovering in anticipation of his arrival, and determinedly grasped his elbow and ushered him up the aisle and into the bench reserved exclusively for the use of the vicar's family. Mr. Underwood had hoped to avoid this, since the 'family' usually consisted of a doting wife and several children, ranged in order of size. Such a position meant that he was now in full view of the entire congregation and could not hope to either slip away early or fall asleep during the sermon. The only advantage he could see was that the Wynter Family pew was directly opposite and he could covertly observe the family.

Sir Henry was, not surprisingly, absent from the gathering, but all the others were present. Charlotte was at the end of the seat, so he had an uninterrupted view of her profile. Next to her were her sisters, then came Harry and Edwin. Miss Chapell, he noticed, had been relegated to the bench behind and looked rather tired and pale. He wondered vaguely if Edwin Wynter had been taunting her again, then dismissed the thought. There was little he could do in her defence without drawing unwanted attention to her. For him to single her out in any way would simply, in the long run, make her life so much more unbearable. He knew the Edwins of the world, and they were nasty, vicious and usually malicious. If she really offended him, Miss Chapell would find that his spite could well follow her, even if she tried to find other employment. Mr. Underwood made a mental note to say something of the kind to her, should he see her alone at any time. It would do her no harm to be warned.

Rev. Underwood, having been a student of human nature for many years, was only too aware that any sermon he might give would be of far less interest to his parishioners than his brother and the new curate, who, mercifully silent, sat next to the altar, he therefore had not bothered to overtax himself in writing a profusion of wisdom which was very unlikely to be heeded. His sermon was short and almost before everyone knew what they were about, they were leaving the comparative gloom of the church and blinking in the sunlight outside.

No one seemed to be in any particular hurry and very soon the area before the porch was crowded and the babble of voices grew louder. Charlotte pretended to chat to Mr. Bellew, but in truth she barely heard a word the poor man said, being more interested in watching the door for the advent of Mr. Underwood. He was a long time in coming and she was beginning to suspect that he had left through the vestry—probably with the sole intention of avoiding her. A pang of humiliation drove the blood from her cheeks as she recalled how she had forced herself into his notice, and how naively she had admitted her feelings for him. She knew, for the first time in her life, how it felt to regret most bitterly her words and actions. She wished she could die, there and then! Oh, to be able to cease breathing, to stop one's heart at will and never have to face the man again! What a fool he must think her, and how she had embarrassed him!

He stepped out of the darkness of the porch at that moment and immediately catching her eye, he smiled warmly at her. Charlotte almost fainted with the flood of relief which swept over her. The smile which she gave him in return hid nothing from those who observed it. There was a softness to her lips, a tenderness in her eyes which caressed every line of his face as she looked at him.

Only two of the gathered company were watching this exchange of glances and it engendered very different reactions in

86

each. Verity Chapell could scarcely bear the pain of realisation. She knew now, without any doubt, that Mr. Underwood would never look at her the way he looked at Charlotte, but she also knew that she would have given all she possessed to have been the recipient. The heavy, ponderous beating of her heart was making her feel sick and faint. She had to get away. Too many people were crushing against her. Miserably aware that her departure would not even be noticed, she walked swiftly down the path towards the lych gate, trying not to stumble over the uneven stone which seemed to rise and fall beneath her feet, blurred by her tear-filled eyes. Only Rev. Underwood saw her go, and he was unable to follow her since tradition dictated that he keep his post until all the rest were gone.

Harry Wynter scowled angrily when he saw his sister ogle the new-comer. He could barely restrain himself from dragging her unceremoniously away from the spot, but the thought of her own fury tempered his decision. Charlotte could be very volatile when she was crossed and was not above grabbing and hurling the first thing which came to hand, without the least care whether it be a cushion or a knife! He had, in the past, ducked and run when Charlotte's ire had been aroused, and he thought too much of his good-looks to risk having them marred by a lucky shot.

No, this was one matter which was going to need careful handling. He fully intended to end this touching little affair, but it was going to have to be done with great delicacy. There was no point at all in provoking the unpredictable Charlotte into elopement!

Greetings having been politely exchanged, Charlotte smiled rather shyly at Mr. Underwood and asked, "Are you feeling better this morning?"

"Oh yes. I'm quite recovered now, thank you. How is your ankle?"

Before she could reply, Harry broke rudely into the conversation, "Well enough for her to go riding! I think my sister has made rather more fuss than the injury warranted!"

Mr. Underwood languidly shifted his gaze to the boy's face, "Fuss? As I recall the fuss was made by Miss Wynter's sisters. She herself showed remarkable restraint and considerable courage in the face of a very unpleasant experience."

Charlotte blushed, but her eyes shone with pleasure as she demurred. Mr. Underwood offered her his arm, "May I escort you to your carriage, Miss Wynter?"

"We have no carriage today, Mr. Underwood. It is Sunday."

Mr. Underwood was used to town and had quite forgotten the strict rulings about what was and was not permitted on Sunday. The Sabbath was not held quite so sacrosanct by town dwellers as it obviously was in the country. He began to realise that the supposed freedom of the countryside was promising to become even more imprisoning than the confining walls of the University.

"Then I shall allow you to escort me to the vicarage gate before I bid you farewell." He tempered hastily.

"Shall I see you tomorrow?"

"Well, I do have a great deal of work to do, but I can spare you an hour. Shall we say eleven o'clock?"

Harry expected a torrent of abuse to pour from her lips at this 'gracious' allowance of one hour of the man's precious time, but to his surprise, his sister took it remarkably calmly. "I shall have the horses ready saddled and you shall show me if you really are the poor horseman you claim!" They exchanged a smile and fell into step beside one another. Harry sulkily followed, feeling like an annoying little boy, and not caring very much for the sensation.

***

The period of quiet reflection which Mr. Underwood was enjoying in the gloomy parlour of the vicarage could not last once Mr. Pollock made his entrance. Underwood started violently as the door flew open and Pollock crossed the room, rubbing his hands together and saying heartily, "All alone Mr. Underwood?"

"I was." He muttered, attempting to sink lower in his chair in the vain hope that he would curl up and disappear entirely.

"Then you'll be glad of some company, I dare swear."

Pollock plumped himself onto a settee raising a cloud of fine dust and causing the legs to creak ominously. Mr. Underwood watched in horrified fascination as the piece of furniture sank beneath the weight. He waited for the whole thing to collapse completely and was sadly disappointed when it merely settled.

"Don't you have anything religious to do, it being Sunday?" He asked hopefully, when he finally decided that nothing was going to break.

"No. Rev. Underwood has told me to take my time over settling in. He says he can manage quite alone."

Mr. Underwood found this utterly unsurprising, "Oh, I think he's just being polite. I'm sure he needs you to do something."

Mr. Pollock laughed, "If I didn't know better, Snuff, I'd think you were trying to get rid of me!"

"Perish the thought!" Replied Mr. Underwood and returned his attention back to the papers which were spread across the table before him.

Pollock rose and joined him by the table which stood under the window, "What are you doing?"

"Planning a murder." Said Underwood with inspired sarcasm.

"Really? Writing a book or something?"

Mr. Underwood sighed and laid down his pen. Obviously he was not going to be allowed to work in peace, "Not exactly, Pollock. Tell me, are you planning to visit any of your new parishioners in the next few days?"

"Yes, as a matter of fact I am."

"Do you think I might tag along with you?"

"Certainly—but why should you want to?"

"Merely interest in my fellow man."

"Are you on the scent of something odd, Snuff?"

Mr. Underwood was rather taken aback, "What do you mean by that?"

Mr. Pollock drew up a chair and sat down, "I seem to remember you had quite a reputation for solving little puzzles, like who was stealing books from the college library, and who broke into the Bursar's office. You always pretended an interest in your fellow man on those occasions too. What's really going on?"

"You recall too much, Pollock! Nothing is going on, and I wouldn't tell you if there was. It would be as good as posting a bulletin on the church door for the whole village to read!"

"That's hardly fair!" Protested the curate, his hands spread in appeal, the very picture of outraged innocence, "I can hold my tongue when it's needed!"

"My dear Pollock, if—and I only say if!—there was a mystery to be solved, it would require tact and delicacy, neither of which, I think you must agree, are your strongest traits!"

"I knew it! You are on to something! Tell me what it is. I could help!"

"Help and you don't mix, Mr. Pollock!"

"Snuff!" Begged the curate, and Mr. Underwood rose to his feet in irritation, "Dammit! Will you stop using that ridiculous name!"

"It suits you!" Grinned Mr. Pollock.

"No it does not!"

Mr. Pollock ignored him, "What time do you want to leave in the morning?"

"As early as you like, but I have an appointment between eleven and twelve."

"With Miss Wynter? I must say Snuff, I never knew you were such a dark horse!"

Mr. Underwood began to gather his papers together, "I shan't pretend to understand what that remark is supposed to mean!"

His companion laughed heartily, "A lovely young filly like that! And you at your age!"

"Am I to assume from that you have counted her teeth as well as my own?"

Mr. Underwood wondered what was happening to him, sarcasm seemed to be the order of the day—and on a Sunday too! "I don't need to look in anyone's mouth to know that you are a lucky old dog!" Countered Mr. Pollock. Mr. Underwood gave him a look which bordered upon loathing, "I'm not exactly in my dotage, Pollock, and a ride together does not indicate a calling of the banns!"

"You don't have an understanding, then?"

"No!" He was being too emphatic, and he knew it. Pollock was grinning in an odiously knowing manner which made Mr. Underwood long to have him back under his tutelage just for a few hours!

"I presume you won't object if I try my hand, then?" Mr. Underwood wondered why everything to do with courtship had to be couched in such coarse terms.

"You presume a great deal too much!"

"Well, perhaps we should let the lady decide? May the best man win?" Pollock held out his hand. Mr. Underwood hesitated only momentarily before he grasped the proffered hand.

"The best man? I don't think I have any contest, Mr. Pollock! Your trouble is that you are too young!"

"Perhaps that is the advantage I ought to press." Replied the incorrigible Pollock with a friendly grin.

Mr. Underwood decided that he required a change of topic and so managed to repress any vague desire to answer this remark, "Have you given any thought to which of your parishioners is to be the lucky recipient of your first visit?" He asked, as he retook his seat.

Successfully sidetracked, Mr. Pollock joined him at the table, "Well, the large house directly opposite the vicarage seemed as good a starting point as any. I understand from your brother that it belongs to a rather wealthy retired manufacturer and his wife. It certainly wouldn't do any harm to flatter them with my first visit!"

His listener could think of several ways in which a visit could do irreparable damage, but he kindly did not voice them.

"I think that is an excellent idea—but I wonder why a wealthy man should retire to this rather out-of-the-way little place?"

"You think that suspicious?" Asked the curate eagerly. Mr. Underwood frowned quellingly, "I think nothing of the kind! I'm merely interested . . ."

"In human nature!" Mr. Pollock completed his sentence for him, "Yes, I know! But I also know there is more to this than meets the eye, and I'm going to find out what it is if it kills me!"

Mr. Underwood eyed him with loathing, "If you don't mind, I shall go back to planning the perfect murder!"

"Feel free, old chap. I shan't disturb you, have no fear!"
With this kind assurance, Mr. Pollock drew a pack of cards from
his pocket and began to riffle them between his fingers in a most
irritating manner, "You don't mind if I try Patience?" He asked
innocently. Mr. Underwood smiled weakly, "Believe me, Mr.
Pollock, it is what you do best!"

CHAPTER ELEVEN

("Festina Lente."—Make haste slowly.)

As Mr. Underwood wandered into the dining room the next morning, sniffing appreciatively at the aroma of hot chocolate, he was rather surprised to be grasped firmly by the hand, "Chuffy, my dear fellow!" The vicar's features were adorned with a smile of pure affection coupled with intense gratitude, and Mr. Underwood could not help but glance over his shoulder to see if he was being followed by the person who should have been receiving this accolade, for he was quite sure he had done nothing to deserve it. Realizing that there was no-one behind him, he decided that his brother was indeed speaking to him and no-one else, he asked tentatively, "Gil? Is there something I should know?"

"Only that you have my eternal gratitude!" Answered the vicar, his voice warm and alive with emotion.

Mr. Underwood allowed himself to be led to the table, made no protest when his brother held his chair for him as he sat, and did not even murmur when he felt his brother briefly, and affectionately, grip his shoulder before seating himself at the other end of the table.

"Why do I feel as though I have somehow missed a very large portion of my life?" he asked diffidently, as he spread his napkin across his knees and began to serve himself from the assembled dishes.

The vicar was evidently in a remarkably good mood, because for once his brother's apparent vagueness did not irritate him, "What do you mean, Chuffy?"

"Well, you seem to think I have, out of the goodness of my heart, done you some kindness. I must say I am delighted that I have been of service, but I cannot for the life of me, imagine how I have done it!"

"You must surely know that in volunteering to escort Mr. Pollock about the village you have removed a great weight from

92

my mind?"

"Have I indeed? That really is most gratifying—I had rather thought you would disapprove."

The vicar heaped kidneys onto his plate, "Why should you imagine that? I was terrified at the prospect of loosing Septimus onto my unsuspecting parishioners!"

Mr. Underwood allowed himself a covert glance in his brother's direction and observing his happy expression did not have the heart to spoil the mood—as a reminder of his reasons would surely do, "Oh, I simply thought you would consider my meddling insufferable."

"Good gracious, no! There is meddling and there is timely intervention—and anything which keeps Septimus Pollock out of trouble definitely comes under the latter heading!"

Since Septimus made his entrance at that moment, Mr. Underwood was spared the necessity of finding an answer. He had to admire his brother for his coolness, when, completely unperturbed, he greeted his curate most warmly, "Good morning, Mr. Pollock, pray come and break your fast. Mrs. Selby has provided a vast repast so I trust you are hungry."

Mr. Underwood, with his literary mind, could not help but notice his brother's musical lilt and his use of rhyme, and thought it denoted a mood of extreme magnanimity.

Mr. Pollock needed no second bidding. "Do you have any plan for us to follow, Mr. Pollock?" Asked Mr. Underwood, when he had recovered from the shock of seeing just how much food the curate was piling onto his plate.

"Plan?" Mr. Pollock looked startled, "What d'ye mean, Plan?" The very idea of actually stopping to think of a scheme before embarking upon anything was a notion both novel and unpleasant to the impetuous Septimus.

"Do not panic, my dear Septimus. My brother does not require drawn maps and written campaigns. He merely wishes to know if you have any particular order in which you intend to make your visits. In short, where are you going first?" The vicar's pleasant smile took away any hint of sarcasm which might possibly have stung the curate—though that was a doubtful eventuality.

"Oh. Well why did he not say so?" Mr. Pollock asked a trifle testily, and returned his attention to his neglected meal, "I told him yesterday that I thought we would try the Renshaw's first, then carry on down the High Street."

"In the general direction of the Wynter Arms?" Guessed Mr. Underwood perceptively.

"That's right." grinned Mr. Pollock. The Reverend waited for his brother to protest, since he was not generally a man who frequented Public Houses, but to his surprise, Mr. Underwood made no demur.

The truth of the matter was that Mr. Underwood was well aware that any public house was a hotbed of local gossip and he would find no better place to hear all the news. For once in his life, he was going to relish the smokey, dim atmosphere of a farming hostelry.

Some time later, Mr. Underwood and Mr. Pollock met at the garden gate and set forth on their journey of discovery. All who saw them thought them strange bedfellows, but neither were aware of anything odd in their alliance. Mr. Underwood could think of no better facade behind which he could hide. Naturally, as a newcomer, Mr. Pollock would be more than fascinated by any information about his new home, and that he should be discreetly guided by the vicar's brother was no surprise to anyone who had already met him.

For his part, Mr. Pollock was simply grateful that he should have company to relieve the tedium of a necessary, but unpleasant task.

Their first port of call could scarcely have been nearer, since the home of the Renshaws' was situated directly opposite to the vicarage. Within moments they had crossed the dusty road and were ringing the doorbell.

An extremely youthful maid answered their summons and looked terrified at the prospect of having to speak to them. Mr. Underwood thought she could not have been more than eleven or twelve and therefore he smiled kindly and bent slightly towards her as he said, "Are your Master and Mistress at home?"

"Yes sir. Oh! No, I'm not supposed to say that am I? Er . . . Oh dear!"

"Perhaps if you ask our names, you could then go and see if they are at home?"

She looked immensely relieved, "Yes. That's right! Could I have your names please?"

The names duly given, she went off, her lips still framing the words, lest she forget them before she reach her goal.

Mr. Renshaw, as the vicar had informed them, was a wealthy man. He had been a very successful manufacturer in Manchester, owning businesses as diverse as a candle factory, a glass makers and various others. Having never been blessed with children, and possessing no other close relations to whom he could bequeath his factories, he had sold them all and now lived very comfortably on the proceeds. Why he should have chosen to retire to Bracken Tor when he had the whole country to choose from, Rev. Underwood did not know. For his own part, Mr. Underwood fully intended to find out!

The little maid returned and showed them into a lavishly decorated drawing room, with the information that both her Master and Mistress would join them presently.

Mr. Underwood winced as Pollock lowered himself heavily

94

into the most spindly-legged chair in the room. It creaked a little but did not break. Pollock was completely unaware of his companion's fears and gazed about the room approvingly, "This is a rum go, Snuff, don't you think?" He asked, making no attempt to lower his tone to anything even vaguely resembling a whisper.

"What is?" Hissed Mr. Underwood, in irritation.

"This place, of course! Look at it! It's huge—and yet he's chosen to build it in this God-forsaken spot, slap-bang in the middle of a farming village, between rows of cottages!"

"Good Heavens, Pollock! Lower your voice, they will hear you! And I'll thank you to remember that this is not a 'God-forsaken' spot! My brother is doing his utmost to ensure that never happens!" Underwood was being quite serious when he made this remark, but Mr. Pollock evidently thought it a grand joke, and guffawed appreciatively.

The door opened and their hosts entered. Mr. Underwood crossed the room swiftly, "Good morning! Pray excuse the intrusion, but Mr. Pollock and I were most eager to introduce ourselves to my brother's parishioners."

The Renshaws were both looking towards Mr. Pollock, seemingly startled by his size and the volume of his laughter, which still rang about the room. Mr. Underwood hastily thrust his hand into Mr. Renshaw's and shook it vigorously. This seemed to bring his attention back to the vicar's brother and he dragged his gaze away from the curate and summoned a smile, "It is a great pleasure to meet you Mr. Underwood. My wife and I have heard a great deal about you."

"Yes, indeed." Murmured his tiny wife, who was almost hiding behind him, "Your brother has made a great impression, Mr. Underwood. Such a charming man."

"Thank-you, Mrs. Renshaw. Shall I tell him you said so?" Mr. Pollock was stunned to hear his erstwhile tutor speak almost teasingly to the woman, and she in her turn giggled shyly and blushed, "Oh dear me, no! I'm a married woman!" Her husband was gazing fondly down at her, smilingly took her hand and pulled it through the crook of his arm in a mildly possessive way, "Shame on you, Bess, for being such a flirt!"

Since the couple could not be a day less than seventy, Mr. Pollock found this interchange rather puzzling, it did not occur to him for a second that Mr. Underwood had handled an awkward introduction with considerable aplomb. His intuition had told him that this devoted pair were rarely apart, and that the way to the man's heart was through his wife's happiness. She had obviously been an attractive woman and in her youth a little mild flirtation would have been her sole pleasure in life. Nothing pleased a woman more than to think she was still a shameless flirt, no matter what her age. Mr. Underwood employed the same trick, very successfully, with his mother. He found he could make her agree to almost anything if he assured her everyone would think her terribly daring.

Mr. Underwood saw nothing odd in the fact that he could flirt quite charmingly with elderly ladies, but was crippled by shyness when confronted by young women. Mr. Pollock thought it very odd indeed, but now was not the time to mention it. The initial difficulties over, they were invited to sit and offered refreshment, an offer which Mr. Pollock wished to take up, but which his companion firmly refused. Conversation flowed easily after that, though Mr. Pollock found it extremely difficult to interject, for almost every time he opened his mouth, Mr. Underwood skillfully interrupted.

When he felt the Renshaws were sufficiently at ease with him, Mr. Underwood risked a few pertinent questions.

"You have a lovely home, Mr. Renshaw, but what made you build it here in Bracken Tor? Surely somewhere nearer to town would have been more convenient?"

"Oh, but Mr. Renshaw was born here, Mr. Underwood! Did you not know?"

"Really? I had no idea you were a local man."

"Yes. I've always felt the need to visit at regular intervals, so it seemed natural to move here when I sold my businesses."

"I can imagine it is a place which possesses you body and soul! I have been here only a very short time, and already I find it fascinating. When one is born in a town or city, one tends to think of the countryside being terribly dull, but nothing could be further from the truth! I understand you have had your share of excitements and tragedies here in Bracken Tor."

"Oh, we manage to keep ourselves occupied." Was it his imagination or did Mr. Renshaw suddenly seem a little wary?

Mrs. Renshaw had no such reservations, "Mr. Underwood, you've no idea! Quite, quite dreadful! Poor Mrs. Hazelhurst!"

"Mrs. Hazelhurst?" Mr. Underwood had been expecting a quite different tragedy to be mentioned, so this rather threw him.

"Yes. Have you not heard?"

"Now, now, my dear! You know I don't like gossip."

"Well, neither do I George! But Mr. Underwood did ask!" Everyone in the room was well aware that Mr. Underwood did not ask, but all kindly refrained from pointing out so small a thing and allowed her to continue, "She was killed by her husband."

"Now Bess! That was never proved! He said it was an accident and the court believed him!"

"Well, I don't! But frankly I thought she provoked him into it! What a bitter, evil-minded woman she was! Never a good word to say for anyone—especially not her husband! And he such a hard worker! I felt terribly sorry for him, I really did!"

"When did all this happen?"

"A few months ago. Hazelhurst still lives at Hill farm, but no-one ever sees him now. He refuses to come into the village, I think he imagines everyone is pointing and staring."

"Which of course they are!" intercepted Mr. Renshaw, with a cynical smile.

"Oh, I don't think so." Countered his wife reasonably.

"Well it would certainly appear that you are no stranger to sudden death! My brother pointed out a poignant little grave to me the other day."

"Do you mean the girl they found in Shady Copse?" Mr. Renshaw's tone was quite sharp. Now Mr. Underwood was under no illusions. The older man was definitely uncomfortable discussing the murder—but why?

"Yes, I believe that was where they discovered her. My brother tells me that the culprit was never caught."

"Not for that crime, no. But who is to say that he did not do something similar somewhere else, and has long been hanged for his crimes! I dare swear he swings on a gibbet even as we speak!" Mr. Renshaw gave the curious impression that he was trying to convince himself as well as his listeners.

"Doubtless you are right, my dear sir! And now Pollock and I must take our leave. Thank-you for your time."

"The pleasure has been entirely ours, Mr. Underwood. Pray call again, and please give my warmest regards to your brother. You must all come for dinner some evening!"

"That would be delightful, thank-you, Mrs. Renshaw."

Mr. Renshaw gestured to his wife to remain seated, "Don't tire yourself, my love. I shall see our guests to the door."

Underwood guessed that the older man had something to say which he didn't wish his wife to hear, and he proved to be correct.

"You'll forgive me for being so direct, young man, but would you mind not discussing the girl's murder again before my wife. She has a very vivid imagination, and I don't wish her to be upset all over again as she was last year."

Mr. Underwood hid the smile which was prompted by his being referred to as 'young man' and his expression could not have been more grave as he said, "Mr. Renshaw, pray accept my humblest apologies. Not for anything in the world would I distress your charming wife! I can't imagine how I allowed the conversation to touch upon so unsavoury a subject. I hold myself entirely responsible and can only promise you that nothing of the kind will every occur again!" The old gentleman's face cleared, as though a great weight had been lifted from his shoulders. He smiled, "Pray think nothing more about it. Good day to you sir!"

The vicar's brother walked down the path towards the gate,

but he still looked serious. He had instinctively liked George Renshaw and his wife, and he had half believed the old man's tale about his wife's nerves on the subject of unknown murderers, but there was something wrong. She had quite happily discussed a man who she believed to be a wife-killer, so why should the other killing frighten her? Mr. Underwood would have liked to have struck Renshaw and his wife from his mental list, but he was sorry to have to place a question mark beside their names. Renshaw openly admitted that he had been born in Bracken Tor, and that he had regularly visited the place over the years.

Would a man of his age have the strength to strike down a young, healthy woman? Mr. Underwood did not know, but he had begun to realize that in this situation, anything was possible.

Mr. Pollock was inclined to be sulky as they traversed the few yards to the first of the cottages which were to be their next destination, "Dammit all, Snuff! I thought this little exercise was designed to introduce me to Bracken Tor!"

"Well, of course it is, Septimus!" Said his companion soothingly.

"One would never know it!"

CHAPTER TWELVE

("Patris Est Filius."—He is his father's son.)

Mr. Underwood now proceeded to display a degree of tact never imagined by his brother. At the next two cottages he made no mention of murders, corpses or even woods. He simply sat back, observing his hosts and allowing Mr. Pollock to dominate the conversation.

In the row of five cottages, which ended in the village shop, there were actually only two men at home, the others being at work in the fields of either Farmer Hazelhurst or one of Sir Henry Wynter's tenants.

The first cottage was the home of Mr. and Mrs. Field, an apt name for a man who had been a farm labourer all his life, as had generations of his family before him. Now riddled with arthritis, Mr. Field was almost housebound and his elderly wife cared diligently though bossily for him.

Next door the Masons were also too old to work and lived on the generosity of Sir Henry. Much as Mr. Underwood disliked the man, he had to give him credit for caring well for his pensioners—it was a great deal more than could be said of many landowners, who thought nothing of casting the old and infirm onto the mercy of the Workhouses and hospitals.

Since the Masons and the Fields cordially detested each other, the only information Mr. Underwood managed to glean from each was about the other, and even Mr. Pollock could not compete with the verbose wives.

When they finally escaped, Mr. Pollock drew his handkerchief from his pocket and ostentatiously mopped his brow, "Phew! Have you ever met women who could talk so much, Snuff? I declare my head is spinning!"

Mr. Underwood shrugged elegantly and made no reply. His own opinion was that it was high time someone had managed to outdo Pollock in the talking stakes. It would have been nice to imagine that he might have been taught a valuable lesson, but

Mr. Underwood had to regretfully admit to himself that such an eventuality was extremely unlikely.

The visit to Mrs. Knowles was necessarily brief since it was her washing day and she was surrounded by five children all under four years old. Mr. Knowles, it transpired, was a shepherd and his visits home were usually short-lived and infrequent. Mr. Underwood, gazing at the toddling, crying, crawling hoard about his feet, could only assume that Mr. Knowles was a man who made the best of his few opportunities—but doubted that he had the strength or inclination for murder. Having said that, perhaps the idea of having yet another mouth to feed might just have been enough to send him over the edge of despair. Mr. Underwood decided that he might like to speak to Mr. Knowles.

Mrs. Hadley was a widow, and apparently the local gossip. There was nothing which passed her window which did not excite her interest and Mr. Underwood made a mental note to return and question her more fully at a later date. There was every possibility that she had seen the girl pass by and if she had been travelling in a recognizable carriage, there would at least be a lead to follow.

Miss Wright lived in the next cottage, and ran the village shop next door, which is where Mr. Pollock and Mr. Underwood found her, when knocking at her front door elicited no response. There was little time for chatting since the lady was continually called upon to serve in the shop—which was unnaturally busy, due to presence of the two gentlemen. Mr. Underwood purchased some comfits as a gift for Miss Wynter, and the two adjourned to the Inn.

There was only time for them to consume one glass of ale each before Mr. Underwood consulted his watch and exclaimed, "Dash it all! I am going to have to hurry if I am not to keep Miss Wynter waiting!"

Don't you mean we?" Asked Pollock with a grin.

"Most certainly not!" Said his companion emphatically, "You were not invited—and you are most definitely not wanted!"

"How do you know? Miss Wynter may be, even at this very moment, cursing herself for having lost an opportunity of seeing me!"

"I very much doubt that!"

"Well . . . If you are afraid to put it to the test . . ." Mr. Pollock allowed the rest of the sentence to fade away and cast a covert glance at Mr. Underwood. A slight clenching of the jaw was the only indication he received that his companion was indeed rising to his bait.

"You had better drink up, Pollock, we have only fifteen minutes in which to reach Wynter Court."

Mr. Pollock obligingly drained his glass, but having gained one point, could not resist a further taunting remark. "I had never noticed you have any particular regard for punctuality in the past, my dear Snuff! As I recall, it was not uncommon for you to be late, or even miss lectures completely!"

Mr. Underwood gave his erstwhile student a quelling glare, "I am never tardy, Mr. Pollock, when I actually remember where I ought to be! Unfortunately I have a poor memory, and frequently forget that I have an appointment!"

"Not forgotten this one, I notice!"

"Quite, but then Miss Wynter has considerably more charm than any of your fellow students! Shall we go?"

Mr. Pollock strode forth at a pace which would have felled a lesser man, but Underwood was now intensely irritated and that fact alone spurred him to greater endeavours than would normally have been the case.

He was quite breathless when they reached the Court, but delighted to notice that they had three minutes to spare. It would appear that Pollock had his uses, for walking at his normal pace, Mr. Underwood could have expected to be at least ten minutes late.

As they walked up the drive, they met young Harry, riding a magnificent black stallion. He reined in and, completely ignoring Mr. Pollock, spoke directly to Mr. Underwood.

"Good morning, Underwood. Looking forward to your ride?" Mr. Underwood turned to his companion, "Pollock, go on up to the house and tell Miss Wynter I shall be with her presently, would you?"

Mr. Pollock obligingly strode on and Mr. Underwood turned his attention to Harry.

"Good morning, Harry. I hope you haven't chosen anything that large for me!" He nodded his head towards Harry's mount, which was decidedly skittish, dancing and blowing in a thoroughly bad-mannered way. Harry controlled the creature with no trouble at all, and Mr. Underwood noticed for the first time just how well-built the young man was, though not particularly tall. He sat the animal well, his thighs well-muscled, his hands and arms quite strong enough to hold his mount in check. Mr. Underwood had to admit that he was a remarkably good horseman for only fifteen, and was rather glad that he appeared to be going off on his own business and would not be there to witness his own rusty efforts.

Harry laughed quite good naturedly, "No, no. Charlotte put herself in charge of selecting your mount. She has found you a quiet old mare."

"Good." Said the older man frankly, not much caring that he was showing a decided lack of spirit.

"You are not interested in impressing my sister with your skills as a horseman then? You wouldn't like to borrow Sabre here, and gallop round to the stables?"

Mr. Underwood looked at Sabre, who just at that moment turned a rolling eye upon him and shook his head. Underwood needed no discouragement of that sort, he had already made a silent vow not to even pat the creature, let alone sit astride it!

"Thank-you for the thought, Harry, but I shall just have to risk your sister not being impressed by me at all!"

"You wouldn't be the first." Replied Harry sympathetically, "Charlotte has left the countryside littered with broken hearted swains." He gazed thoughtfully down at Mr. Underwood before adding tentatively. "Would you be offended if I offered you a little advice, Underwood?"

Mr. Underwood imagined that the advice was going to consist of some secret knack of handling a horse, so he smiled and answered, "Not at all, pray continue."

"This is not an easy thing to say about one's own sister, but I think you should be wary, Underwood. Of course she's the sweetest little thing ever born, and I adore her, but she really is a heartless tease. Normally I mind own business and let the chaps get on with it—but I can't help feeling you are different."

"Different?" There was a coldness about his tone which Harry seemed not to notice, "I presume you mean older?"

"Well, not just older, but more serious. I think you could be hurt and it is only fair that you should be warned."

"It wouldn't be the first time and I think I'm old enough to make my own decisions, but thank you for the thought Harry." There was no hint of gratitude in his voice, but Harry was well satisfied with the outcome of their chat. No matter how hard he tried, Underwood would not be able to forget the things Charlotte's brother had said to him. The relationship was doomed before it ever began.

Harry said nothing more, and without bidding Underwood farewell, he suddenly let Sabre have his head and left the older man in a swirling cloud of dust.

Mr. Underwood stood staring thoughtfully after him, then drew his snuff box from his pocket and slowly inhaled a pinch. When he replaced it, he not only dusted his front, but his sleeves and breeches too. Black was not a good colour to wear when was one likely to be covered in dust. He decided there and then that he might have some new clothes, and resolved to ask Gil if he knew of a good local tailor.

It was almost unbearably hot in the stable courtyard. Charlotte was stood beside Mr. Pollock, laughing up at him. She turned her head swiftly when she saw Mr. Underwood and waved cheerily to him, "Good morning, Mr. Underwood! Isn't it a delightful day?"

"Lovely." He responded, "Are we ready to leave?"

"In a moment. Abney is still saddling up and I have sent Miss Chapell indoors to change into her riding habit. Papa would

throw a fit if I went out alone with two such eligible bachelors!"
She laughed again and Mr. Underwood experienced a sudden
feeling of melancholy. Such loveliness did not come to a man in
his fortieth year—or at least not without a price—and would he
really be prepared to pay it?

He was spared any further dismal thoughts by the arrival of
Miss Chapell, who smiled shyly at him and bade him good day.
There was an air of subdued excitement about her which made
him square his shoulders and mentally shrug off his negative
attitude. She was obviously prepared to simply enjoy a ride in
the sunshine and he ought to do the same. Nothing had
happened, nothing had changed. Why not leave the worrying
until something did?

As Harry had predicted, Charlotte had chosen a quiet bay
mare for him, with four neat little socks and a resigned look in
her eye. Miss Chapell's mount was of a similar ilk, but Pollock
had elected to take on a stallion who was nearly as wild looking
as Harry's mount had been, and Charlotte was again mounted on
the chestnut.

They walked the horses out of the courtyard and Charlotte
led the way round the house, along the gravel drive and towards
the road. As soon as the path widened sufficiently to allow it,
Mr. Pollock spurred his horse until he was beside Charlotte. Mr.
Underwood noticed the manoeuvre, but did nothing. He was not
about to involve himself in an unseemly scuffle for prime
position next to Miss Wynter. He did not notice when Miss
Chapell's mare fell into step beside his own, and was completely
unaware that she was watching his face as he observed Pollock
and Charlotte happily chatting and laughing in front of them.
Verity was struck by an almost physical pain as she saw the
expression of desolation in his eyes. Damn Miss Charlotte Wynter
and Mr. Septimus Pollock! Did they have no thought at all for
the feelings of others? She resolved to distract Mr. Underwood's
attention from their junketings, and spare him further distress.
As it happened, she had been wanting to see him, because she
had several interesting things to disclose.

"Mr. Underwood." He withdrew his gaze from the pair in
front and turned his head towards her , "Miss Chapell. I do beg
your pardon, I didn't notice you there."

"I wanted to speak to you, Mr. Underwood, but I could
think of no way of visiting you alone."

He smiled rather sadly, "Convention can be a little wearing
on occasion, can't it? We really must think of some legitimate
reason for you to visit the vicarage."

"Do you have any suggestions?"

"No. Oh, wait a moment! Perhaps I have! Have you ever had
any particular desire to learn Latin or Greek?"

Her manner brightened considerably, "Mr. Underwood! How

did you guess? All my life I have dreamed of speaking Latin! How clever of you to know! And how kind to offer to tutor me!"

They laughed together and Miss Chapell was immensely relieved to notice that his dark mood seemed to have lifted slightly.

"Tuesday and Saturday afternoons are officially my free times, though I am occasionally given other time as well."

"Are you sure you want to give up your time to learn Latin, merely as a cover for my investigation?"

"Well, I don't have anything else to do."

"Very well. Shall we say Saturday, then, three until four, and take tea with my brother and I afterwards."

"That would be delightful. Thank-you, Mr. Underwood."

"Now, you said you had something to tell me?"

"Yes, though I am not sure how significant it is, I have been asking a few discreet questions amongst the staff at the Court, and I have discovered something which may be of interest to you. Toby Hallam discovered the body at 5.30 in the morning, but Abney told me he had passed the exact spot at midnight and there had been nothing then."

"Are you quite certain?" Mr. Underwood was extremely interested in this disclosure, though he did not explain why to Miss Chapell.

"Yes. Abney was quite emphatic. He says that it is something which has always bothered him—that he almost ran into the murderer—and might even have been able to prevent the crime."

"He can rest assured on that point! He might have been able to prevent the mutilation, but she was already dead when her body was brought to the wood."

"Naturally I did not mention that to him. It would have looked very strange had I known a detail like that!" Her discretion was amply rewarded by his smile of warm approval. "Quite! Well done for remembering that fact! I can see you are going to be of invaluable help to me, Miss Chapell! Tell me, did Abney mention why he was out wandering the grounds at midnight? And did he see anything unusual? Any strange vehicle on the road perhaps?"

"Oh!" She sounded disappointed, "I never thought to ask him that!"

"Never mind. Your behaviour in every other respect has been exceptional! I shall find an excuse to talk to Abney myself —and Toby Hallam. Thank you, Miss Chapell!"

She blushed slightly at his praise, and feeling suddenly shy, began to search in her pockets. "I wrote a brief resume of my interviews with the other staff members, so that you can read them at your leisure." At last she located the errant scrap of paper and leaned across to hand it to him. Without even glancing at it, he thrust it into his own pocket, "Thank you once again,

Miss Chapell."

"Verity." She corrected with a shy smile.

"Verity." He repeated, with a smile which made her heart pound.

The spell was broken by Pollock who, seeing that they had reached a stretch of open moorland, now turned in his saddle to challenge the stragglers to a gallop. Verity's eyes glowed with excitement at the very thought, but Mr. Underwood firmly shook his head. He was sadly lacking in practice, he explained, not having ridden at all for several years. Verity readily accepted the invitation and spurred her mount on, but Charlotte oddly refused to be drawn. She declared her intention of dismounting and taking a rest, but happily encouraged Verity to race Mr. Pollock, and if at all possible, to beat him. Neither party needed a second bidding, and within minutes the thundering hoofbeats had faded into the distance, leaving Charlotte and Mr. Underwood alone.

He dismounted, suppressing the groan which rose to his lips as his body began to protest at the unfamiliar exercise. He ached, despite the sedate pace which had been set, but not for the world would he acquaint Miss Wynter of the fact. Tethering his mare to a convenient bush, he then glanced towards her, "Do you require assistance?" He asked, rather surprised that she should suddenly seem so helpless. Actually, Charlotte was quite capable of dropping the considerable distance to the ground, and had often done so without hesitation or fear, but it seemed to her that having a gentleman to help might be rather more pleasant.

"If you wouldn't mind." She answered almost diffidently. He approached her and held up his arms to catch her. She leaned forward and placed her hands on his shoulders, then allowed herself to slide gently into his grasp. To her intense disappointment he made no attempt to retain that grasp, but set her immediately and firmly on her feet, then he walked away from her, leaving her to tether her own beast before joining him.

He had found a comfortable patch of sheep-cropped turf and had seated himself on his outspread jacket. As she approached he was refreshing himself with a pinch of snuff.

"May I try some?" She asked.

"Certainly not! It is a most unladylike habit!" He stated firmly, quite overlooking the fact that he had once offered Miss Chapell his box without a second thought. In his mind Miss Wynter and Miss Chapell were worlds apart. Charlotte was quite firmly set upon a pedestal, Verity a colleague in employment and a sister in class. Fortunately Charlotte was unaware of this minor hypocrisy, and took the refusal with equanimity. She sat beside him and for a few moments they were silent, he wrapped in his own sombre thoughts, she covertly examining his features and wondering vaguely what ailed him. At last, unable to bear the hush any longer, she gathered her courage and asked, "What was in the note you took from Verity, Mr. Underwood?"

He looked so startled that the suspicion which had begun to form in her mind immediately took substance and she hastily added, "Never mind. It is none of my business—but I wish you had told me!" She rose swiftly to her feet and began to walk back towards her horse.

He rose equally swiftly and catching her by the arm, swung her round to face him, "You wish I had told you what, Charlotte? What the devil are you talking about?"

There were tears in her eyes, but her face was marred by an angry frown, "You should have told me that your interest was in Miss Chapell and not in me! You have let me make a complete fool of myself and I hate you for it!"

His dismay at this vehemently spoken diatribe was comical to behold, but Charlotte was too irate to notice. She simply thought his hesitation in answering was an admission of guilt and not caused by the stunning impact of so many accusations in two short sentences! The fact that he had never thought of Miss Chapell as anything other than a pleasant companion was enough to make her assumption of a romance ludicrous, but to add she hated him was astounding to him. No-one had ever told him he was hated; he was not the sort of man to engender so strong an emotion in anyone—and certainly not in a woman. "Hate? Me?" The tone of his voice grew steadily more incredulous. "Great Heavens! Why should you hate me?"

She was furious. Two spots of colour on her cheeks were only cooled by the tears which began to fall. "You dare to ask me that? Let me loose! I don't want your hands on me." She tried to wrench her arm from his grasp, but his fingers merely tightened. "If I am to endure such abuse, I think I deserve to know the reason!" He was growing a little hot of temper himself. He had had to watch her spend the past half hour flirting with a half-witted curate, had endured the discomfort of the saddle merely to please her, and now she had the gall to accuse him of some unspecified wrong-doing. Dammit was the woman ready for Bedlam, or was he?

"You and my governess pass love-letters behind my back, and you expect me to ignore the fact—or did you think I would not notice?"

"Love letters?" His sudden burst of laughter did little to calm her, "Foolish child! That was not a love letter!"

She was unconvinced, but she ceased to struggle, "Do you expect me to believe that? What other reason could there be for Verity to pass notes to you?" He suddenly released her, his anger dying as swiftly as it has risen. "You may believe what you wish, Miss Wynter, with my blessing, but I think I have never given you cause to doubt my word!" She had never expected to hear such hurt and anger in his voice and she was stunned by the display. She had always seen him very much in control of his emotions, and had childishly imagined that because he did not show his passions as she did, then he must simply not experience them.

It rather frightened her to see this unknown side to his character. She looked at him and his eyes met hers squarely. Her gaze dropped first, and she lifted a hand to her face to brush the tears impatiently from her cheeks. "Do you swear there is nothing between you and Miss Chapell?" She spoke almost in a whisper, as though ashamed of what she asked, but felt compelled to ask it.

"Do I need to?" His voice was low too, but had an underlying strength which made her quail. She briefly shook her head.

"Come here." It never occurred to her to disobey, though she was generally headstrong and unused to being ordered and not asked. She stepped towards him, her head still down. He took her chin between gentle fingers, lifted her face and kissed her on the lips. It was a swift movement, he barely touched her, but her eyes flew wide with shock and her intake of breath was sharp.

"Now behave yourself." He said calmly, then glancing past her shoulder, added, "Miss Chapell and Mr. Pollock are upon us, wipe your tears and blow your nose."

With that unromantic remark he left her and went to untether his mare.

CHAPTER THIRTEEN

("Horresco Referens."—I shudder as I tell it.)

Miss Chapell's list began with a short letter of apology, which Mr. Underwood quickly scanned, being eager to get on with the more important document;
"Dear Mr. Underwood,
Pray forgive the untidiness and lack of order in the following: Due to circumstances, I was forced to try and remember everything of importance and write my notes later. It would have looked very strange had I taken down notes of everything which was said in the Servant's Hall!"
There was a list of staff members, with a brief description of their duties, followed by snippets of conversation. Mr. Underwood was most impressed. Miss Chapell had compiled an excellent report under difficult conditions, and he could see that she was going to be of invaluable assistance to him.
"Brownsword—Butler, has been with Sir Henry for over twenty years. Never married, no children. Shows a great deal of respect for Sir Henry's title and position, but is unforthcoming on his opinion of the man himself. I rather gather he thinks he brings the family into disrepute, though his loyalty is such that he would never openly critisize his master.
Mrs. Gregg—Cook, served longer than Brownsword, and was kitchen maid under Sir Henry's father. Never married, no children, her title is mere courtesy. Blindly loyal to Sir Henry, since she remembers him as a young man, and considers that he has been the unfortunate victim of a succession of ambitious women. She holds the highest position among the female staff, since Sir Henry does not waste his money on employing a Housekeeper. That position is filled by whichever of his daughters is currently the eldest unmarried. The staff feel that now Maria is married, Jane will probably hold the position indefinitely. Sir Henry shows a marked inclination to pass over her in the marriage stakes and keep her at home.

Sally Peters—Housemaid, two years service (There seems to be a constant stream of housemaids coming and going, no one would tell me why, but I gather Sir Henry in his cups has an eye for a pretty young girl!) Sally is very pert and pretty, and seems to hold out hope of marrying Abney's son Alfred—he shows no reciprocation of feeling!

Alfred Abney—footman. Five years service. Much to Abney's disappointment he hates horses and the outdoor life, so assiduously avoided following his father into the stables. Extremely taciturn, one might almost say sulky! Impossible to draw him into the conversation.

Jacob Mullin— Under footman and bootboy. Shy and somewhat slow—witted. Likes to feign knowledge he does not actually possess. He says he heard the Master quarrelling with Charlotte in the library the evening before the body was found, but no one else seems to believe him. Charlotte is undoubtedly her father's favourite, being most like him in temperament, and it is rare indeed for them to exchange cross words. He vents the worst of his spleen upon Maria, Jane and poor little Isobel.

Poverty Yates—kitchen maid. An orphan who came from the poorhouse, hence her rather unkind name. She has been with Sir Henry only about eight months and the apex of her ambition is to rise to the dizzy height of Cook. She takes Mrs. Gregg as her example and works herself to the bone, poor little creature! Since she is rarely allowed out of the kitchen, and even more rarely allowed to express an opinion, I gathered little information from her.

There are other staff members, who do not live in, to whom I have not yet spoken, and I have also to interview the outdoor staff. I shall let you know as soon as I have more information."

Mr. Underwood turned to the second sheet of paper.

"I managed to bring the conversation around to the required subject by mentioning Charlotte's reluctance to stay in the woods alone on the day you rescued her from the trap. As I had supposed the staff gathered for their midday meal were only too glad to have something gory to discuss over dinner! It is very odd, is it not, how people always relate important happenings to themselves. They always seem to remember what they were doing, and why, when they hear the news! Sally Peters began by expressing her own dread of the wood and casting longing glances towards Alfred. No-one would catch her in the woods alone after dark, she declared, in a tone of voice which told everyone who was listening that she only meant ALONE! Alfred ignored this rather obvious invitation and shovelled food into his mouth, as is his habit! I can't imagine why Sally finds him so irresistible! Mrs. Gregg chastised her roundly for her boldness, then embarked on her own version of events. She could remember it like it was yesterday, she said. Roused from the

109

sleep of the just by the screaming and carrying on downstairs. She met the Master coming out of his bedroom, fully dressed, with his hair all ruffled, looking as though he had thrown his clothes on in his agitation. Toby Hallam was almost jabbering with shock, trying to tell the Master what he had seen, but almost incoherent. For a moment Sir Henry looked as though he were going to strike the man. Miss Maria stood on the landing in her shift, looking like death warmed up (Mrs. Gregg has a rather dramatic turn of phrase!) not saying a word, just staring ahead as though she were seeing a ghost. The other girls joined her presently, all demanding to know what had happened. Maria seemed to come to herself then, and shooed them all back to bed. They have never been told the full story and know only that the girl was found in the woods—no mention of the head, so pray do not confide that detail to Charlotte! Harry never stirred. He said he never heard a thing, but he could sleep though an earthquake!

Brownsword took up the story here. He recalled how he too had joined the throng, delayed by the fact that he had insisted on dressing before appearing in front of his employer and staff. (Brownsword has very definite ideas of what is done and not done!)

He was the one who suggested that the doctor ought to be called, but Toby Hallam interrupted, almost hysterical, "There's no point in calling the doctor to her, you fool! I tell you there's no help for her!" Brownsword was not at all pleased to be called a fool by one of the outdoor staff, and his dignity was wounded. He pointedly ignored Toby and informed Sir Henry in frosty tones that the doctor must be called anyway. That, he said importantly, was how things should be done. Sir Henry seemed confused and agitated, and turned aggressively on them all, "For God's sake! Let a man think, can't you?" He started downstairs, then turned back to speak to Brownsword. "Fetch a bottle of brandy to the library—and don't let anyone do anything until I give you word! Do you understand?" Naturally no-one argued with him. His hands were shaking, and his face had lost its usual high colour. Mrs. Gregg said that she thought he was on the verge of collapse. He went into the library, took Maria in with him, and didn't come out again for nearly an hour. He had drunk all the brandy, but it didn't seem to have had the normal effect upon him. He seemed sober, and was still deathly pale. Maria looked ghastly, and almost fainted when she came out of the room. Mrs. Gregg said the Master had given her all the details—about the missing head etc., and she was terribly shocked. When the doctor was finally sent for, he had to see her and give her something to help her sleep, she was in such a state. Apparently he told Sir Henry what he thought of him for thrusting the knowledge on his most sensitive daughter. "If you had to tell someone." He was heard to roar, "Why didn't you confide in the brutal little lout of a son! He has the stomach for death and mutilation—sees it all the time on the hunting field!" Sir Henry was furious and growled at Dr. Herbert to mind his own damned business."

There ended Verity's report and Mr. Underwood's face was grave as he finally laid the paper down. There was something strangely evocative about it, knowing, as he did, most of the characters mentioned. He could picture each one, see their probable reaction to the stunning news that there was a murdered girl, lying, mutilated beyond recognition, within the walls of their estate. He was glad that Charlotte had not been the one to hear her father's drunken description of the body, but he was also furious that he had forced it upon Maria. Damn the man, he had no soul! Instinctively he applied a Latin tag to Sir Henry and his son 'Arcades ambo'—two of a kind! He carefully refolded the notes along their original creases and returned them to his pocket. It would never do for any of his carefully garnered information to fall into Pollock's reckless possession. It would be completely beyond his capabilities to keep anything a secret, and it was becoming more and more vital that this remained confidential, and not only for Gil's sake. Mr. Underwood was beginning to feel that there might be a great deal more to this little mystery than had at first been apparent.

Suddenly feeling the need to talk to his brother, he went in search of the vicar, but was unlucky at first. The vicarage seemed deserted. Mrs. Selby was the only living soul he encountered and he had to go out into the garden to find even her. She informed him that she rather thought the vicar was in church.

Mr. Underwood was loth to pursue his brother and disturb him, when he was, presumably, at prayer, but he was also a great believer in doing things as and when they occurred to him, so he swiftly overcame his scruples and followed the Reverend gentleman across the churchyard.

Gil was indeed kneeling at the altar, so Mr. Underwood slipped into a convenient pew and waited patiently. It occurred to him that his brother would have been disappointed that he did not follow the cleric's example and turn his thoughts to higher things, but Mr. Underwood had his own reasons for doubting the existence of a loving and just God—and he had no intention of arguing the point with his brother. Instead he stared unseeing at the coloured patterns cast upon the stone floor by the stained glass window, and cogitated upon the story contained in the missive handed him by Miss Chapell.

Presently the vicar rose to his feet and was startled to see his brother sitting in a pew, obviously deep in thought.

"Hello!" His tone reflected his surprise at the other's presence.

"Is there something amiss?"

"Not at all," Replied Underwood, "I merely wanted a private word with you and the church was the only place I could be sure of not running into Mr. Pollock."

"But he is a clergyman!" Protested the vicar faintly.

"Do you think he is aware of that fact?" Asked Mr. Underwood scathingly, displaying a degree of cynicism which was most unbecoming.

Rev. Underwood made no attempt to dispute this unkind comment, but he rather felt that Underwood was a little hard upon the unfortunate Pollock. He seemed to find something to critisize in everything the poor young man said or did. However, he did recognize that though his brother denied the suggestion, his health was not at its best, and he had taken a Sabbatical with the express purpose of avoiding his boys for a considerable period of time. It must have come as rather a shock to him to find Pollock suddenly installed with him for an unspecified amount of time.

"What did you wish to discuss?" The vicar joined his brother on the pew, closed the little door which divided the seat from the aisle, and prepared himself to hear something unpleasant—he always seemed to hear something unpleasant from his sibling!

Strangely, having gone to great lengths to search out his brother, and then wait for him, Mr. Underwood now found it impossible to put his thoughts into words. He toyed nervously with one of the signet rings he wore on each of his little fingers—one deeply engraved with his initials, the other a plain gold band, like a woman's wedding ring. Actually that was precisely what it was—the ring his fiancee would have worn had their wedding ever taken place. It was this ring he twisted and though the vicar noticed it, he said nothing, merely waited with infinite patience for his brother to speak.

"Gil, what do you know of Miss Wynter's character?"

"Charlotte?" He managed to inject just the right degree of surprise into his tone, but in truth he was not as stunned as he wanted to appear. It was a conversation he had been expecting, but he knew his brother would detest the idea that he had been in any way transparent!

"You must understand that I do not really know her well, and can only give you my opinion."

"There is no man whose opinion I value more, Gil. Pray give it."

"Well, she is a little spoiled." He began diffidently.

"She is horribly spoiled!" Stated Mr. Underwood brutally, "But will she grow out of it?"

"I expect so." Gil could not repress a smile. Now he knew his brother was in love! He would have noticed nothing about Charlotte at all, had she not engaged his interest very firmly indeed, "She is essentially a nice-natured, bright and vivacious girl."

"You sound as though you are giving an end of term report!" Complained the love-lorn Underwood.

"Well, I don't know what else you expect me to say. You can see for yourself that she is beautiful!"

"That is a vastly over-used word!"

"Then you dispute that it could be applied to Charlotte?"

"I did not say so!" Underwood sounded testy and his next comment told his brother why. "But if I can see her beauty, so can every other young buck in the County! Her brother intimated that she has no shortage of heart-broken swains dying for love of her—is she a flirt, Gil?"

Gilbert considered this question carefully before answering, "I have never noticed any particular evidence of it, but it would be a most unusual girl who did not allow her popularity to go to her head a little!'

Mr. Underwood waved his hand impatiently. "That is not what I mean! Dash it all! I don't mind her enjoying her loveliness! Who am I to stop her? She can trample on the heart of every man she meets, if she wants to—but the question which plagues me is this; does she mean to trample on mine too?"

"I can't possibly answer that! After all, is that not what love is all about—taking a risk?"

Underwood returned his attention to his ring. He turned it between his fingers, and for a moment the vicar thought he was about to wrench it from his finger. He almost put his hand out to prevent such an action, knowing it had never been removed since the day it had been placed there.

"I can't do that Gil! I can't risk my heart again! I have to be sure!"

Gilbert did reach out his hand, but he merely placed it over his brother's, "Then you will have to stop now, Chuffy! There are no guarantees! You will have to decide whether or not to trust her, and then take the consequences."

"Mr. Underwood drew in a deep breath, "Of course you are right, Gil. Thank you."

Rev. Underwood rose to his feet, "Shall we have some tea?" He asked rousingly. Mr. Underwood managed to summon a smile to his solemn countenance, "As long as you make it!"

***

As they trod the path which led to the vicarage, Mr. Underwood spoke again, but it was an entirely different subject.

"Gil, what do you know of the circumstance surrounding the

113

death of Mrs. Hazelhurst?"

"Now, Chuffy! Hazelhurst was acquitted by a Court!" The vicar stopped and turned to confront his brother, "You are not going to drag all that up too!"

"Calm yourself, Gil! Why must you always place the worst possible complexion upon everything I do or say? I know Hazelhurst was found not guilty and it never occurred to me that he would have any connection with our other little problem, but his name was mentioned to me and I should like to know what happened."

The vicar looked unconvinced, but he fell back into step beside his companion. "There is a very steep, craggy outcrop of rock near the Hazelhurst Farm and Mrs. Hazelhurst apparently fell over it and broke her neck. Her husband found her. It was one of those occasions when the truth was obscured by gossip and conjecture. Unfortunately for Hazelhurst it was well known that he and his wife did not get on. In the absence of any witnesses, there were three possible conclusions; one, that it was a genuine accident and the woman had fallen, but in that case, what was she doing up there—she had never shown any interest in walking before, and certainly not to Boar's Hollow. Two, that her husband, or someone else, had pushed her to her death, either at home, for example down the stairs and then moved the body, or there on the rocks. Then you have the problem of how she was lured to her death. Thirdly, that she had gone to crag with the express intention of throwing herself to her death. Hazelhurst swore he knew nothing about it, and was convinced himself that it had been accidental. Sir Henry, as local Magistrate, believed him and he was acquitted. Since there was no proof that she had committed suicide, I was able to prevent those who wished to have her body buried at the crossroads from having their wishes fulfilled!"

"Good God! Do they still do that?" Mr. Underwood was shocked and his brother smiled slightly, "Not in my parish! But I am afraid that it has not been easy to wean country people away from some of the age old superstitions they have lived by for centuries, People who live and die by the soil tend to be a little primitive on occasion."

"Gil, this conversation has given me a very worrying notion!"

The vicar's smile swiftly slid into a frown, "What do you mean?

"Perhaps I have been totally wrong about the reason for the girl's murder."

"In what way?"

"Well, I was so sure I was right, I had not left open any other possibilities. I have been assuming that her head was removed to prevent identification—but what if there was quite a different reason?"

"What other reason could there be—besides my theory that the crime was committed by a madman?"

"Superstition. Was she killed as some sort of sacrifice? Did the ancients not believe that the soil had to be fed with human blood?"

Gil hesitated for a few moments before shaking his head in firm denial, "No, I refuse to believe any such nonsense!"

"Why?"

That was a question the cleric in Gil found very hard to answer. He looked into his brother's eyes, his own clouded with worry.

"Chuffy, if I had to believe something like that could happen in my parish, could be carried out by people I know and respect, I would have to leave the ministry."

This was not the reaction Underwood had been expecting, for his own excitement at finding an alternative theory had blinded him to his brother's very different approach to life. His own expression became very troubled as he watched his brother walk away from him.

***

Even Mr. Pollock's famed good humour was beginning to wear a little thin by the time the irrepressible Mr. Underwood had dragged him around the entire village. Underwood refused to rest until every home had been visited, and Pollock was awash with tea, his head buzzing with the accumulated gossip of the parish. He began to wonder what devil was driving Underwood, for he could see nothing even vaguely interesting in anything which had been said and done, but Underwood spent his evenings writing copious notes, drawing complicated diagrams, and generally being infernally secretive.

Unknown to Mr. Pollock, Underwood actually found very little of interest, but he tried his best to discover what he could and to draw the most tenuous of connections between the village and the murdered girl.

He came up with nothing. No one admitted to knowing her, no one admitted to seeing her and, not entirely unexpectedly, no one admitted to having murdered her.

His greatest hope had lain with Toby Hallam and Abney—the gamekeeper who had found the body, and the groom who had told Miss Chapell that he had passed the spot where she was found only hours before and had seen nothing.

Toby Hallam had seemed exceptionally embarrassed to have to admit that he had discovered the body, and rather to

Underwood's disappointment he had a perfectly valid reason for being in the woods at five thirty in the morning. Underwood, who knew very little about country ways, was astounded to hear that a game keeper was a stranger to regular hours. Poachers kept odd hours and therefore so did the man whose job it was to catch them.

Hallam was not a squeamish man—no one who trapped and culled could be, but he did not scruple to tell Mr. Underwood that he had vomited when he had seen the mutilation inflicted upon the corpse. Very clumsily done, was his verdict. Underwood found himself feeling a little nauseated and hastily changed the subject.

Abney was even less use. He had been in the Wynter Arms until eleven thirty, having had words with his wife, and had taken rather more than was good for him. Yes, he had passed the spot, and no the body was not there then, but he had failed to notice the presence or indeed absence of any vehicle which might have contained the body. He had, in short, failed to notice anything at all, including the ditch into which he had fallen, and out of which he had sheepishly dragged himself, giggling inanely, and hoping no one had seen him fall.

Soon there was only the dame school run by the two Misses Dadd left to visit, and at this point Underwood took pity not only upon Pollock, but also, he felt, upon the two Misses Dadd. He understood from his brother that they had already met Pollock and been inexpressibly shocked by his frank and candid mode of address. Since he felt sure that there was very little these two little old ladies might be able to tell him, Underwood decided to grant himself a short rest and visit them at some later date.

All that remained now was to sift the interviews and decide which of the villagers warranted a second, and more pressing, questioning.

CHAPTER FOURTEEN

("In Partibus Infidelium."—In heathen places.)

Helen Herbert scanned the letter in her hand with incredulous delight. It would seem that her plan was working beautifully! Verity could not keep her appointment for tea on Saturday afternoon because she was studying Latin with Mr. Underwood.

"Francis, my dear, what do you think of this?" She handed the missive to him and was surprised when he seemed quite unmoved by the contents. "Did I not tell you that Verity and Mr. Underwood were absolutely made for each other?"

Dr. Herbert tossed the letter disdainfully into the centre of the table. "My love, I should not read too much into that if I were you!"

"But why ever not? Verity must have some reason for this sudden interest in Latin."

"Well, what ever it is, it is not so that she can carry on an intrigue with Underwood! I assure you that his interest lies in an entirely different direction, and Miss Chapell is well aware of the fact!"

His wife was at once agog for more information, "Oh Francis, who is it? Do tell, pray!"

"It is no secret, so I see no harm in voicing popular opinion. It would appear that he and Charlotte Wynter are smitten with each other—though for some strange reason, they are both being extremely coy about it!"

"Charlotte! I don't believe it!"

"Why do you sound so astonished? Charlotte is a remarkably attractive girl."

Helen was irritated that he should think so, and even more annoyed that Underwood should prefer the superficiality of a pretty face above the myriad virtues she knew her friend possessed.

"I would not go so far as to say 'remarkably' attractive." She

117

argued, with a haughty lift of her chin. "And though I can understand Mr. Underwood being attracted to her physically, I question whether she has the mental equipment to keep him interested! What on earth does she see in him? Oh, I admit he is a charming creature, and that smile quite melts ones bones, but I should have expected Charlotte to go for the knight in shining armour type of man, all brawn and very little brain! One has to face facts, Francis, and the truth is Mr. Underwood has a great deal more to offer intellectually than physically, and Charlotte is quite the opposite!"

"Perhaps, my dear, that is precisely what both of them are searching for!" Suggested her husband with a smile.

"Nonsense!" Helen have a short and, for her, a rather unkind laugh.

"Charlotte has not the faintest interest in the erudite! I don't suppose she has opened a book since the day she was released from the schoolroom! If they marry it will be an unmitigated disaster! Within months they will find they have not the least thing in common!"

"As I recall, dearest girl, that is exactly what was said about us!" Dr. Herbert reached across the table and laid his hand affectionately upon hers. Her face softened into a loving smile, "Yes, I believe Mama did think you were far too clever for me!"

"Neither she nor I ever suspected that you would turn out to be far too clever for me!"

Helen giggled appreciatively.

"Anyway, I expect he melted her bones with his smile!" He added teasingly, returning his attention to his newspaper. Helen tapped him playfully, "Oh you!" She said.

***

Perfect peace reigned in the study of Bracken Tor vicarage, kindly lent by the vicar to facilitate the learning of Latin by Miss Verity Chapell. Mr. Pollock had been dispatched to Beconfield with a hired hack to execute various errands for the inmates of the parsonage and was not expected to return for several hours.

A selection of Latin textbooks lay spread upon the desk, and Miss Chapell's dark head was bent industriously over a sheet of writing paper, but regretfully she was not engaged in conjugating verbs, but in studying Mr. Underwood's neatly written resume of the last known movements of Mary Smith—or at least as much as they had been able to piece together. It was unfortunately very short.

The problem which faced them was to discover where

118

exactly she had gone when she left the coach in Beconfield. Until someone came forward and admitted to having seen her, they could not even know the general direction she had taken. How, and with whom, had she spent the day and evening prior to her brutal death? As far as Verity and Underwood were concerned she had stepped off the stage and into a mist of mystery, only to emerge as a headless corpse in a wood.

Mr. Underwood was continually frustrated by this enigma. Whilst the whole affair was shrouded by the silence forced upon him by his brother, the task of tracing her movements was an impossible one. Miss Chapell looked anxiously at him, "You are not going to give up now, Mr. Underwood?"

He managed to summon a bracing smile, despite his fear that his investigation was doomed to failure. "No, Miss Chapell, 'Dum spiro, spero'—while I breath, I hope! I am not yet utterly defeated, but it is tedious, all these politely framed, hidden questions! I cannot help wishing I had not promised Gil to preserve secrecy! Some awkward questions to frighten the culprit into rash action would be most useful!"

"I suppose it does rather slow us down, but perhaps it will work in our favour—anyone who has something to hide must surely be taken off guard by our cover."

"I hope you are right—to quote yet another Latin phrase, 'gutta cavat lapidem,' the constant drip of water wears away stone. May our perseverance be rewarded—even if we have to spend the rest of our lives badgering the residents of the district, we will solve this crime!"

"Of course we will!" She told him warmly, "We owe it to poor little 'Mary' don't we?"

"Indeed we do!"

"So what is the next step?"

"Well, I intend to follow very closely the four rules given by the great Rene Descrates for true, scientific enquiry."

"And what are they?"

"One) Never accept as true anything that cannot be seen as such; Two) divide difficulties into as many parts as possible; Three) Seek solutions to the simplest problems first and proceed step by step to the most difficult; Four) Review all conclusions to make sure there are no omissions."

Verity was most impressed and showed it, "It sounds wonderful." She said, "But how do we implement all that?"

"I have absolutely no idea—but I'm sure it is the most excellent advice!"

Presently, in order to give the ring of authenticity to their assignation they laid 'Mary Smith' aside and turned their attention to Latin.

Underwood was under no illusions as to the unpleasant aspects of character present in his fellow man. The likes of

Edwin Wynter would not hesitate to read evil into the situation, besmirching Miss Chapell's name and his own—though he was, at that moment, more concerned for her than himself. It would give Edwin enormous pleasure to test Verity's knowledge of Latin in order to be able to prove her ignorant of the language.

They worked solidly for over an hour and Mr. Underwood was startled when he heard the clock in the hall strike four. He could scarcely believe the time had passed so swiftly. Of late he had begun to find teaching a chore, tedious and unrewarding, but Verity's quick mind and superior understanding had made the tutoring a rare pleasure. He wanted to tell her so, but the memory of Charlotte's accusation of favouritism towards the governess prevented him. If Charlotte had noticed evidence of favour, then it was possible others had also. He had quite enough to contend with in his life without adding further complications.

Instead he determinedly closed the books and allowed himself the luxury of a full stretch, "Enough Miss Chapell. 'Nunc est bibendum'!"

"I'm afraid I am not yet able to translate, Mr. Underwood."

He gave his most boyish grin and folded his hands behind his head, "I merely remarked, 'Now is the time for drinking,' and though a glass of 'aqua vitae' would be most welcome, I fear the shock of my asking for it would kill my brother! We shall have to settle for tea, though thanks to Gil, it is a most superior brew!"

"Tea would be more than adequate."

Gil was in the parlour and was already in the throes of the tea-making ritual. Verity watched him in amused fascination. "Does he always go to that much trouble?" She asked her companion in a low voice.

"He does." Asserted Mr. Underwood, as he gently guided her past the over-crowded furniture and found her a comfortable spot by the fire.

"However it is well worth the wait!"

Verity, upon tasting the beverage, quite agreed, and there followed a most convivial half hour, during which much tea was drunk, many crumpets and slices of fruit cake consumed, and the conversation was bright and amusing.

With much regret the young lady rose at last to leave, and when Mr. Underwood returned from escorting her to the vicarage gate, he spoke thoughtfully to his brother, "Do you know, Gil, she is an excessively charming girl! You could do much worse for yourself than to court her."

Gil looked extremely startled, "Miss Chapell? Good Heavens, Chuffy!"

"Now, what is wrong with that suggestion? She may not be beautiful, but she certainly isn't plain! And besides, no vicar wants a dashing wife—causes too many problems!"

Gil relaxed back into his chair, his lips pursed into a thin line of disapproval. "There are times, my dear brother, when you are incredibly obtuse!"

"Dammit!" Protested the sorely-abused Mr. Underwood, "What the devil have I said now?"

"Not a thing! Pray don't tax your intellect any further!"

"What is that supposed to mean?"

"Only that anyone with half an eye could see that Miss Chapell's affections are already engaged!"

"Do you really think so?" Underwood sounded unconvinced.

"I know so!"

"You seem very sure. Has Verity told you so herself?"

"That is not the sort of thing young ladies confide!"

"Well, since you seem so certain, perhaps you know who the fellow is? Perhaps you could have a chat with him and hasten the calling of the banns?"

The vicar sighed heavily and closed his eyes, as though driven beyond endurance, "Pray forget I ever mentioned the matter."

"Certainly—but I should not let this fellow, who ever he is, put you off. Verity cannot be so very taken with him if she has not mentioned him to me."

"Perhaps not. Thank you for the advice."

"Think nothing of it, Gil. What are brothers for, if not to offer help to each other when it is needed!"

***

By the following Monday both brothers were feeling in need of all the help they could get, from whatever quarter. Rev. Underwood had received one of their mother's closely written, rambling, much crossed epistles and with barely disguised panic he exclaimed, "Angels and ministers of grace defend us!"

Underwood was on his way out of the door, but this outburst gave him cause to hesitate, "Anything amiss, Gil?"

"That rather depends upon your point of view! Mother has written to say that she is coming to visit."

"Mother? Here?"

"Yes, here! Where else? She arrives in Beconfield the day after tomorrow."

"Oh my God! When is the next coach back to Cambridge?"

"You are not leaving now! You are going to stay and face her with me!"

"Gil, have a little compassion!" The vicar was completely unmoved by his brother's plea for mercy and shook his head firmly, "Chuffy you stay!"

"But you know Mother is only coming here to persuade one or the other of us into getting married."

"Well, you will be able to give her some good news in that direction, won't you?" Rev. Underwood smiled pleasantly, but there was a determination in his voice which his brother recognized and dreaded.

"Gil . . ."

"There is nothing more to be said. If you want mother to cease her campaign to marry us off, you will have to tell her that you have an understanding with Miss Wynter."

Mr. Underwood was not amused, "I find that remark in distinctly poor taste! The subject of marriage has never been raised between Miss Wynter and myself and it is doubtful that it ever will be."

"Nonsense! It is obvious to everyone that Charlotte is utterly infatuated—you need only speak the words and she would marry you tomorrow!"

Mr. Underwood could not suppress his natural vanity and there was rather an inane smile upon his face as he asked diffidently. "Do you really think so, Gil?"

"Yes! So why not put us all out of our misery and ask her?"

"Mainly because I would have to face her father first!" He admitted frankly.

The vicar's usually serene expression was marred by the scornful look which momentarily passed across his face. "Sir Henry Wynter would give any one of his daughters to passing gypsies, so I can hardly imagine his objecting to your suit!" He said with a sneering cynicism which was most uncharacteristic. His brother reached for his snuff box whilst he considered this remark.

"I would have to resign from the University." He said, almost to himself, the Reverend gentleman was inclined to take this as an extremely hopeful sign, since his brother had never before even entertained the vague possibility of leaving Cambridge.

"Well, Father did not exactly leave any of us penniless, did he? And there are plenty of excellent schools looking for tutors. You could even start your own school—persuade Sir Henry to fund a charitable institution!"

"Very droll!" Said Mr. Underwood, but he appeared to be considering the suggestion with interest. "I suppose there would be life for me outside the hallowed walls of the University—but what of Charlotte? Would she be content as a mere schoolmaster's wife?"

"There is only one way to discover the answer to that question, brother, and that is to ask the lady!"

Mr. Underwood inhaled deeply of his pinch of snuff and replaced the box in his pocket. "Would you like me to go and meet Mother?" He asked.

"We will go together, I think." Replied the vicar, well aware that this swift change of topic meant that his brother felt the matter had been discussed enough and was now closed.

***

Mr. Underwood's investigation now took on a somewhat feverish intensity. He was desperate to gather as much information as he could before the arrival of his mother, who, he knew, would be totally undemanding, thereby engendering a degree of guilt in her offspring which would ensure their complete attention throughout the course of her visit. He was quite determined to at least have something to think about whilst he was doing his filial duty.

He asked Mrs. Selby, who had lived all her life in the village, who, in her opinion, was the greatest gossip she knew, and was surprised, though he should not have been, to hear her name not a woman but a man—old Tom Briggs, the former Blacksmith. From his bench outside the forge, which his son now utilized, there was little his eyes and ears missed, and when the seat was vacant, it could be safely surmized that he was occupying his regular spot by the inglenook of the Wynter Arms.

Mr. Underwood, unaccompanied by Pollock, who had been set several tasks by the vicar, amongst them to write a sermon suitable for the ears of the Reverend gentleman's mother, sallied forth in search of the redoubtable Mr. Briggs.

It was, as always, dim and smoky in the tap room, due, no doubt, to the foul-smelling tobacco which seem to be the universal favourite, and to the fact that summer or winter, a fire always burned in the huge grate. It was the landlord's boast that the fire had never been allowed to go out in four hundred years, and that was probably not far from the truth. The stone flagged floor, the thick walls and tiny windows ensured daylight never pierced the interior, leaving it always chilly. The fire was a necessity, not a luxury.

Underwood approached the landlord, whom he recognized from his previous visit, and handing him a goodly selection of silver coins, asked to be directed to Tom Briggs, adding that he desired neither his own glass nor Tom's be allowed to stand empty for the duration of their conversation.

Jonas Blackett made a swift calculation of the sum he held and then raised his head to smile toothlessly at this obviously well-to-do customer, "Certainly Sir. That's Old Tom over there by the fire."

He nodded his head in the direction of the inglenook and its sole occupant. Mr. Underwood wasted no further time but crossed the room swiftly and in the same breath, introduced himself and invited himself to join the older man.

Tom raised shrewd blue eyes to his face and gave a friendly grin.

"You'll be the Reverend's brother?" Underwood had long since ceased to struggle against the inevitable and merely acknowledged the truth of this statement with a nod of his head.

"I'm told you are the foremost authority on life in Bracken Tor, Mr. Briggs. Would you care to share a flagon of beer and swap stories?"

"Nothing would please me more—but why should a gentleman like you be interested in the likes of us?"

"The countryside always fascinates town dwellers, Mr. Briggs."

"Well, you'd be the best judge of that—and the name is Tom."

The landlord approached at that moment and filled Tom's tankard then placed a glass before Mr. Underwood. The beer looked very dark and strong and he had to steel himself to take the first sip. Surprisingly he found it rather pleasant, so he took a deeper draught and settled himself to listen Tom.

The first half hour passed swiftly. Tom, given free rein for the first time in months, was verbose, the ale was strong and Mr. Underwood found the combination of the old man's voice, the alcohol and the heat of the fire extremely soporific. It was with great difficulty that he dragged himself from the edge of sleep and begin to throw in comments and questions which would eventually bring the conversation to the subject he required.

Once he was brought to death and burial, Tom waxed positively lyrical and Underwood wondered anew at people's fascination with the hereafter. It was a subject he personally avoided with a vengeance.

He had begun to fade gently away again when Tom mentioned something which brought him briskly to his senses, though he showed no physical change of attitude.

" . . . of course the vicar frowned on the idea of burying the Hazelhurst woman at the crossroads, but murdered or suicide, either way she was going to walk, wasn't she?"

"Walk?" Inquired his apparently sleepily puzzled audience. "How could she 'walk' if she was dead?"

"Ah!" Commented Tom, as though his companion had made a deeply profound remark, "There you have it."

"Have what?"

"The problem. How do you discourage the spirit from walking after death?"

"I have no idea—how do you?"

"Well, of course the best way is to bury them at the

crossroads—causes confusion, you see. They rise up, but then don't know which road to take."

Mr. Underwood resisted the temptation to point out that if the crossroads was known to the person in life, then there was no reason why the way should suddenly be forgotten after death. He was more interested in hearing what other gems of folklore might issue from Mr. Briggs.

"Failing the crossroads—since it seems to upset the clergy so much—what other methods are there?"

Tom looked somewhat shifty as he glanced about to ensure they were not overheard. "This must go no further—especially not to your brother."

"You have my word." Mr. Underwood assured him, leaning conspiritorily closer.

"You drive an iron spike through the body into the earth below."

This Mr. Underwood had not been expecting and he was extremely taken aback. It was several seconds, during which Tom slaked his thirst and held up his tankard to Jonas to be refilled, before he recovered sufficiently to ask, "Was that really done to Mrs. Hazelhurst?"

"Aye—and others. Murdered or suicides."

"But why those in particular?"

"The murdered come back looking for revenge, the suicides from remorse. It's a mortal sin, you see."

Of course, a mortal sin meant immediate and permanent banishment from Paradise. That being the case, there was not much else to do but return to earth and wander about scaring the wits out of simple country folk! Underwood knew his private thoughts were unkindly cynical and mocked at strongly held beliefs, but he felt that as long as he never voiced them to the credulous Tom, there was no harm in them.

He now felt rather inclined to leave the matter well alone, but having come this far, it seemed rather a pity to abandon the line of questioning.

"So the murdered girl would have been treated thus, also?"

Tom did not feign ignorance and ask to which girl his companion referred, he merely glanced shrewdly at Underwood over the rim of his tankard before lowering it and replying, "Not just her, my friend."

"Who else?" Tom's voice was a barely discernible whisper, "Lady Wynter, for one." At the sound of the name, every muscle and sinew in Underwood's body stiffened, as though preparing for flight, "What!"

"You heard me well enough, I think."

"But what possible reason could there be in her case? I understood she died in childbirth."

"That's the story Sir Henry would have everyone believe, but there were those who didn't believe it then, and they don't believe it now! He made no secret of the fact that he was tired of her, and was sick of her constantly giving him daughters instead of the son he longed for."

"But she had given him a son, finally."

"Aye, but too late. He had taken a fancy to a young piece from over Beconfield way and he was out of his mind to marry her. She wouldn't give in to him, you see, and he wasn't used to being refused." The Henry VIII and Anne Boleyn story, thought Underwood, suddenly realizing how easy it was to believe all this of Sir Henry. He had been aptly named! He dragged his attention back to Tom, who was still deep in his reminiscences, "Of course, he was not short of mistresses, and there are several children born the wrong side of the blanket, but she would not even look his way, so he thought he could persuade her if he promised her marriage. He thought she hankered to be a lady."

"But he never did marry her?"

"No, the minute the boy was born and the mistress dead, he took off to London with the child. He said he wanted the best care for his son. Said he was sickly and needed special treatment. He didn't even stay for the mistress' funeral. Left the girls in the charge of the housekeeper and didn't show his face here for over two years. When he came home, the boy was the bonniest little lad you ever saw, already steady on his feet. Whatever the London treatment was, It certainly seemed to work, for the lad hasn't ailed a day in his life since."

"He is a remarkably fine specimen." Admitted Mr. Underwood thoughtfully, "What happened to the young lady from Beconfield?"

"Ran away to marry a soldier. We never saw her again."

"She could not possibly have been the corpse in the wood?"

"No, too old. The doctor said the girl in the wood was probably under twenty. All this happened fifteen years ago, Alice Mills would be more than thirty by now."

"Tell me something about the Renshaws. I understand Mr. Renshaw was born here. Did you know him as a young man?"

"Oh aye. He did very well for himself. He inherited a small farm from his uncle, sold it to Hazelhurst's grandfather, and took the money to start a business in Manchester. I hear he could do no wrong where business was concerned and was worth a fortune by the time he was forty. They had one child—a son, but he died of consumption when he was only in his late twenties."

"Was the son ever married? Were there any grandchildren?"

"Well, he never married, but that doesn't mean there were no children, does it? Not if Sir Henry is anything to go by!" Tom laughed wickedly, but his companion found it hard to even raise a smile. He had been given a suspect for his murder and he did not like it. Could Renshaw's son have left an illegitimate child

126

who had come to demand her rights of the wealthy Mr. Renshaw? Was that why the man had been so uncomfortable at the mention of the girl?

Mr. Underwood had desired to tax his brain, and had been amply supplied. All that remained was for him to sift what he had heard and decide what was true, what was conjecture, what was malicious gossip and—the truth must be faced—what might be Tom Briggs' idea of a joke, He would probably think it highly amusing to fool a gullible town dweller with his fanciful tales.

When he had done all that, he had to decide where it left him with his own self-inflicted little riddle.

He thanked Tom for his time and the information he had given, then rose rather unsteadily to his feet.

Tom watched him stagger towards the door with an affectionate smile upon his face, "I see you gave him the unwatered, Jonas!" He called across to the landlord. Jonas was swiftly on the defense, spluttering indignantly. "You'll find no watered ale here, Tom Briggs, and I'll thank you to mind your tongue!"

Mr. Underwood stumbled, blinking, into the sunlight, to the sound of a hearty quarrel issuing from the dark doorway behind him. He leaned against a convenient post for a few moments until his head ceased to swim, then he began to make his unsteady way back to the vicarage.

CHAPTER FIFTEEN

("Labor omnia Vincit."—Work conquers all things.)

Dr. Herbert was about to turn into the lane which led to the school of the two Misses Dadd when he caught sight of Mr. Underwood, staggering very slightly, in the general direction of the vicarage. He hailed the vicar's brother with a shout and a cheery wave, "Hello there, Underwood!"

Mr. Underwood seemed to have some difficulty in focusing his eyes correctly; but when he finally recognized the doctor, he waved back.

"Good day to you, Francis."

As they drew level, Underwood stumbled on the uneven road surface and the doctor's hand shot out to catch his arm and prevent him falling full length in the road, "Are you all right, Underwood?" He asked with some concern. Mr. Underwood laughed, "I'm ashamed to have to admit that I am rather foxed—I believe that is the current phrase!"

"If you mean drunk, my friend, you are quite right! Good God! I never had you marked down as a drinking man!"

Mr. Underwood drew himself up to his full height and attempted to gather the shreds of his dignity about him, "I am normally abstem . . . abste . . . I do not normally drink at all! This was all in the name of research! And I did not drink more than two pints to Tom Briggs' six, but the ale was of a rather stronger type than I expected."

"If you have been drinking with Tom, I'm surprised you are still on your feet! Come on, we had better get you off the street before someone sees you. Your brother won't thank you for causing a scandal!"

Mr. Underwood was inclined to argue this point, so the doctor dragged him bodily to the vicarage, which, very fortunately, was only yards away.

Once indoors the vicar's brother flopped into the nearest chair, and Dr. Herbert went in search of Mrs. Selby. He returned to find the abstemious Underwood fast asleep. He called to tell the housekeeper that the coffee was no longer required and left to return to his neglected round of visits.

It was not the last he was to see of Mr. Underwood that day, however, for much later he answered a knock at his front door and was surprised to see an elegantly attired Mr. Underwood standing on the step.

"Good evening, Francis. My brother was taking me to dine with one of his clerical friends, but I persuaded him to leave a little early so that we could stop here for a few moments. There was something I wanted to ask you."

"Oh, then please come in—but should we not ask the vicar in too?"

"Don't worry about him—he'll be quite all right in the carriage."

Having thus, heartlessly, disposed of his brother, he walked into the doctor's hall way. "This is your study, is it not?" He asked, pointing at one of the many doors leading off the hall. The doctor nodded and they both entered the room.

"As I said, Francis, I don't have very much time, so I am not going to hide what I have to say behind pointless pleasantries."

In the, admittedly short, time Francis had known Underwood, he had never noticed him hide anything behind pointless pleasantries, but it seemed infinitely simpler to allow this remark to pass.

"Do you know anything of a rumour that Lady Wynter met her end by anything other than natural causes?"

The doctor looked uncomfortable, but he refused to be drawn into unseemly speculation.

"Tom Briggs is a mischief-making old gossip!"

"Then you have heard it?"

"Yes." the answer was short and to the point—just the way Mr. Underwood liked his answers!

"Do you believe it?"

"What I believe is totally irrelevant. I was barely out of short-coats when Lady Wynter died."

"Come now, Francis, don't be coy. Do you have doubts or not?"

The doctor seemed reluctant to speak, but the barely concealed impatience of his guest made him nervous and caused a flood of ill-considered information to pour from his lips.

"Well, it is true Sir Henry did not send for the doctor to attend his wife. She was left to the tender mercies of the local mid-wife, who was, from all accounts, none too clean and over fond of the bottle. She was also the mother of one of Sir Henry's mistresses. It is quite possible that Lady Wynter could have been saved by better nursing—but that does not mean she was deliberately murdered!"

"Who was she?"

Dr. Herbert turned away from his friend and walked towards the window. "She's been dead these ten years and more! What is the point of raking up the past?"

"Who was she?" Underwood's voice was low, but it seemed to pierce the man who stood before him. His shoulders straightened as though in preparation for the carrying of a heavy load. "She was Hazelhurst's mother."

"Hazelhurst?" Mr. Underwood sounded as though he had been expecting the name to crop up again, "And the mistress was Hazelhurst's sister?"

"Yes."

"Where is she now?"

"I have no idea. She took her child and went to Manchester, I think. She hasn't been home for years—in fact I think she left before Lady Wynter's death, so you see, there would have been no need for her mother, or anyone else, to kill Lady Wynter. Everyone knew Harriet had an illegitimate child. She could not have married Sir Henry—he would not have so demeaned himself!"

"He might not have demeaned himself to marry her, but he didn't mind demeaning himself to bed her!" Underwood was angry and his anger made the doctor realise that he had said too much. "It is not our place to judge others." He reminded his guest gently. Underwood gave a rueful grin, "The trouble with spending one's life in the purified air of Cambridge is that it turns one into an insufferable prig!"

"Don't be so hard on yourself." Advised the doctor calmly. "Very few men are saints—and that includes you and Sir Henry Wynter!"

There was a gentle knock at the door and Helen came in, "Hello, Mr. Underwood." She said, with a charming smile, "I thought I heard your voice. Do I intrude?"

"Good evening, Helen. Not at all. I was about to leave."

"A very short visit! But you have saved me a journey. I wanted to invite you and your brother to dine on Friday evening. I have asked Miss Wynter and Miss Chapell and a few other young people, so I thought we might dance later."

"That would be most pleasant. But my brother and I are expecting a visit from our mother."

"Well, she must come too, of course!"

"Thank-you."

Mr Underwood returned to the waiting carriage and found his brother growing restive, "Do hurry, C.H. We shall be late! I abhor tardiness!"

"Very well! There is no need for apoplexy! I am here now."

The carriage jerked into motion as Mr. Underwood took his

130

seat, causing him to fall heavily backwards, and raising a muffled protest from his companion, who was unfortunate enough to be partially underneath him when he fell.

"So sorry, Gil."

"Good God! What have you been eating! You weigh as much as a horse!"

"Don't exaggerate! And I would have thought you would delighted that Mrs. Selby's cooking is doing me so much good!"

"Not when all that goodness lands right on top of me!" Grumbled the vicar, straightening his clothes and hat rather huffily, "Now will you tell me what you wanted to ask the doctor?"

"No. As it happens, I wasn't able to finish the conversation, we were interrupted by Mrs. Herbert. By the bye, she invited us to dine on Friday—with Mother, naturally."

"Very neighbourly of her."

"She has also invited Miss Chapell, so you can initiate your courtship!"

The vicar refused to dignify that remark with a reply, and the rest of the journey was covered in silence.

Mr. Underwood had been reluctant to attend the dinner to which his brother had insisted upon taking him, but he was pleasantly surprised to find that he spent a fascinating evening in the company of a clergy man who had made ancient tradition and folklore his hobby and passion. Someone had had the foresight to place two gentlemen next to one another at the table and once their conversation was set in motion, it was beyond the capabilities of anyone present to stop it.

For the first time since his arrival in Bracken Tor, Mr. Underwood was afforded the luxury of asking any question at all without having to fret about the consequences. His companion, the Rev. Josiah Blackwell, was surprised and delighted to find someone who seemed to find his pastime utterly fascinating and who could not hear enough of his researches.

Underwood's interest centered mainly upon the superstitions surrounding death, but encompassed all other country traditions, so Rev. Blackwell was given no cause for alarm.

"Is it true that suicides are believed to walk after death?"

"Oh yes. Of course the traditional remedy was burial at the cross roads, and since burial upon consecrated ground was frowned upon for those who had committed mortal sin, there was rarely any reason to deny the tradition."

"I had heard that another method was to drive a stake through the body, effectively pinning it to the ground."

"Well, that was more usual in the case of those who were suspected of having practised witchcraft, but I have heard of it being used in the case of suicides."

"What about the murdered?"

131

"Those who have met death violently, under any circumstances, are often believed to 'come back,' so to speak; either for the purpose of revenge or simply from confusion as to their position."

"Position?"

"I'm sorry, I phrased that rather badly. I simply meant that if death overtakes a person suddenly, their spirit may not actually realize that it has 'passed over.' Many people believe that such spirits continue to appear in their usual 'haunts' simply because they do not understand that they should actually be elsewhere. Simple people are terrified by the thought that they might be plagued by such spirits, so they take some rather archaic precautions to prevent it. Metal—especially iron, is believed to have special significance and power."

"Is there any particular reason for that?"

"Well, St. Dunstan is the patron saint of Blacksmiths and legend has it that he overcame the Devil with red hot pincers. However, I am inclined to believe that the mystic power of iron goes back a great deal further. The ancient peoples who inhabited these islands would have been easily overpowered by invaders who carried metal weapons."

Mr. Underwood was impressed, "You make it sound as though, if investigated deeply enough, any silly superstition may well have a sensible reason at the heart of it."

"I think that is probably true."

"And do many of these tradition survive?"

"Many more than one would imagine. Do you yourself ever 'touch wood' for luck?"

Mr. Underwood was forced ruefully to admit that he had indeed, on occasion, 'touched wood' to ward off misfortune.

"That is a legacy from our Celtic ancestors. They were, of course, tree-worshipers. They also believed in the power of the head, considering it to be the seat of all power and intelligence. They often beheaded the vanquished and cast the heads into wells and rivers."

Underwood was particularly interested to hear this, but managed to hide his eagerness behind a laugh, "Great Heavens! I hope that is a tradition which has long died away."

"I sometimes wonder." Answered Rev. Blackwell seriously, and Mr. Underwood knew a moment of intense discomfort. Could it be that he was on completely the wrong track where 'Mary Smith' was concerned? Could it really be that she was an unknown unfortunate who just happened to be in the wrong place at the wrong time, and had become the victim of some remnant of a strange and murderous cult which had used her in a weird sacrifical killing? Could there still be pockets of ancient beliefs left untouched by the onset of Christianity over hundreds of years?

If a clergyman believed it possible, then could he simply dismiss the idea as so much nonsense?

Underwood was more troubled than he cared to show. What had seemed a straightforward case was beginning to show aspects which he had never envisioned, but despite the fact that every question he asked seemed to engender a dozen more complex ones, he was still determined not to be swayed from his purpose. He would find the killer of Mary Smith if it took him until doomsday!

He absent-mindedly accepted the port decanter as it was passed to him, refilled his glass and passed it on to Rev. Blackwell.

"Believe me, Blackwell, I have no wish to question your word, but I really find it very hard to believe that such superstitious nonsense is still practised today! The world is changing, there are new inventions every day which make life easier for all, so why should people hark back to their ancient pasts?"

Rev. Blackwell smiled slightly, "You are a town dweller, aren't you Underwood?"

"Yes, but what has that to do with anything?"

"Everything, my friend! You have the town dweller's romantic vision of the countryside—the greenery, the sunshine, the flowers, the birdsong! Let me tell you that living in the countryside means that one rarely has the time or the inclination to sit about admiring Mother Nature in all her glory! Agriculture is a life of grinding poverty, sheer hard work, bitter chill in the winter, wet, miserable and dirty! And those new inventions which you so laud are the cause of even more misery! Small towns, villages and hamlets are being deserted in droves by the young people heading for the big towns in the hope of easier work and better pay—and that means that the ones left behind have to work twice as hard to produce double the food for these new town inhabitants. Whence do you think all the workers for these new-fangled Mills come? The countryside, of course! Is it any wonder that poor, ignorant peoples find some comfort in strange, half-forgotten rites which are the only stable thing in a changing world?"

"I suppose not—but what form do these rites take?"

"It is not easy to discover that! Naturally they are surrounded by deep secrecy—since in the past participants have been persecuted, tortured and put to death, is it scarcely surprising they have become very coy about disclosing anything of interest."

"Do you think they would go as far as human sacrifice?"

"It is a distinct possibility—but as a clergyman, I would like to think not."

"Do you know my brother's parish of Bracken Tor?"

This apparent change of topic did not seem to surprise Rev. Blackwell. "Indeed I do—and it is just the sort of remote place which tends to harbour the exact superstitions we have been discussing!"

It was Mr. Underwood's turn to smile, "Don't let my brother hear you say anything of that kind!"

"I wouldn't dream of it—but you don't seem at all shocked. May I ask why?"

"On the condition that it goes no further, I shall tell you."

"My lips are sealed."

Underwood did not begin to speak immediately, but twirled the wine in his glass and gazed thoughtfully at it. "There was a murder in Bracken Tor just over a year ago. A young girl. No-one knows who she was because her body had been decapitated. I have set myself the task of finding her murderer."

"Why?" Underwood raised puzzled grey eyes to Blackwell's face. "Of all the questions I expected you to ask, 'why' was not one of them! Of what interest are my motives?"

"They are of a great interest to me, Mr. Underwood, because I don't think you have quite considered what the consequences of your actions might be."

"If I succeed, I bring a murderer to justice! What other consequence could there be?"

"Justice? Have you considered what 'justice' means in this particular case? The culprit will be hanged—and you will have brought him to the scaffold! I know your type, Mr. Underwood, bookish, dreamy and incurably romantic! Are you going to be able to live with yourself, knowing that you have brought about another's death—be it justified or not!"

Mr. Underwood continued to find the wine in his glass utterly fascinating. It seemed he could not take his eyes off it. "As you have correctly assumed, Blackwell, I am not a violent man. I abhor violence of any kind. I don't think I can recall any occasion when I have raised my hand to another human being. I have never beaten any of my students, though God knows they have deserved it at times! And whilst I personally do not agree that to hang a man in any way atones for his crime. I also feel, very strongly, that no one should be allowed to take another human life and escape punishment. It is a dilemma which has tortured me."

"Then why put yourself through that torture? Why not simply mind your own affairs and leave matters like this to the authorities? If one believes in a just God, then one has to believe that sinners will be punished—in the next life if not in this one."

"And if one does not believe in God at all—what then?"

Underwood expected his clerical companion to be shocked by this quietly spoken question, but Blackwell was made of sterner stuff than that. He gave a slight, but infinitely kind smile. "What tragedy in your life has led you to that conclusion, my friend?"

Though Mr. Underwood managed to ask, "Now what makes you think I have suffered any tragedy?" his slightly shocked expression told Mr. Blackwell that his assumption was quite correct.

"There is no mystery to arriving at such a judgment, Underwood. It was a simple deduction. Your brother is a clergyman, and you are obviously close, you presumably had a similar upbringing, but something caused a parting somewhere along the way. Your brother never lost his faith in God, but you have, therefore the reason must be intensely personal."

Mr. Underwood grinned ruefully, "You have, of course, hit the correct solution on the first try."

"It gives me no pleasure to be right in these circumstances, my dear fellow. Do you mind if I ask, is it that past which drives you now?"

Blackwell felt, almost physically, his companion's withdrawal, "I have no wish to be rude, but I have never discussed what happened with anyone—not even my brother."

"Perhaps you ought to—but certainly not here and now. Let us leave the matter by saying that should you ever decide to take my advice, I would be only too willing to hear anything you wish to confide, and offer any counsel it is in my power to give."

Mr. Underwood merely nodded.

CHAPTER SIXTEEN

("Mater Familias."—The Mother of a family.)

Mrs. Underwood was blond like her eldest son, but had the calm demeanour of the younger. She alighted from the London stage with not a hair out of place and seemingly completely unaffected by the eighteen hours of rocking and bumping over largely unmade roads that were now behind her.

She kissed both her sons with equal affection, but the very observant might have noticed that there was an especially worried expression in her grey eyes as they scanned her elder child's face.

"How lovely of you both to come and meet me. Such an unexpected pleasure."

"Nothing could have kept us away." Asserted Mr. Underwood, with his most charming smile. His mother was well aware that she was being teased, and tapped his cheek with mock annoyance, "Behave yourself!"

There was a thud on the ground behind them as her luggage was unceremoniously thrown off the top of the coach, raising a cloud of choking dust, and Rev. Underwood ran to retrieve it, throwing an irritated glance in the direction of the unheeding coachman.

Whilst his attention was thus distracted, Mrs. Underwood took the opportunity to have a private word with her eldest, "Are you well, my son? I have been worried about you."

Underwood smiled and placed a comforting arm about her shoulders, "I have told you often enough, Mother, that you should not waste your thoughts on me! There is absolutely no need, I promise you! I should concentrate on Gil if I were you. You have sent him almost to the point of apoplexy with your little announcement!"

"Oh dear." Said his mother absently, not sounding in the least concerned, "What announcement was that?"

Mr. Underwood was well aware that his mother's apparent

abstraction served exactly the same purpose as his own—in fact it was very useful device for drawing attention away from subjects which were inconvenient. Being a master of this particular trick, he was not about to be taken in by his mother.

"The news of your forthcoming nuptials!" He explained patiently.

"Oh that!" She declared dismissively, drawing her gloves on and fixing them firmly by the simple expedient of pressing her index finger between each other finger, Well, I don't see why that should have upset Gil! It is not as though either of you live at home any longer, is it?"

Gilbert rejoined them at this moment and asked brightly—rather too brightly, thought Underwood, "Shall we be on our way? There is still some distance to travel, and I know Mrs. Selby will be eager to welcome you Mother."

From this Underwood assumed, correctly, that the vicar had known exactly what their conversation entailed and felt it entirely inappropriate that it should take place in the yard of the Crown Inn, Beconfield.

Presently, all the luggage safely stowed, the family were speeding towards Bracken Tor in the dilapidated carriage owned by the vicarage, drawn by on one of Tom Briggs' hired hacks. The Rev. Underwood did not keep a horse, though the vicarage did boast a stable, for he could not justify the expense of an ostler when he so rarely needed transport.

He was fond of walking, and there were very few of his parishioners who lived beyond his range. That his brother was not fond of walking and was finding the lack of a carriage an extreme inconvenience, was of absolutely no concern of his.

The vicar was handling the reins, very inexpertly in his brother's opinion, but he kindly said nothing on the subject, but turned his attention to his mother.

"How are the rest of the family, Mother?" This question was not prompted from filial devotion, but from an awareness that Mrs. Underwood could quite happily discuss her family for hours on end without drawing breath.

"Uncle George is suffering rather badly with gout." She answered.

"Serves him right!" Intercepted the vicar, in a most unChristian tone of voice, "He drinks too much! I told him often enough that his over-indulgence would end in some such way!"

"As I recall, he called you a priggish young puppy when you delivered that particular sermon!" Said Mr. Underwood, with a wry grin.

"Now, now boys! Enough of that. Uncle George is my favourite brother!"

"Uncle George is an outrageous old rip and if you knew half the things he has done in the past . . ."

"Tut tut!" Intercepted Underwood hastily, "Gil, kindly remember you are a man of the cloth!"

The reverend gentleman had the grace to blush and sank into a rather sulky silence.

Underwood, remembering that there were very few of their relations of whom the vicar approved, decided that it was altogether too unsafe a topic and guided his mother's conversation along other lines.

"Are we to be allowed to know to whom you have promised yourself in marriage, Mother? Your rather cryptic missive held no hint."

He saw his brother's shoulders stiffen, but it was too late to change tactics now—and it was something which was going to be discussed sooner or later, so let it be sooner!

To the surprise of both brothers, Mrs. Underwood began to laugh, extremely heartily, "Oh dear!"

"Perhaps you would care to let us join in the jest, Mother," Said the vicar rather testily, "I own I see nothing funny myself!"

"You would if you had seen General Milner struggling up off his knees after he had made his proposal!"

"Good God! General Milner must be ninety if he's a day!" Exclaimed Mr. Underwood.

"Nonsense, Chuffy! Don't be unkind!" Chided Mrs. Underwood, with great dignity, "He is exactly the same age that you dear father would have been, had he lived!"

Since the brothers had always thought of their father as the relatively young man he had been at the time of his death, this came as rather a shock and they both needed a few moments to digest the information.

"So you actually intend to go through with this folly?" Said the vicar, in a tone which he had tried hard to disguise, and immediately regretted when he heard the hiss of his mother's intaken breath.

"Gil!"

In his anguish he simply dropped the reins and turned to his mother, "I'm sorry!"

"Dash it all, Gil!" Yelled Underwood, making a dive for the reins and hoisting the pony to a standstill, "Are you trying to tumble us all into a ditch!"

Gil was too busy trying to take Mrs. Underwood's hands in his own to take any notice of his struggling sibling.

"Mother, I apologize. That was unforgivable."

"Yes, it was, Gil, but I do forgive you. I understand that this has all come as a terrible shock to you, but I think you should try to see my own dilemma. I rarely see you both—you have your own lives, after all, but I do feel horrible lonely sometimes, and General Milner has always been exceedingly kind."

"But you know you are more than welcome to come and live

with me, Mother! I've asked you often enough!"

Mrs. Underwood smiled and patted his cheek, "Now, Gil! You know how I despise women who hang onto their sons' coat tails! And if I was about to look after you, you would never feel the need to marry! No, I'm quite determined to see my grandchildren out of shortcoats before I die—though you two are making it less and less likely!"

Mr. Underwood had by now succeeded in bringing their errant steed under control and felt confident enough to take his brother's place and speak at the same time. "Mother, I have absolutely no doubt that you will live far longer that either Gil or myself, so you can take that pathetic expression off your face and stop trying to force us into matrimony."

"I don't know how I managed to raise two such rude and disrespectful boys!"

"Mother you know perfectly well that you raised 'par nobile fratum!' "

Gil laughed, "That's very good, Chuffy! A noble pair of brothers! Very apt!"

"It is not apt!" Said Mrs. Underwood, "You are an ungrateful pair of wretches, and I don't know why I have travelled all these miles merely to be insulted!"

The vicar cast a wicked glance in his brother's direction and confided, "Comfort yourself with the thought that you may not have to wait so very much longer for your heart's desire, Mother."

Mrs. Underwood brightened visibly, "My dear Gil! Don't tell me you have found yourself a girl?"

"Not I, Mother."

He had the satisfaction of seeing his mother quite bereft of the power of speech. Her mouth dropped open in a most unladylike fashion and several seconds elapsed before she was able to say, "Chuffy? I simply cannot believe it! Who is she? When shall I meet her?"

Underwood was glaring at his brother in a manner which boded ill for the time when they would be alone together. "Don't get yourself too excited, Mama! The young lady concerned has made no indication that she would welcome my suit—nor, may I add, has her father!"

"Not welcome your suit!" Mrs. Underwood was clearly highly offended that there should be any doubt at all that her precious son was a fit husband for the highest lady in the land. "If the young lady is too foolish . . ."

"Now, now, Mama! There is no need to fly into a pet! I merely meant that I have yet to ask for her hand. There are reasons for my reticence, I do assure you."

"What reasons, my dear? You must not let what has gone before ruin your life any longer!"

There was an awkard silence at this, albeit veiled, mention of Mr. Underwood's past, until the gentleman concerned managed to force a serene smile to his lips, "I am not, Mother, I promise. That was not the reason to which I referred. The problem is with the child herself."

"Is she not strong? Does she suffer from some progressive disease?"

"If you would cease to interrupt, perhaps I could explain the matter!" Mr. Underwood was clearly losing patience and his mother tried very hard to hold back the flood of questions which continually sprang to her lips.

"There is absoulutely nothing wrong with her. She is lovely, vivacious and in rude health—she is also, however, extremely young, and I hesitate to ask her to tie herself to a man who is considerably older than herself."

His mother snorted in contempt of his qualms, "Great Heavens, Chuffy! Is that all? God bless my soul, what does age matter? I'm surprised at you, silly boy!"

Mr. Underwood was not reassured and could not prevent a hint of sarcasm entering his voice as he asked. "Do you not think that a man has a responsibilty to ensure the future happiness of his bride by at least endeavouring to survive the wedding by perhaps a few years?"

"Now you are being pessimistic in the extreme, Chuffy! There is absoutely no need to think that you will not live to a great age and enjoy the best of health for years to come! It seems to me that you are simply finding excuses not to ask the girl!"

The vicar entirely concurred with this view but had not, so far, had the courage to voice the opinion, so it was with a rather unkind grin that he greeted his mother's remark.

Mr. Underwood turned from his mother and with great dignity clicked the pony back into action, "When—and if!—I feel the time is right, I shall make my proposal. Until then, I'll thank you both not to meddle in my affairs!"

The vicar and his mother exchanged a glance but wisely decided to make no further comment.

***

Mrs. Underwood had almost as great a talent for faux pas as her elder son and the next occasion when she succeeded in embarrassing every one about her was on the following Friday evening at the residence of the good Doctor and his wife.

With the vicar's almost fanatical preoccupation with punctuality, they were the first arrivals and were comfortably ensconced when the rest of the party arrived.

140

Hearing voices he recognized in the hall, the vicar leant towards his mother and whispered, "Chuffy's intended has just arrived, Mother. Prepare yourself to meet your probable future daughter-in-law!"

Charlotte swept into the room, looking extremely decorative in a white gown with an overdress of gauze sewn all over with tiny pearls, behind her came Jane, Emma and Eliza. Verity Chapell followed them, looking, for the first time in weeks, something like her old, cheerful self. Her eyes, when they came to rest upon Mr. Underwood, shone with a brilliance which lent her face an unaccustomed beauty.

Mrs. Underwood, catching the look and seeing a young woman who quite obviously adored her son, immediately rose to her feet and crossed the room, "My dear! How pleased I am to meet you! How wicked it was of Underwood to hide you from me!"

Verity blushed to the roots of her hair but could see no other course but to accept the salutation bestowed upon her. The Rev. Underwood, as always, sprang swiftly to the rescue, "May I present Miss Verity Chapell to you Mother. As you know, she has become Underwood's best pupil! And these are the daughters of Sir Henry Wynter, Charlotte, Jane and Eliza.'

Mrs. Underwood gave no indication that she had made any error, but kissed Charlotte as warmly as she had Verity, and accepted the introduction to the other sisters.

Underwood stood impassively by the piano, and attempted to greet no one at all. Fortunately his rather churlish behavior went competely unnoticed and presently Helen diverted everyone's attention by offering refreshments and drawing Verity and Charlotte to the instrument and begging them to play and sing respectively.

When all the company were engrossed in the entertainment, Underwood took the opportunity to slip out into the hall, observed only by Helen, who swiftly followed him.

"You are not leaving, Mr. Underwood?" She asked quietly, thus arresting his proposed flight. He turned and forced a smile, "Not if you wish me to remain." He answered.

"Of course I do." She told him warmly, "And what is more, I require you to put that silly incident out of you mind. Charlotte is far too overdressed for the occasion, and it is not surprising that your mother thought her . . . well . . ."

Thunder rolled ominously and a flash of lightning lit the hall to sudden brilliance.

"My mother thought her far above my touch—and she is undoubtedly right!" Underwood finished the sentence which hung painfully in the air.

"That was not what I intended to say." Said Helen gently, "Besides, what does it matter what anyone else thinks? It is how

Charlotte and you feel that is the only important thing."

"And how does Charlotte feel?"

"Only Charlotte can answer that question, Mr. Underwood. Would you like me to send her to join you in the study?"

He looked at her without answering and Helen experienced the strangest sensation as she met his eyes. In the novels she had read, she had often seen the expression 'her heart was wrung' and until this moment it had seemed rather silly, but the pity she felt for Underwood when she saw the years of misery and loneliness etched upon his features created an almost physical pain within her breast. She found herself promising violent retribution upon Charlotte should she give this man cause for yet more agony.

When at last he broke the silence, it was not the answer she had been expecting, "Not just now, Helen. I would rather talk to you for a few moments, if you can neglect your guests for a while . . ."

For one horrid moment she panicked, thinking that he was about to make an embarrassing admission to her, then just as swiftly she dismissed the thought. He was quite obviously in love with Charlotte, and anything he had to say would reflect that fact.

"Of course." She said, her voice bearing an added warmth to make up for the unworthy thought she had so briefly entertained.

There was a fire in the doctor's study, but it had dropped low in the grate. She was glad of an excuse to turn away from him, and busied herself with the poker, hoping to stir a little life into the embers. Thunder crashed again and made her start violently, "Good Heavens! The weather has certainly turned with a vengance, hasn't it?"

The first odd drops of rain rattled against the casement, and Mr. Underwood turned his head, "I suppose we should not complain, the weather over the last few days has been remarkably warm for May. I had been led to believe that I faced constant rainfall once I travelled northward."

"We have an entirely unwarranted reputation for rain, Mr. Underwood! I hope you are going to speak up on our behalf when you return to Cambridge."

He turned back to her, "I may not be returning to Cambridge, Helen. That is one of the things I wish to discuss with you."

She gestured towards a chair and seated herself at the same time, "Not return? But what else will you do? Despite your complaints of their behaviour, I rather thought you would be lost without your boys!" She smiled and was pleased to notice that it was returned.

"Oh, I think I could get used to living without them—in fact I would have to, if I was to marry. Wives are rather frowned upon in College—altogether too distracting!"

"I could imagine a wife like Charlotte being very distracting indeed!" Asserted Helen, somewhat stunned by the mental image she had created. Dear God! Charlotte Wynter alone among hundreds of men and boys! Not something to be foisted upon the long-suffering Mr. Underwood.

"Yes, upon reflection, I think it was probably a very wise ruling." Agreed Underwood, "But as you must see, it causes me a considerable problem. Is marriage worth the sacrifice of my career?"

Helen, who adored her husband, had no doubt, "A happy marriage certainly is!"

"But if I am wrong? If my marriage is not destined to be happy?"

"You are asking for guarantees, Mr. Underwood!" She protested hotly. "No one can possible assure you of happiness! If you are not prepared to take a risk, then no, I do not think you love Charlotte enough to make a happy marriage! I think you would always be harking back, blaming her for lost opportunities. If you have any doubts at all, then you should not even consider asking Charlotte to marry you. I can envision no worse misery for her than to be tied to a man who could not trust her with his heart."

Underwood looked shocked by her vehemence, but was still unconvinced, "She is very young, Helen. Do you think she fully understands what damage she could inflict upon that heart? I'm too old to withstand the anguish engendered by a fickle wife!"

Helen softened as she looked into his eyes, "Oh, Mr. Underwood! Yet again you are asking for sureties! Believe me, I do understand your reluctance, but if you love Charlotte, you must trust her!"

He rose to his feet and began to pace about the room in agitation, "Great Heavens! What do I know of love? But for a brief engagement years ago, I have spent my life away from the company of women. My only experience of love was the agony of loss! All I know of Charlotte is that she forced me to look into eyes which were filled with adoration for me and in doing so turned a heart of stone back into a beating, living organ! Is that love?"

"Yes, Mr. Underwood, I think it is." Answered Helen gently, "Wait here, I shall send Charlotte to you."

With that she was gone. Underwood walked across to the window and stared out into the rainlashed darkness. The storm had moved away now, and the occasional flashes of lightning and rumbles of thunder were growing distant.

When he heard the door open he turned and saw Charlotte framed in the doorway. The pearls on her dress shimmered as she walked towards him, creating an aura of light around her and reflecting the radiance in her eyes as she looked at him. There was a strange constriction in his throat and he had to swallow deeply before he was able to speak.

"I'm sorry I missed your song."

She smiled, "I'm not, I was so nervous of your Mama, I made a terrible mess of it."

"I doubt that—and you really have no need to worry about my mother. She is a very sweet person when you get to know her."

As they had been speaking, they had been moving towards each other, and now they met almost in the centre of the room. He took her hand and raised it to his lips. "It would seem I have several apologies to make. Do you mind if I get them over with?"

She gave a nervous little laugh, "I can't imagine what they are, but please do continue, if it makes you happy."

"No man is ever happy to apologize, my dear!" Her heart skipped excitedly as his slow smile reached his eyes, "Firstly, I was uncivil enough to neglect to greet you when you arrived, then I was careless enough to allow my mother to embarrass you. Both unforgivable sins, but can I hope you will overlook my transgressions?"

The colour crept gently into her cheeks and she lowered her eyes, "Pray don't . . . think any more about it. I understood competely. Naturally your Mama must think I'm altogether too young and silly to be considered your friend. Verity is so much clever than I, you are bound to have much more in common with her."

"Charlotte . . ."

She raised tragic eyes to his, "No please let me finish. There is something I have to say to you. I know I was sulky and stupidly jealous the other day, but I have had time to think about things and what happened tonight convinced me of the truth. I must have embarrassed you horribly by throwing myself at your head. I should have known you were only being kind to a silly girl. Even your Mama can see that Verity is the wife for you . . ."

"Are you refusing to marry me?"

Her blush grew deeper, "How can I? You have not asked me."

His eyes seemed very dark and deep as she looked up into them and she wondered how she could ever have imagined that grey eyes were cold. His were like smoky embers burning into her flesh.

"I'm asking you now."

Before she could answer he leaned forward and laid his lips gently against hers. She needed no futher encouragement. With a joyous cry, she flung her arms about his neck and returned the kiss with enthusiasm. Once his initial shock had subsided, he found himself grasping her waist and drawing her closer against him. For a few precious moments they kissed and clung, discovering the delight of each other, then the door opened and Helen glanced in. Guiltily the lovers sprang apart, hovering between confusion at the interruption, and relief that it was only the doctor's wife who had seen them embracing.

Her smile was wide and delighted as she announced. "We are waiting dinner on you both!"

Hand in hand they left the study, and still hand in hand they entered the dining room. One look at their faces left no one present in any doubt at all that all had been settled between them and they were greeted with a chorus of congratulation and felicitations.

Mrs. Underwood was the first to rise and kiss them both, and Verity Chapell was the second.

CHAPTER SEVENTEEN

("Amor Vincit Omnia."—Love conquers all.)

Mr. Underwood was not normally a man much influenced by convention, but he could not help but feel that in view of the extreme youth of his prospective bride, he had committed the ultimate solecism in asking for her hand before having sought the permission of her father.

In an effort to correct that failure, he therefore made up his mind to visit Sir Henry before another day was passed.

Accordingly, he rose early next morning and would have been on his way to Wynter Court before nine had struck on the case clock in the vicarage hallway, had not his brother gently informed him that Sir Henry was invariably a late riser, unless he was attending a meet, which, to the best of the vicar's knowledge, he was not on that particular day—neither brother was knowledgable enough in hunting lore to realize that it was out of season.

Underwood had to suppress his impatience until a much more reasonable hour. It was not an interview to which he was looking forward, and he had hoped to have it over and done with as early and as quickly as possible.

However, all too soon he was venturing out into the wet and misty morning, still grey and chilly from the rain of the evening before. The street was unusually empty—as it had been on the day he arrived, but never since—and he met no-one with whom he could exchange friendly greetings. Normally this would not have concerned him in any way, but today there was a slight depression hanging over him which only a merry smile could have dispelled. He squared his shoulders and set his feet on the path, comforting himself with his thought that he would soon be seeing Charlotte. Her smile would be more than merry enough for any man!

As he drew nearer the moors his mood grew even more despondent. The heather looked dull and lifeless, the lowering clouds had an ominous darkness which betokened more rain. It was with immense gratitude that he turned his back on them and took the path which led down towards Wynter Court. He hoped that once in amongst the trees he would be able to shake off his mood, but the silence was oppressive and the drips which fell from the branches seemed to be aimed directly at the back of his neck and slid icily down his spine. This was no way to approach his future father-in-law and he knew it!

Apparently the servants had been told to expect him, for he was shown directly into Sir Henry's study and was presently facing the man across the expanse of his enormous desk—a desk which was not merely decorative, but at which Sir Henry worked exceedingly hard, running his estate with knowledge and precision, and studying the cases he was called upon to try with an impartiality which was legendary.

Sir Henry leant back in his chair and appeared to take the measure of the man before him, his eyes narrowed shrewdly as if to mentally weigh the good and bad points of his discomfited visitor. For the first time Underwood saw the Judge and not the drunkard and bully.

"I shall put you out of your misery, Underwood, and tell you that Charlotte has warned me of you intentions."

"There was no need for her to have done so. I am perfectly capable of speaking for myself." Underwood's tone was quiet and measured, as though, even at this early stage in the conversation, he was trying not to let the older man betray him into a display of irritation.

"Speak then," Countered Sir Henry with a grin, "convince me that I should hand my daughter into your care—for I do assure you, she will be entirely in your care, once you have her, for I have no intention of paying anything other than a token dowry."

"I have never supposed otherwise, Charlotte will want for nothing, I assure you of that!"

"Good, I'm more than ready to admit that I have little time to spare for my daughters, but if I have a favourite, it is she."

"I'm sure she is signally aware of the honor." Underwood tried hard, but he could not keep the note of sarcasm from his tone. He took a deep breath and added, rather coldly, "Do you wish me to acquaint you more fully with my financial situation?"

"There's no need, I'm really not interested. As long as you feed, house and clothe her decently, and don't come whining to me for handouts, what you have or don't have is your own affair."

"Do you wish to know where we will be living?" Underwood began to understand the depression which had haunted him all morning. Sir Henry's indifference was genuine and complete! He leaned forward so that his elbows rested on the desk, and his chin rested on his now interlocked fingers.

"Would you find it shocking if I answered no to that question? Frankly I have no interest in your arrangements whatever. Doubtless Charlotte will visit from time to time, and that is all I require of her. You obviously think me an unspeakably callous parent, but should the day ever dawn that you have six daughters for whom you have to find suitable husbands, you will understand when one of those daughters takes it upon herself to find her own husband, albeit not the man you would have chosen for her yourself!"

It was as much as Underwood could do not to ask in what way he fell short of Sir Henry's exacting standards, for he was wise enough to know that the older man would have no compunction in telling him, and in doing so very probably convince him of his own unworthiness. Instead he summoned a smile, although a rather humourless one, "Well, there we find ourselves of one accord, Sir Henry, for if I am not your choice of husband for Charlotte, you are most certainly not my choice of father-in-law!"

Sir Henry laughed, "Whatever else I may think of you, Underwood, I have to admit that you are always painfully honest! There are not many men who would have said that to their prospective father-in-law! Aren't you even a little afraid that I shall throw you out of my house and warn Charlotte that she must never see you again?"

Charlotte's father spoke as though he were joking, but Underwood sensed he was being tested and answered with perfect gravity, "Not in the least. I have great faith in the Romeo and Juliet syndrome. I should merely ask Charlotte to elope with me—in fact the idea has several points which heartily recommend it, foremost among them being the complete absence of relatives at the wedding!"

The older man roared with laughter. "I've a mind to put you to the test, Underwood! I don't believe for a moment you have the courage to arrange an elopement, much less carry it through!"

"Believe me, Sir, I most certainly have!"

Suddenly Sir Henry seemed to lose interest in the subject and he flung out a inviting hand, "Sit yourself down, Underwood. We'll close the agreement on a glass of brandy and you can tell me what sort of a cricketer you are."

Mr. Underwood was rather stunned by the sudden veer in the conversation and he sank obediently into the seat he had been gestured towards and asked faintly, "Cricketer? I can still knock up a half century, but what has that to do with anything?"

"There is a match next week and we are a couple of men short. Will you play?"

"Certainly, I'd be delighted, but what is the occasion?"

"Oh, it is an annual match between Bracken Tor and Calden.

Dr. Herbert captains Calden, and I, naturally, captain Bracken Tor. Competition is fierce and at the moment we are running neck and neck. Bracken Tor needs to win this match to make the score even. Do you think you are up to the challenge?"

"I sincerely hope so," Underwood answered automatically, his thoughts elsewhere.

"I hope so too. If you let the side down, I shall have to seriously reconsider your marriage to my daughter."

Mr. Underwood smiled again, "Speaking of your daughter, do you think I might be allowed to see her now?"

"See her whenever you like." Underwood considered himself dismissed and left Sir Henry to his celebratory brandy which he was destined not to share.

The maid Sally was in the hall when he entered it, and he wondered vaguely if she had been listening at the door. There was an extremely pert smile on her face. He decided to ignore it and asked, "Could you tell Charlotte that I would like to speak to her please?"

"She's out in the paddock on Merryman, Sir. Shall I send Abney to fetch her?"

No, that won't be necessary. I shall go out to her myself."

Merryman was always a mettlesome beast, but today, as Underwood approached the paddock, he seemed even more spirited than usual. Charlotte was obviously having some difficulty in holding him, her face quite pink with exertion, and beads of sweat shining on her nose and brow. Underwood's blood ran cold at the thought of what damage so huge a horse could do, should he manage to unseat his rider. Very sensibly he did not call out to Charlotte, or distract her in any way, until she brought the wheeling animal under some sort of control.

"Phew! He is feeling his oats this morning!" She called brightly, sliding deftly from the saddle. The glimpse he caught of her long slim legs made Mr. Underwood unworthily think the horse was not the only one!

She led the skittish Merryman behind her as she walked towards him, and Underwood could not help but notice how small she looked beside the great beast.

"Do you think it quite safe to ride that animal?" He asked diffidently.

She laughed up at him, her eyes sparkling with glee, "Does he worry you, Mr. Underwood?" she asked softly, "There's no need really! He's an absolute lamb!"

Underwood warily eyed the now softly blowing Merryman, "A wolf in lamb's clothing, perhaps!"

"Just like Papa! And speaking of Papa, have you seen him?"

"Indeed I have." He took her hand and kissed it, "Our betrothal is now formally acknowledged by all, and my mother bids me bring you back to the vicarage for a celebration luncheon."

Some of the sparkle died from her eyes, "Oh Underwood! She terrifies me so!"

"My mother? My mother could not terrify anyone!" He answered her softly, "And she would be most distressed to hear you say so!"

"But if she does not like me!" cried the anguished Charlotte. "Maria's Mama-in-law makes her life a perfect misery, constantly causing dissent between her and Edwin. I could not bear it if she were to cause quarrels between you and I, simply because she hates me!"

"Calm yourself, sweet child! There is no possibility at all that my Mama will not adore you as I do . . ."

Charlotte raised tear-drenched green eyes to his, "Do you?" She whispered.

"Do I what?"

"Adore me?"

"I suppose I do." He answered softly, and lowered his head to kiss the pretty lips which were raised invitingly to his.

Merryman, sensing that his mistress was too preoccupied to pay attention to him, nudged Underwood rather roughly aside with his muzzle. They laughed and Underwood said, "I think we had better save that until we are completely alone!"

"We have the whole morning before us. Why do we not walk through the woods to the vicarage and you can tell me all about yourself. That way, if your mama asks any awkward questions, I shall be able to dazzle her with my knowledge of her son!"

"Very well."

As they strolled towards the house, leading Merryman, Charlotte suddenly spoke, "By the bye, I understand you expressed an interest in the Hazelhurst family?"

"Only in a very general sense." Answered Underwood guardedly, "Why do you mention it?"

"Oh, I simply thought you might wish to know that Hazelhurst's sister has come home."

"Has she really?" Mr. Underwood was very interested indeed by this disclosure, but managed to sound rather bored. "How came you to know that?"

"Papa and Harry were riding over that way the other day and happened to meet her on the road."

With his awareness of the past, Underwood doubted strongly that any meeting between Sir Henry and Miss Hazelhurst was accidental, but naturally he made no such comment to his fiancee.

"Why were you asking about the Hazelhursts?" She asked after a moment, obviously trying to instill the same level of boredom into her tone as he had, but scarcely succeeding. She had heard of the beauty of Miss Hazelhurst and had been

150

tortured by the thought that Underwood knew of it too. His evasive answer did nothing to calm her fears.

"Did I ask about them? I don't recall having done so."

"Helen Herbert told Verity that you had asked the doctor about them."

"And Verity told you?" Underwood's tone was a little sharp, caused by surprise and disappointment in Verity's apparent careless talk.

Charlotte bit her lip rather guiltily, "Well, she did not exactly tell me—I sort of overheard them talking!"

Underwood smiled, "In other words you were eavesdropping?"

"Certainly not!" Protested the young lady, but she made no further comment. How could she admit that she had been passing an open door, had heard his name mentioned and had not been able to resist the lure of hearing him discussed, even in so obscure a manner? Men were quite vain enough without being told things like that!

Once Merryman had been handed over to Abney, and Charlotte had changed her dress, the newly betrothed couple were free to wander in the general direction of the woods, which would finally lead them to the road and thence the vicarage.

Since they had, as Charlotte had said, the whole morning before them, their steps were unhurried, and their conversation animated. There was much they had to discover about each other.

"Tell me about your father." She asked him, "Was he like you?"

"No. He resembled Gilbert more than I. Dark hair and eyes. He was a merchant and spent much of his time abroad—China, India, you know. We saw him very infrequently really, hence our closeness to our mother. I think he was rather disappointed that neither Gil nor I showed any inclination to follow in his footsteps, though of course it was due to his success that he was able to ensure a good education for us. He died of a recurring fever he caught while he was away from home."

"How old were you when he died?"

The sympathy in her voice made him smile. She was obviously imagining a small boy bereft of his father.

"I was rather older than you are now, my dear, but it was not a pleasant experience. During his illness, he spent more time at home than he ever had before, and Gil and I had chance to grow very fond of him. When we were small, he tended to be a passing visitor who brought very exciting gifts. We did not appreciate him until it was almost too late. My mother adored him. She took his death very badly."

By this time they had almost reached the spot where Charlotte had suffered her accident with the trap, and since it had been that moment which had first drawn them together, she could not help but bring his attention to the fact.

She was unaware that her companion was interested in the spot for quite another reason, so was extremely gratified when he insisted upon stopping to look around, having first received her assurance that her papa had had all traps cleared from this section of the wood.

There was, of course, no trace left of that past tragedy, no bloodstains upon the grass, no imprint of a body amongst the now dying bluebells. He would not ask Charlotte to point out the exact place, desiring her to have no knowledge of his macabre investigation, but when he saw the flat rock, still bearing the strike marks of an axe or some similar implement, he knew he could not be far from the place the body had lain.

Looking down into Charlotte's happy face renewed the depression which he had fought so vainly to banish that morning. What manner of monster could snuff the life from a living, breathing girl? Who could bring themselves to cruelly douse that spark of fire which raised man above the animals? It took a kind of madness which Underwood had no desire to understand or forgive.

With a sudden fierceness which quite startled Charlotte, he drew her into his arms, pressing her against his chest. They remained thus for a few moments, then Charlotte gently said, "I'm very touched by this display of affection, but you are crushing my ribs, I can scarcely breath!"

Her prosaic attitude broke the spell. He laughed, rather self consciously. "I do beg your pardon. I was overcome with a sudden desire to protect you, but instead I almost managed to do you an injury!"

"Protect me from what?" She asked, taking a deep breath, and brushing her now dishevelled hair from her face.

"Life, I suppose. Come, we have lingered long enough. Gil detests tardiness."

If she was puzzled by his curious behaviour, she made no remark upon it, but happily allowed him to lead her back towards the path. She was feeling much more confident about meeting his mother again now, strangely enough because of that same curious behaviour. Never before had he, unprompted, embraced her and suddenly she realised that he did indeed love her, and was not, as she had been imagining, being courteous in not rejecting her advances. She felt suddenly very old and wise, no longer an apprehensive little girl, but a woman who was worthy of being loved by a man like C. H. Underwood.

Chapter Eighteen

("Terrae Filius."—A son of the soil.)

Mrs. Underwood was determined to atone for her clumsiness in mistaking Verity for Charlotte, so accordingly she made a special effort to make the girl feel warmly welcome at the vicarage. Since she possessed her elder son's charm in full measure, it was not long before Charlotte was quite as enchanted with the mother as she was with the son.

Gilbert, delighted to see his brother looking so happy, was also in sparkling form and the luncheon proved to be a very merry affair.

Charlotte felt so relaxed by the end of the meal that she was even brave enough to voice the question she had been longing to ask. "Please, Mrs. Underwood, won't you tell me what Underwood's name is? He absolutely refuses to disclose it, but how can I marry a man whose name I don't know?"

She threw a flirtatious glance in Underwood's direction, but he merely smiled calmly and waited for his mother's reply.

Mrs. Underwood drew her handkerchief from her cuff and made a great play of dabbing her eyes, "My dear Charlotte, you have managed to hit upon the one subject which quite mortifies me! How can a mother live with herself when she realizes that her child so detests the name she gave him, that he absolutely refuses to use it!"

"But surely it cannot be so bad as all that!" Protested Charlotte, quite shocked that Underwood had been heartless enough to castigate his poor mother for her choice of name.

"It is!" Intercepted Mr. Underwood wryly, "And I can assure you that my mother is under very strict instructions not to tell you or anyone else what it is!"

"Oh, but this is terrible! You can't possible mean to keep such a thing from me!"

"Indeed I do!" Asserted Underwood, "But I am prepared to allow my mother to tell you why she bestowed the name upon me, and if you can guess what it is I promise to tell you if you are right or wrong."

With this Charlotte had to be satisfied.

"Very well."

Mrs. Underwood looked rather startled, "Good heavens, Chuffy! You must be in love! You have never gone so far as that before!"

Underwood continued to smile his infuriatingly serene smile and Gil thought he knew the reason. Charlotte was very far from being bookish, and the chances of her knowing any Greek Mythology was extremely remote.

"Well, why did you name him so, Mrs. Underwood?" Prompted the now impatient Charlotte, feeling quite confident that she should soon know her loved one's Christian name.

"My husband and I travelled abroad after our marriage. We happened to be in Greece when . . ." She blushed daintily, "When we became aware that a child was a possibility. We were in Rome when we were sure."

Charlotte would normally have blushed furiously at so indelicate a discussion, but she was so eager to solve the problem that she simply asked, "So his first name is Greek?"

"And his middle name Roman." Inserted the wholly British Gilbert with a grin.

"Are they the only clues I am to receive?" Asked the now clearly disappointed Charlotte. Gilbert was quite right, she knew nothing of Greece at all, and even less of Rome.

"No, I shall give you one more. The gentleman for whom I am named married Harmonia, the daughter of Aphrodite." Since Aphrodite and her daughter were famed for their beauty, Underwood intended that Charlotte should take this as a compliment, but her blank look told the assembled company quite plainly that even these meant nothing to her and Gilbert began to feel rather sorry for her. Would she and his brother really be happy together? There seemed to be little common ground between them. Charlotte might seem young and innocently amusing now, but would her husband grow to despise her ignorance of the things which fascinated him? For the first time the vicar began to have qualms. Perhaps he had rushed his brother into a decision which might, one day, cause great unhappiness for them all.

To hide his own fears and worries, he hastily changed the subject and the former happy mood soon returned.

By mid-afternoon Charlotte had regretfully decided that she must take her leave, and when Underwood did not offer to see her home, the vicar gallantly filled the breach.

Underwood was quite unaware that he had, in any way, shown a lack of concern for his betrothed. The truth was that he had been thinking over what Charlotte had told him of the

154

Hazelhursts, and it was bourne upon him that a visit to their farm was long overdue. As always when he had a specific goal in mind, all else was forgotten, including Charlotte and his mother.

As soon as Gil and Charlotte were gone, he gave his mother a hasty kiss and bade her tell Gil not to wait dinner upon him.

"But where are you going?"

"Oh, just for a walk. I feel the need to blow the cobwebs away."

"Shall I come with you? I haven't set foot out of doors today."

"Not this time, Mother, if you don't mind. I would rather be alone."

"Very well, dear."

As Underwood reached the door, she called him back, "She is quite, quite lovely, my dear." She said. He rewarded her with his most boyish grin, "She is, isn't she?" With that he was gone and his mother was left with her own thoughts—and not all of them happy.

***

Underwood turned left out of the vicarage gate, past the church and left again when he reached the blacksmith. He had made it his business to know where each and every villager lived, but he had never actually travelled along this particular track, so it was with great interest that he looked about him.

Presently he reached the large house which was used by the two Misses Dadd as a school. All was quiet so he assumed the young ladies were all indoors at their lessons. His brother had told him that the Misses Dadd took in the daughters of clergymen and other respectable but generally impecunious gentlefolk, hence the far-flung situation of the school. Hill Farm, the home of Hazelhurst, was their nearest neighbour—and not a particularly friendly or helpful one, if the two elderly ladies were to be believed.

The track began to climb rather steeply and Underwood found the going increasingly difficult. It was not for nothing, then, that Hazelhurst's place was called 'Hill' Farm!

When he stopped briefly to catch his breath, Underwood was surprised to realize just how high he had gone. Bracken Tor was laid out below him like a child's toy village, he could see every detail, from the church and graveyard to the trees which marked the boundary of Sir Henry's property. He was rather glad that the mist of the morning had lifted, for all this would have been lost to him. As it was he could scarcely make out the tops of the hills, which were still mantled with low cloud.

155

He was beginning to think that he had been misdirected by his brother, for apart from the stony track beneath his feet, there was no indication of any dwelling place in this inhospitable spot. Even the sheep were few and nervous, running wildly at his approach. At last a single stone gatepost, set askew, proclaimed the presence of Hill Farm up ahead.

Presently Underwood found himself in the muddy courtyard of a large, stone built farm house and allowed himself the luxury of a well-earned rest upon a conveniently low stone wall. He was still puffing and blowing when he heard a woman's voice ask, "Are you all right?" and he was obliged to face the fact that he was quite obviously even more out of condition than he had previously thought.

He lifted his head and managed to summon a smile, "I shall be when I have regained my breath!"

She looked him up and down with a half smile and a look in her eye which Underwood was more used to seeing in the eyes of men when observing pretty wenches. Much to his chagrin he found himself growing red.

"You do know you are trespassing, don't you?" She asked, her hands upon her very shapely hips. Underwood could not help but let his eye rove over her. If she was, as he suspected, Harriet Hazelhurst, he could quite understand what Sir Henry had seen in her. From her dark hair to her slim ankles she was perfection—not his type, of course, but that did not stop him from understanding her allure for other men.

He did not answer her question, but asked one of his own, "Are you Miss Hazelhurst?"

"I am. And who might you be?"

"My name is Underwood."

"Good God! You're not the vicar?" Her disgust was obvious and Underwood was rather glad his brother did not have to hear it.

"His brother." He told her swiftly.

"Not much better!" She returned equally swiftly, "What do you want with us?"

"I don't want anything at all! I just happened to be walking in this direction and growing rather tired, I hoped to beg a drink of water."

She gave that same half smile he had noticed before—one which clearly said, "I don't believe a word you say."

"Just happened?" She mimicked unkindly, "My dear sir, no one 'just happens' within five miles of Hill Farm! It is the God-forsaken end of the earth! If you have taken the trouble to walk up here, then you must have a reason!"

He spread his hands and shrugged his shoulders, "I'm prepared to admit that I had not realized that the road led only to here, but I promise you there was no other motive!"

156

She seemed to hesitate, then spat, extremely venomously, "Are you sure you have not listened to village gossip and come up here to try your luck with me? Oh, I know what they say about me, and I don't give a damn!" The fact that she felt the need to voice this remark told Underwood that she cared very much indeed what was said about her, but he felt it rather safer to keep that opinion to himself.

"Miss Hazelhurst, you may believe me or not, as you wish, but I am very happily betrothed to Miss Charlotte Wynter. No other woman holds any interest for me whatsoever—now, do you think I could beg that drink of water?"

The mention of the name Wynter, as he had supposed it would, appeared to shock her and it was several seconds before she recovered sufficiently to speak again. "You had better come in, I'm about to make tea for my brother, and I'll not have it said I was ever unmannerly to a visitor—albeit an uninvited one!"

He followed her across the yard, through a door and so into the kitchen. There was nothing very different here than any of the village cottages, except that the room was considerably larger. The floor was stone slabbed, the fireplace equipped with hooks and spits for cooking, and before it stood two wooden settles, high-backed and uncomfortable, but the only seats the room offered. Down the center of the room was a vast wooden table, clean-scrubbed and worn with years of use. To one side of the fire was a basket which contained a greyhound bitch happily suckling several puppies.

Miss Hazelhurst indicated that he should seat himself on one of the settles while she hoisted a huge kettle towards the fire. He immediately rose and insisted upon helping her with her burden, and she reluctantly allowed him to do so, apparently not being used to such consideration. They were still involved in this rather unseemly tussle when her brother appeared at the doorway, scraping the thick mud from his boots on a cast iron scraper set in a niche in the wall.

"Who's your friend, Harriet?" He asked, glancing at Underwood with little interest and even less amity. Underwood observed him with fascination. In his voice and demeanour there was something vaguely familiar, something which caused his visitor to frown slightly as he tried to place it. The source of the resemblance eluded him and he was forced to conclude that in such a small community there were bound to be relatives living all around the district. Probably Hazelhurst would turn out, prosaically, to be a cousin of someone residing in the village.

"Vicar's brother on a walk." She answered shortly, finally forcing Underwood to relinquish his claim upon the kettle and fixing it over the fire.

"Odd place to take a walk."

"That's what I told him—still it wouldn't do if we were all

157

alike, would it?" She seemed almost happy now that the task was accomplished, and actually smiled at Underwood, who was hovering by the fire, wondering whether to walk across the kitchen and offer his hand to his unwilling host. He was reluctant to do so, because he rather suspected Hazelhurst would be rude enough to refuse to shake hands and he was unwilling to allow himself to be made a fool of before the woman.

As it happened Hazelhurst was not quite as churlish as he at first appeared and actually offered his hand to Underwood before seating himself.

"My sister and I are not churchgoers, as you will already have noticed, but I have heard good reports of your brother, so for his sake you are welcome."

Underwood was beginning to get rather sick of hearing how saintly his brother was—it was very difficult for him to see saintliness in the annoying little brother who had been the bane of his youth.

"Thank-you." He said, a little stiffly, adding swiftly, "I could not help but notice how high up you are here. Farming must be very difficult on such barren terrain."

"We have mainly sheep, a few cattle for milk and meat and hens for the eggs. We manage to live comfortably—but no man on a hill farm is ever going to die rich!"

"I suppose not."

"What is your own business, Underwood?"

"I tutor at Cambridge—or at least I did." Underwood frowned slightly as he realised how unsettled his life had become. He could no longer even tell another man how he earned his living.

Hazelhurst accepted a cup of tea from his sister, "What changed?" He asked bluntly.

"I'm going to get married." Answered Underwood, in an almost awed tone of voice. It was the first time he had actually allowed himself to speak the words and he was surprised to realise that the very sound of them terrified him.

Hazelhurst seemed to be aware of his thoughts, for he grinned broadly, "You must be ready for bedlam, giving up your freedom at your age!"

Underwood was rather offended. He had often congratulated himself on not looking his age.

"Anyone we know?" Added the incorrigible Hazelhurst.

"Charlotte Wynter." Said his sister quietly, handing Mr. Underwood his tea.

Hazelhurst spat copiously and accurately into the heart of the fire, causing a loud sizzle. "It's advice I know you'll not take, Underwood, but I shall give it anyway! Stay away from the Wynters! That family is a curse and a blight!"

Underwood maintained his calm demeanour, "You sound as

though you know them well, Hazelhurst."

"Well enough!" Growled the farmer, shifting his position in his chair, obviously uncomfortable with the knowledge that he had spoken carelessly.

"What manner of man is Sir Henry? I own I have seen little in him to recommend him to me, yet I have to make the attempt for Charlotte's sake." Underwood sipped the tea Harriet had given him. It was a strong and hearty brew, not in the least like the delicate tea favoured by his brother, yet he found himself glad of its downright flavour.

His host shrugged non-committally, "It depends on what you mean. As a Magistrate he is hard but fair—as a man . . ."

"Yes?"

"As a man," Interrupted his sister suddenly and very bitterly, "He is selfish, ruthless and incapable of affection. He uses people without thought for their feelings, and he casts them off when they no longer amuse him or are of no use to him!"

"Harriet!" Her brother spoke quietly, but she reacted as though he had screamed her name, starting violently and subsiding into blushing silence.

"He seems very fond of his son." Suggested Underwood, almost diffidently. Somehow it did not seem a very good idea to suggest that Sir Henry had any good points to these two, but in fairness he felt he had to make the attempt.

Harriet laughed harshly, "He's proud of him, aye, I'll admit that, but let's face facts! He has ruined the boy! He'll grow to be as merciless and arrogant as his father!" Underwood wondered vaguely why she should care. Harry was nothing to her. Perhaps as a mother, she could not bear to see any child being raised badly. This thought prompted another. Surely Tom Briggs had mentioned that she had had a child—by Sir Henry, if gossip was to be believed. He longed to ask her what had become of her child, but there was no way he could mention it without disclosing the fact that he knew the very village gossip he had previously denied. Yet again he was going to have to leave a place without asking any of the vital questions which plagued him. Fighting a stifling feeling of utter frustration, he rose to his feet.

"I have strayed long enough, abusing your hospitality with my uninvited presence. Thank you for the tea, Miss Hazelhurst."

"I'll walk you to the gate." Said the farmer, rising also, and accompanied Underwood out of the door.

Half way across the farm yard, he glanced behind him, as though to ensure they were not being followed, then he spoke quietly to Underwood, "You must forgive my sister's outburst, she feels she was treated very badly by Sir Henry."

"In what way?" Asked Underwood, maintaining the illusion of complete ignorance.

Hazelhurst's lined and ruddy features split in an unkind grin, "Village gossip must be failing badly if you do not know that my sister had a child by Sir Henry Wynter!"

Underwood considered the moment had arrived for him to admit he knew a little of their affairs, "I had heard something." He said a trifle cagily. "But you must understand that my brother does not encourage gossip."

"No, I can believe he does not. Well, since you are about to throw in your lot with the Wynters, I should like you to know the true story from me!"

"I would be very interested to hear it."

"Have you been married before, Underwood?" Hazelhurst asked the question bluntly, and though Underwood could not see what connection the answer might have with what they were discussing, still he answered it, "No. I was engaged once before, but never married."

"You cannot know, then, what it is like to be shackled to another human being for twenty years—bad enough if there is something to bind you, but intolerable if the partner you choose is the wrong one, in every possible way!"

"Is that what happened to your sister?" Underwood asked diffidently.

"Not to my sister—to me! When Harriet came home and told us she was pregnant, my wife screamed abuse at her, and threw her out of the house. And I was too much of a coward to stop her! I despise myself now, but then all I wanted was a peaceful life—and I thought Wynter would help her. He paid for her to go to Manchester, but that was about all he did! Harriet had to scrape a living, doing whatever she could to survive—do you wonder that she hates Sir Henry?"

"And the child? What happened to the son or daughter she had? I saw no evidence of another presence here with you—only two places set at the table, only two cups in frequent use on the dresser." Hazelhurst looked rather startled that his guest had noticed so much in a relatively short period of time, "I declare you do not miss much, Underwood!" He said in reluctant admiration, "she lost the child. Several years ago now. It was a blessing really, even if she doesn't see it that way."

"Was it a boy or a girl?" Persisted Underwood. The farmer hesitated for a few seconds before saying, "A girl."

Underwood parted company with Hazelhurst at the perilously leaning gatepost and barely noticed his surroundings on the homeward journey, so deep and confused were his thoughts. He wondered exactly how long ago 'several years' was, and if a man could grow so tired of his virago wife that he could bring himself to thrust her over a precipice.

160

CHAPTER NINETEEN

("**Amantium Irae Amoris Integratio Est.**"—
Lover's quarrels are the renewal of love.)

The morning of the cricket match dawned clear, with high, fluffy clouds and the promise of sunshine later in the day, much to the relief of all concerned.

Since the thunderstorm of the week before, the weather had been intermittently wet and misty, and all had feared a ruined day. It was to be the best day of the year, second only to the Harvest home, with every man given a day away from his labours, and every woman and child leaving their spinning and weaving untouched by the fire.

Mr. Underwood might not have looked forward to the match quite so gleefully had he known just how many of the players were baying for his blood. Two of Charlotte's erstwhile suitors were members of Sir Henry's eleven, not to mention her brother and the rejected Mr. Pollock.

Calden's team were not much better disposed towards him, having been told that the newcomer was Cambridge's ace batsman and a killing bowler.

Happily unaware of all this ill will, Underwood calmly took his place and was stunned when the ball hurtled past his ear, missing him by a fraction of an inch. Unfortunately for the man who bowled it, this seemingly deliberate attempt on his life merely gave Underwood the anger, strength and determination to hit the next ball bowled at him for an incredible distance, much to the delight of the crowd. The sight of Charlotte clapping happily and dancing excitedly on the spot was enough to convince Underwood that his heroism must continue, sadly, it also raised the ire of the four men who were out to prove him a fool before the obviously infatuated Charlotte. From there the match descended into carnage.

Underwood had easily knocked up his promise half century before it was bourne upon him that this was rather aggressive play for a simple village match. When his opening partner was

161

lost and Harry joined him at the stumps, Underwood hoped things would calm down a little, but he was destined to be disappointed. Harry's first action was to slash at a ball and yell "YES!" at the top of his voice. Since only an idiot would attempt to run a single at this juncture, Underwood wisely held his ground and Harry found himself out to his first ball. Since his intention had been to run Underwood out, his fury knew no bounds and the entire village had the pleasure of seeing Sir Henry's spoilt boy grow red in the face and throw his bat viciously in the general direction of the Vicar's brother. That gentleman neatly sidestepped the missile, then stood with one foot negligently crossed over the other and elegantly helped himself to a pinch of snuff whilst his new partner hurried across the field. The crowd went wild.

Things calmed a little when Abney came in to bat and Underwood was able to have a well-earned rest, since Abney was one of those shy batsman who would not dream of tapping anything beyond the odd single.

Sir Henry scored a very respectable twenty, and by the time the first innings were over, Underwood looked forward to his tea with a stunning ninety three under his belt. Charlotte flew onto the field to meet and congratulate him, and Pollock, Harry, Lithgoe and Radcliffe glowered at him from the sidelines.

"Have you any idea why not only Calden, but half of Bracken Tor were trying to kill me out there, Charlotte?" He asked, smiling down at the young woman who positively bounced as she clung to his arm. She had the grace to giggle shamefacedly, "Well, Mr. Radcliffe and Mr. Lithgoe both cherished a hope that I might accept their offers of marriage, and even Mr. Pollock had shown an interest before you came and swept me off my feet."

"I do think you might have warned me that I was going to be facing half a dozen rejected males! Jealousy is a terrible thing."

"Do you think they are jealous?" she asked ingenuously, her green eyes peeping mischievously sideways at him. Underwood looked at her lovely face, the burnished thickness of her hair, "Oh, yes." He murmured, "I think they are very jealous indeed—and with every good reason!"

A magnificent repast had been laid on trestles under the trees which skirted the village green where the match was being played. Sir Henry had not stinted, and there was not one female in the village who had not added a pie, cake or savoury to the haunches of roast meat Sir Henry had provided. It was a merry gathering, with food to spare and barrels of ale for any who wanted it.

Underwood was just downing his glass of ale when a voice behind him almost made him choke.

"I'm looking for a Mr. Underwood!" The voice was loud and boisterous, the voice of a young man who was vain and arrogant, and well used to getting his own way. Underwood turned, "I am Underwood." He said shortly, "What can I do for you?"

"It's what I can do for you that counts!" Answered the young fellow, grinning and making no attempt to lower his voice, "You advertised in the London papers for any information concerning a young woman who was murdered here last year." Underwood did not look about him, but even so, he was painfully aware that complete silence had fallen over those who were near enough to hear what was being said. He made no reply, but waited for the man to continue, "I'm here to claim the reward you offered, my friend, you see, Mary Smith was my wife."

There was a ripple of bemused comment, but Underwood refused to be shocked. "You have taken a great deal of time to come forward and claim her." He said evenly. The man who claimed to be the husband of poor dead Mary was not in the least moved, his grin remained firmly in place, "I'm a sailor." He answered, "I've been at sea for over two years. A friend presented me with the newspaper on my return and I came straight here on the overnight mail coach."

Underwood became suddenly aware of the many interested listeners and hastily drew the conversation to a close, "We cannot discuss this here and now. Are you planning to stay at the Inn?"

"I wasn't planning to stay at all. I came to collect my money and go!"

"I'm afraid it isn't quite that simple. I'm not such a gull as to hand over fifty guineas to the first man who tells me his tale. I suggest you bespeak a room and I shall meet you at the inn later this evening, say nine o'clock. Does that meet with your approval?"

"Certainly." He looked about him, "Do you object to my staying and watching the rest of the match?"

Underwood objected strongly, but could hardly say so. He nodded curtly and turned his attention back to Charlotte, who, he found, was looking up at him with worried eyes. He led her to a spot some distance from the crowds and invited her to sit upon his spread coat.

"What was that man talking about?" She asked quietly. Underwood did not immediately answer her, but addressed himself to his full plate. He chewed methodically for some time then swallowed and spoke almost casually, "It was just as he said. I advertised in the London papers for information."

"But why? I don't understand. What has all that to do with you?"

"Nothing. I simply found it untenable that anyone should be murdered and little or no attempt be made to find the culprit."

Though she did not move, he felt her withdraw from him, "Are you suggesting that my papa did nothing to bring the murderer to justice?"

He glanced down at her stiff face and hastily reviewed the answer he had been about to offer, "I was not here to see what effort was put into solving the mystery, I only know that it was unsuccessful."

"My papa prides himself upon his sense of justice! If there had been any way of finding that girl's murderer, he would have employed it."

"I have no reason to disbelieve you." He said, and determinedly took another mouthful of food, hoping that such an action would effectively cut short the conversation. For several minutes the ploy seemed to work, for she fell silent and he ate.

"Is this why you have been asking so many questions about the village?"

He nodded curtly.

"You cad!" She spat viciously, "How dare you!" She leapt to her feet and he was forced to grasp her wrist to prevent her leaving.

"Come, Charlotte! Be reasonable! How have I deserved this abuse?"

She glanced contemptuously down at him, her cheeks a furious red.

"You have used us all! We welcome you into our community, we gave you hospitality and respect, and all the time you were seeing each and every one of us a potential murderer!"

"Not you, my dear!" He protested. She wrenched her hand from his.

"Am I supposed to thank you for that?"

The hurt look upon his face gave her cause for hesitation, "I'm sorry you choose to see things in this light. Since you have obviously made up your mind to hate me, there is little I can say in my defence."

Her anger receded as quickly as it had risen, but she could not admit that to him so she said, rather gruffly, "I suppose I should hear your defence, if you think you have one!"

He did not speak for a moment, and she waited in silence for him to begin, trying not to be a distracted by the way the sunlight glinted on his bright hair, and how dark his eyes seemed when they gazed into her own.

"It was her grave, so small, overgrown and neglected. It wrung my heart to see it. No one should die like that, forgotten and uncared for. I simply couldn't rest until I had righted the wrong and found a name to carve upon the stone. As for my secretive behaviour—that was at Gilbert's request. He thought I should not investigate the matter for fear of rousing unpleasant memories, so I had no choice but to keep the reason for my

164

questions to myself."

The sadness in his eyes told her that he was speaking the truth, and she felt herself, almost unwillingly, sinking back onto the ground beside him.

"Does that mean I am forgiven?"

She looked steadfastly as her hands, interlinked in her lap, "I . . . I don't know what to think. Half of me can understand why you have done what you have done, the other half is still angry you should have so deceived us all.'

"That is understandable."

"Do you have nothing else to say? Nothing that can make me forget my anger?"

"No."

His matter-of-factness was unanswerable and suddenly Charlotte felt laughter welling up inside her, "You are impossible!" She said, but the laughter burst through and she could not control it, though her head told her that she had never felt less amused in her life! He put his arm about her to support her lolling body, which suddenly seemed quite heavy and helpless. Her laughter ceased abruptly when he kissed her, and she found herself responding with more passion than she had ever shown before. It was several dizzying seconds before she realized that they were in plain view of the entire village and that her behaviour was that of a hoyden. She pushed him weakly away.

"Come, Mr. Underwood. You have now to shine as a bowler, and you have not yet finished your tea!"

He released her and returned, with renewed vigour, to the plate of rapidly staling food. Charlotte went to fetch him more ale, and he hoped that it would not so affect his eyesight as to make his bowling a thing of amusement. There were too may younger men hoping and praying to see him fail!

As soon as Charlotte departed, Dr. Herbert took the opportunity to join Underwood and have a quiet word.

"Congratulations on your innings Underwood. I don't think we have ever had a higher score to chase."

Mr. Underwood, who was making up for lost time, did not answer because his mouth was full, but he nodded in acknowledgment of the other man's compliment.

Francis settled himself on the grass beside his friend and added softly, "Devilish unfortunate, that fellow turning up and shouting about his affairs to all and sundry. I'm afraid any attempt at secrecy is now doomed. How did Charlotte react?"

"Badly, at first." Responded Underwood shortly, he had suddenly realized how very hungry he was, and did not intend to have his meal disturbed yet again.

"You managed to explain it away, then?"

"No, I told her the truth."

165

"Gad! that was courageous! Are you still engaged?"

"Only just. She took my actions as a personal affront to her father."

"Well, I suppose in a way they are!"

"In every way!" Asserted Mr. Underwood wryly, "And I should not be at all surprised if he does not have something to say to me too!"

***

Mr. Underwood had been hoping for a little peace and quiet, in order to prepare himself for the meeting with the stranger who claimed Mary Smith as his wife, but it was a forlorn hope. No sooner had he entered the house than Mrs. Selby informed him Mr. Renshaw had been waiting in the study for over half an hour, hoping to speak urgently with him.

Underwood could not imagine what Renshaw wanted with him, but he resignedly entered the study and found an extremely agitated Renshaw pacing the room.

"You wanted to see me, Mr. Renshaw?"

The older man was white and shaking and Underwood immediately took pity upon him. Without waiting to ask he poured his guest a brandy from the rarely used decanter.

"Thank you." Renshaw took the glass and drained it instantly. It seemed to steady him a little for he was able to meet Underwood's eyes and say, "What I have to tell you is not pleasant, Mr. Underwood, and I want you to believe that I am not proud of myself, but when that young man turned up today and began to tell all assembled at the green that the girl in the wood was his wife, I knew I could not keep my secret any longer."

Underwood remained impassive, Mr. Renshaw had no idea how his belated confession was affecting his companion, and so he continued.

"I met the girl, only hours before she was killed, and I . . ."

A dull red crept into his cheeks and Mr. Underwood compassionately finished his sentence for him. "If she did not claim you as her kin, then the only other thing she could have done to cause you such embarrassment was to solicit you. Which was it Mr. Renshaw?"

Mr. Renshaw looked confused, "She made no claim of kinship. Why should you think she would?" Mr. Underwood did not bother to answer the question, but asked, "You made love to her?" The older man nodded miserably only too aware how sordid Underwood must think the incident, "I have no excuse—she offered, and I could not resist accepting. It was a

166

fumbled exercise, in a dark wood, on the cold ground and I need not scruple to tell you that it was largely unsuccessful . . ."

"Where did you meet her?"

"I overtook her just outside the village. I was on my way back from Beconfield and I stopped to offer her a ride."

"Where did you go?"

"She told me she knew of a quiet place we could go. It turned out to be Shady Copse."

"Did you kill her, Mr. Renshaw?" The question was quietly asked, but its effect upon the older man was dramatic. "Dear God, no! That is why I have come to see you! I realize now that I have been a fool to keep quiet so long, but I was scared witless when they found her the next day! Can you imagine how I felt, knowing that I had been the last person to see her alive? And what would my wife say if she knew what I had done? We have had an exceptionally happy marriage, Mr. Underwood, despite the tragedy of losing our only son! How could I admit that I had been unfaithful with the first little slut who offered herself for a few shillings?"

"Don't call her a slut, Mr. Renshaw. We are all what life has made us, and she seems to have paid rather heavily for her loose morals!"

"Yes, yes, I suppose so. But what am I to do now?"

"Answer one last question, could you provide me with an accurate description of her?"

The older man shook his head, "I'm sorry, but it was dark, I only ever saw her in the light of a horn lantern, I only know that her hair was darkish, but I could not give the exact colour for it was covered by a bonnet."

Underwood looked thoughtful and Mr. Renshaw unconsciously twisted his hands as he waited for him to speak again. When the silence became too much for him to bear, he asked diffidently, "You do believe me, don't you, Underwood?"

Mr. Underwood roused himself from his reverie and glanced at his companion. "I think I probably do, Mr. Renshaw, but you must let me think about what is to be done next."

Mr. Renshaw seemed pathetically grateful for this lukewarm assurance and he left looking a great deal happier than he had when he arrived.

He would not have done so had he realized what effect his tardy confession had had upon Mr. Underwood. There was something which troubled him greatly, and that was the significance of Renshaw's own words. He had said he was the last person to see her alive, but the last person to see the girl alive was surely her killer? Had Renshaw used his words carelessly in his agitation, or was his subconscious mind taking the opportunity to admit to the killing? Underwood was not a happy man. He had instinctively liked Mr. Renshaw and his wife, but he could not ignore the old man's determination that his spouse should never know of his brief infidelity. In trying to clear his name, Renshaw had weaved a mesh about himself that might ultimately lead him to the gallows!

***

When Mr. Underwood entered the inn that evening to keep his rendezvous with the stranger, his reception was somewhat mixed. On the one hand the entire village was delighted that he had, almost single-handedly won the match for them, having ended the second innings with three wickets and a superb catch, but that was rather negated by the news that he had been secretly investigating the murder of the year before. It was not something of which Bracken Tor was proud and they deeply resented this outside interference, which they took to mean that they had somehow failed to do their duty in allowing the culprit to go free.

He received a few half-hearted slaps on the back, but no one rose to offer to buy him a drink. This did not disturb him unduly, since he had more than his normal allowance immediately after the match.

The stranger was sitting by the inglenook, in the company of Tom and seemed to be conversing quite happily with the old fellow. This vision did nothing to comfort Underwood, for he had intended to ask several questions in order to discover whether or not the girl had really been known to him, and now there was the slightest chance that Tom had given away information which could be of use, if the man proved to be nothing more than a mercenary hoaxer.

As he approached the stranger rose, with that self-confident grin which Underwood had come to despise, despite their very short acquaintance.

"Good evening, Mr. Underwood."

"Good evening . . . er . . . Smith, I assume?"

"No, Blake, actually. Frederick Blake, late of His Majesty's Navy."

"Oh. Your wife was travelling under the name of Smith. Why was that, do you suppose?"

"Women do strange things sometimes." Since he accompanied this remark with an extremely meaning wink, Underwood was prompted to reflect that his initial opinion of the man was not to undergo any sudden alteration. Due to the successful day, the inn was considerably more crowded than usual, and it was obvious to Underwood that their conversation had little chance of remaining private, he therefore asked, "Shall we find somewhere a little less congested for our discussion?"

"Where do you suggest?"

"Your room here, or the Vicarage perhaps?"

"I think the Vicarage. I might need the vicar to support me should you decide not to give me the payment you promised!"

"I can assure you that if you are who you say you are, there is no need to worry that I will not fulfill my obligations! But let it be the vicarage by all means."

They left the inn together and were very soon entering the front door of the vicarage. Gil had been told to possibly expect a visitor, so had retired to his room, leaving his study at his brother's disposal.

Once he was happily ensconced in one of the more comfortable chairs in the study, Blake became positively expansive on the subject of 'Mary Smith.' He told Mr. Underwood how they had met, how long they had been married, how his wife had hated his long trips away at sea. Since Underwood had absolutely no way of proving or disproving any of this information, he allowed Blake to talk himself to a standstill before asking, "Could you describe your wife to me, Blake."

Blake laughed, but for the first time he seemed a little uneasy.

"Well, what the devil do you think I have been doing?"

"No, I meant her physical appearance. What was the colour of her hair, for example?"

The sailor was not quite so unprepared as Underwood had supposed, he gave his infuriating grin. "But I was led to understand that your corpse was headless, so how would you know whether or not I was right or wrong?"

"And if I were to tell you that I had found the head and now knew the colour of her hair?"

"I should ask you what it was, then tell you whether or not it was my wife!" Countered the not unintelligent Blake.

"Touche!" Commented Underwood, "It would appear we have reached an impasse! You can't prove my corpse is your wife, equally, I cannot prove it is not."

"So it would seem."

"Perhaps you knew her height?"

"Considerably shorter without her head!" Jibed the now irritated Blake.

"It was possible for the Doctor to estimate her height in life, despite the missing parts!" Returned Underwood coldly. He was now fully convinced of Blake's imposture, but it was imperative that he prove it beyond any doubt—not an easy thing to achieve when he was almost as ignorant as the fraudster!

"She stood about so high." Said Blake, sketching a hasty swing of his hand, which could have been anything between five feet and five six.

Underwood had a sudden notion, "Damn it all!" He cried, as though impatient with himself, "I forgot the birthmark. Naturally, if you tell me where the young lady's birthmark was situated, there can be no doubt that you knew her intimately." This was a shot in the dark, for he remembered no mention being made of a birthmark, but since almost everyone had one, it would be an easy thing to check the matter with Dr. Herbert.

For the first time Blake's grin slid from his face and stayed away.

An imperious hammering on the front door caused a look of relief to pass over his features. At least he should be allowed some time to think whilst Underwood answered the summons.

Mr Underwood was more than content to leave him for a few minutes, now being quite sure that he had asked a question which the arrogant young man definitely could not answer.

Abney stood on the doorstep, breathless and agitated. "Begging your pardon, Mr. Underwood, but Sir Henry has sent me to fetch you and the other gentleman. I've been all the way to the inn, but they told me you had come back here."

"He wants to see us now?" Asked Underwood incredulously.

"Yes sir. I have the carriage waiting."

Underwood desired nothing more than to tell Abney to tell his Master to go the Devil, but it was not in his nature to cause trouble for those who could not defend themselves, so reluctantly he caught up his coat, then fetched Blake from the study. "We have been invited to Wynter Court for an interview with the local magistrate." He informed the now seriously discomfited Blake.

"Magistrate? What the devil for? I haven't done anything wrong!"

"Nobody said you had! Now stop whining and come along. Sir Henry is not a patient man!" Underwood was already beginning to see how the situation could be turned to his advantage in breaking Blake's story and he was now quite looking forward to this tardy visit to Wynter Court.

CHAPTER TWENTY

("De Mortuis Nil Nisi Bonum."—Speak only well of the dead.)

It was after eleven when the carriage drew up outside the front door of Wynter Court. Most of the household was in darkness and Underwood assumed, correctly, that the family was in bed. Sir Henry had chosen the time for their interview well, there would appear to be little chance of their being disturbed.

Abney himself showed them to the library, then left them along to face his drunk and furious employer.

"What the devil do you mean by it, Underwood!" He growled, causing Abney to skip swiftly to the door and shut it hastily behind him. He had no desire to hear his master castigate the unfortunate Underwood.

That gentleman refused entirely to be intimidated and simply walked across the room, settled himself into a chair and gestured Blake to do likewise, "I assume we still live in a free country?" He asked, negligently helping himself to a pinch of snuff.

"What the hell has that to do with anything?"

"Quite a lot!" Swiftly Underwood rose to his feet and leaned menacingly across Sir Henry's desk, his face thrust within inches of the older man's, "It means I am free to do precisely what I like, and I certainly do not have to answer to you! You may be God Almighty to the peasants, but believe me, you do not frighten me! Now, if you wish to discuss this problem in a civilized manner, I am quite prepared to do so, but I swear if you speak to me in that way again, I am going to punch you right on the nose!"

It would be difficult to say which of the gentlemen was most stunned by this outburst. Underwood was a peace-loving man and he had never before felt the desire to strike another human being, let alone voice a threat to do so! Blake sat with a silly grin on his face, between amusement and astonishment, but for once speechless, unable to decide which man he judged to be the more insane.

As for Sir Henry, he grew very red, and spluttered inarticulately for several seconds before subsiding back into his chair. Underwood took this deflation as tacit surrender, and drew himself up to his full height. "I think we understand each other. Now, perhaps you will tell Mr. Blake and myself exactly why you wanted to drag us out here at this ungodly hour?"

Sir Henry still seemed to be recovering himself and did not immediately answer, instead he dragged himself out of his chair and headed for the decanter of brandy which stood on a tray with several glasses on an occasional table. He poured a very large tot with an unsteady hand, slopping more onto the tray than landed in the glass. He drank it greedily, watched by a longing Mr. Blake; Underwood could not help but notice the young man's expression of yearning and silently crossed the room, poured two more glasses and handed one to his companion. He tossed his own off in one swallow, feeling rather in need of sustenance since the magnitude of what he had done began to come home to him.

Sir Henry stood before the fireplace, his back to the flames, and the interview began. Underwood explained briefly how he had become interested in solving the mystery of the unknown murder victim (though he gave no reason for that interest; a man of Sir Henry's obvious insensitivity was hardly likely to identify with his own feelings of pity for the poor girl) and how he traced her coach journey from London. He told of the newspaper advertisement and the promise of monetary reward for information. He then turned to Mr. Blake, as did Sir Henry, and both gentlemen waited patiently for him to add his side of the story. Blake had been seriously disconcerted by the events of the past few minutes, so that when he tried to speak, his voice was a hoarse croak. He choked, took a sip of brandy and tried again.

"I don't know what you expect from me! I've told you that the woman you call Mary Smith was my wife, now I just want my money so I can go!"

"A wedding license would be helpful for a start!" Said Sir Henry, making no attempt to disguise the skepticism in his tone. Underwood almost dashed a hand against his forehead; what a fool he was! Why had he not thought of that? It might not prove who Mary Smith was, but it would certainly prove whether or not Blake had ever actually been married!

"I don't carry it around with me." Answered Blake smoothly.

"Then I suggest you go back to London, and when you have it, you can bring it to show us!'

Blake's tone took on an unpleasantly whining quality which Underwood found even more odious than his previously arrogant one.

"That's hardly fair! It has cost me a small fortune to get here! You can't mean to send me back without the reward!"

"Then you had better come up with some much more convincing proof, my friend!"

"I'm tired!" Protested the young man, "I can hardly think straight! I have travelled for eighteen hours, and barely slept for twenty-four!"

"Very well, we will continue this conversation in the morning. Be here at eleven thirty sharp!"

Feeling themselves dismissed, Blake and Underwood made for the door. Sir Henry allowed Blake to enter the hall before laying a restraining hand upon Underwood's sleeve. "I think you will find," he said confidentially, "that young man will have pranced back to whichever cesspit he rose from, by eleven tomorrow morning!"

For Mr. Underwood it seemed to be going against nature to actually agree with anything said by Sir Henry Wynter, but on this occasion he was forced to concede that the magistrate was very probably correct.

He nodded, then followed Blake into the hall.

Sir Henry, however, had one last shock to release upon them, for as his two guests approached the front door he said, "I told Abney he could retire, since it was so late, so I'm afraid you will have to walk back to the village." With that he went back down the passageway and shut the library door upon them. The two men exchanged stunned glances, "Does he mean it?" Asked the exhausted Blake rather bleakly.

"I'm very much afraid he does!" Sighed a resigned Underwood, "Damn the old goat!"

Mr. Underwood would have preferred, from a distance point of view, to have taken the short cut through the woods, but knowing Sir Henry's predilection for protecting his property with man-traps, he decided that, though longer, the drive itself was infinitely safer.

They began the long tramp in silence, their way lit only by the moon and a small horn lantern which Abney had kindheartedly left for them. Blake was quite obviously growing more and more disheartened. He could plainly see his fifty guineas drifting further and further from his grasp, added to which he had already spent considerable sums on clothes, travel and staying at the inn. To say that he was disillusioned by his first voyage into fraud would be to vastly understate the matter.

Underwood could only be grateful that his companion showed no inclination to talk, and in fact had fallen slightly behind, presumably to discourage conversation.

He abhorred violence of any kind and the strain of the past twenty-four hours was beginning to play upon his nerves. He still could not quite believe that he had played in such a blood thirsty game of cricket, and then actually threatened to strike his future father-in-law. He wondered vaguely how Charlotte would react when she was told of it.

Slowly, though, the tension in his body began to relax and he found himself rather enjoying this unexpected late-night stroll. It was a glorious evening, with a clear sky and all manner of fragrant odours wafting from the still damp earth. Neither man was hurrying, mainly from absolute weariness, and Underwood found himself breathing deeply of the clean air and looking happily about him. It was full moonlight, with not even an occasional wisp of cloud to obscure the light. Though they did have a small horn lamp, provided by the ever thoughtful Abney, it was not really necessary for it was quite incredible how much could be discerned in the silvery haze. The faintest breeze rustled the leaves above their heads and he found himself smiling slightly; he had always considered the sound of wind-stirred leaves to be the most cheerful of noises, giving one the same feeling of joy and well-being as the burbling of a brook or the distant sound of children's laughter.

He thought he heard some animal snuffling amongst last year's leaves and he wondered what it might be. The sight of a badger shambling out on its nightly forage, or a fox darting in the moonlight, its eyes glinting coldly as it stared at them, would be the final perfection.

Suddenly a shot rang out and Underwood instinctively shied. Behind him Blake crashed to the ground with a sickening thud, the breath forced from his body by the impact.

It was several seconds before Underwood could gather his shocked wits sufficiently to understand what had happened. Blake lay, face upward, his arms thrown outwards, his eyes open, staring, shining slightly with reflected moonlight. A dark stain spread across his body, Underwood knew he was dead, but he forced himself to try and find a pulse in the neck, the wrist.

As he knelt there, alone in the moonlight, vainly trying to find some evidence of life in the young man who had some few minutes before been complaining of his utter weariness, Underwood was struck by a dizzying nausea, which he had to close his eyes against and fight. He could not pass out here, for one thing he was not safe. Whoever had shot Blake could even now be reloading his gun. With a supreme effort he found the strength to stagger to his feet and set off at an unsteady run back to Wynter Court.

With little thought for the sleeping inmates of the house, he raised the great knocker and hammered it against the door with all his might. The sound reverberated through the house and presently the light of a single candle could be seen through the windows on either side of the door gliding in a ghostly fashion down the stairs.

Brownsword, his coat drawn hastily over his night-shirt, opened the door to the ashen-faced Underwood. The latter stumbled into the hall and sank into a convenient chair, "Fetch help. There has been an accident!"

Roused by the noise several members of the family now began to descend the stairs, Charlotte amongst them. Seeing the pale and obviously shaken Underwood, she rushed to his side, only to recoil in horror when she saw his blood-soaked sleeve, "Good God! What has happened to you, Underwood!"

"It is not my blood." He said soothingly, but she shook her head.

"Yes it is! Your coat is torn and I can see the wound!"

Underwood glanced down and saw she spoke the truth. The material of the upper arm of his coat was jaggedly torn, and blood oozed from the flesh beneath. The shot which had killed Blake must have first skimmed past him, catching his arm. He had felt nothing then, but now his face drained completely of colour, he closed his eyes and slid gracefully to the floor in a dead faint.

Charlotte shrieked at Brownsword to fetch brandy, a doctor and anything else he could think of, whilst Jane sensibly hoisted the inert Underwood into a sitting position and gently slapped his cheeks until he opened his eyes.

Presently, the situation explained, Underwood was led by a solicitous Charlotte into the parlour where he was persuaded to lie on the sofa and await the doctor's arrival, while Abney and two footmen were despatched to search the woods and bring back the body of the unfortunate Blake. Harry, who had arrived rather belatedly on the scene was sent to fetch Dr. Herbert.

Brownsword was sent to rouse the master of the house, who had, apparently, slept through all the noise. Knowing him to be drunk, Underwood was scarcely surprised that he had heard none of the hysteria which had taken place directly beneath his room.

Charlotte seated herself on a foot-stool at Underwood's side and alternately held his hand, and bathed his brow with cold water. Underwood lay with his eyes firmly shut, hardly aware of his loved one's ministrations. A dull ache had now set into his arm and he was suffering from severe shock, brought on not only by his injury, but by the increasing certainty that he had brushed as close to death as he was ever likely to without succumbing. A matter of inches had saved him and condemned Blake.

He fully realized that it was his startled movement when he had heard the shot which had probably saved his life—but had it been an accident? Some poacher who had seen an unexpected movement in the moonlight and assumed he was seeing a deer? Or was his own sinister suspicion the truth, that someone had meant to kill him and that the unlucky Blake had received a shot meant for him?

He sat bolt upright as another thought struck him, making

Charlotte jump nervily before recovering herself and gently forcing him back into a prone position.

Had the shot actually been meant for Blake—had he known more than he told? Did he perhaps know who had killed the woman who had called herself Mary Smith, and had that murderer killed again to ensure that his secret was never revealed? Where had Mr. Renshaw gone after he left the vicarage?

Underwood allowed his features to relax into the serenity of sleep, but behind the expressionless mask his mind was a swirling, bubbling eddy of confused thought, with the occasional piece of flotsam thrown to the surface, to be caught, retained and examined further at a later date.

CHAPTER TWENTY-ONE

("Littera Scripta Manet."—What is written is permenant.)

Though he would never have thought it possible, Underwood did fall into a light doze and was aroused only by the arrival of Dr. Herbert.

"What have you been doing to yourself?" He enquired, in that hearty tone which was meant to take the patient's mind off their trauma. The glance which Underwood cast at him left him in no doubt that this was the wrong approach for this particular sufferer. He hastily sent Charlotte to fetch water and cloths and carried a chair to the side of the sofa.

"I assume I made no mistake and the man is beyond help?" asked Underwood, as the doctor sat beside him.

"You made no error, my friend. I'm sorry."

"For him, or for me?"

"For both of you, if you must have it! He may be dead, but your experience cannot have been altogether pleasant!"

"Not altogether."

Francis bade him shift into a sitting position and helped him remove his coat, saying as he did so, "You are a lucky man, Underwood."

"More fortunate than Blake, certainly!" Agreed Underwood bitterly.

The doctor deftly cut away the material of his shirt, exposing the injury to view, "A mere scratch. Nothing to worry you there." Underwood forced himself to look and was humiliated to see that his wound was indeed a mere scratch. To have fainted on account of it was mortifying, but the circumstances were rather exceptional, and he had no way of knowing that it was so minor.

"I understand you heard only one shot, so I suppose the bullet must have brushed past you before it hit poor Blake."

"I suppose so."

"What a damnable thing! A tragic accident! No doubt it was

177

some poacher who mistook your movements for a deer."

"Francis!" Protested Underwood, "It was almost as bright as day out there this evening! I could see individual leaves upon the trees! And I have yet to see a deer carrying a lantern! Any man who was a good enough shot to hit a man in the heart, was blessed with sight good enough to know the difference between man and beasts!"

"Are you trying to say that you don't believe it was an accident?"

"I have my doubts!" Further conversation was halted by the arrival of Charlotte with a basin and ewer of hot water. Dr. Herbert relieved her of her burden and said, "I think you had better wait outside, Charlotte. It would be unseemly for you to remain with Underwood stripped to the waist!"

"Oh nonsense! We are to be married, and I have seen Harry thus hundreds of times!"

"And when you are married, Underwood will be your business, until then—Out!" She went sulkily out, but not before flashing a pert smile in Underwood's direction.

Francis said nothing more until he had helped his patient out of his shirt, then he began to clean the wound with water Charlotte had brought, "I don't know what answer to give you. I find it hard to believe that anyone would make an attempt on your life!"

"What other explanation is there? Blake lies dead and but for a chance movement, it would have been me!"

"But who could possibly have known you would be there, and at what time?"

"Unfortunately any number of people. Sir Henry sent for us. Abney came, but called at the inn first, thinking we were there. As you can imagine, the inn was particularly full this evening due to the success of the cricket match. It is going to be almost impossible to prove or disprove any one's knowledge of mine and Blake's whereabouts—as for time, well, they need only hide amongst the trees, knowing that sooner or later we would have to pass—though they must have been expecting us to return in the carriage—I certainly was!"

"Sir Henry did not offer you a carriage in which to return to the vicarage?"

"On the contrary, he told us he had sent Abney to bed and we would have to walk!"

"So, Sir Henry was the only man who knew you were on foot?" Underwood stared at Francis for several minutes, a faint frown creasing his brow. At last he shook his head, as though to dislodge an unworthy thought, "He was drunk when we left him. He couldn't have hit a barn door—and Abney knew also, of course."

"Of course we are assuming that this is all connected with

Mary Smith. We could be quite wrong."

"What do you mean?"

"Well there was more than one man who was lusting for your blood this afternoon!"

"Charlotte's disappointed suitors, do you mean? No, I refuse to believe any one of them feels strongly enough to commit murder!"

"That may not have been the intention! Perhaps they hoped to frighten you into leaving Bracken Tor. It is the sort of hot-headed stupidity for which young men are renowned! A warning shot which tragically found a target."

Underwood had to admit that his friend had found a plausible theory, but he was tired and could not find the necessary energy to even think about it. He winced as the doctor tied the final knot in his makeshift bandage.

"I suggest you accept Sir Henry's hospitality for the night. Perhaps things will look different in the morning. I shall call back to make sure there are no further problems and that you have no fever, then you can go back to the vicarage."

"Thank you Francis." The doctor smiled and gripped Underwood's good shoulder in an affectionate hand. "I'm very glad to be able to be of service."

Reluctantly Mr. Underwood allowed Charlotte to arrange for the bed in the Blue room to be made up and warmed, then accepted her assistance in climbing the stairs. He tried not to think that whilst he was enjoying the warmth of a feather bed, Blake was laid on a sheep hurdle in an empty stable, a hole in his heart and his lifesblood staining the embroidery of his new waistcoat.

He wished now he had given the man fifty guineas and sent him back to London on the first available coach.

***

Charlotte allowed him to sleep late the next morning, then brought him a tray piled high with cold meats and a pot of coffee. Underwood had never felt less like eating, but was making a valiant attempt when there came the lightest of tapping upon his bedroom door.

It was Verity Chapell, who entered like a thief, looking about her as though she expected hidden observers in every corner. Mr. Underwood watched these actions with some amusement before asking,

"What exactly are you doing, Verity?"

"I need to speak to you." She told him in hushed tones.

"Then speak, and stop looking about you like that! You have

179

a most unpleasantly cunning expression upon your face!'

"Well, I don't want to be caught in here! How would it look?"

"It would look precisely how it is! One of my friends coming to enquire after my health! Now, for Heaven's sake sit down!" She did as she was asked, but still seemed ill-at-ease.

"What did you wish to see me about?"

"Last night. I'm so relieved you were not hurt badly!"

"Thank you, but I cannot help wishing Blake had been as fortunate! I feel very responsible."

"You cannot blame yourself for that!" She protested, "Blake was simply in the wrong place at the wrong time!"

"Yes, but it was I who brought him here!"

"Nonsense! Greed brought him here, nothing more! I don't believe for a moment that he was married to our girl, do you?"

Underwood was forced to admit that he did not, "But he paid a very high price for his greed!" He added rather bitterly.

"Where do we go from here?" She asked, ignoring his last remark.

"I'm not sure we go anywhere, Verity. I cannot help feeling that we may have reached the end of the road."

Verity was appalled, "You cannot mean that, Underwood! Who ever killed Mary Smith probably killed Blake too! You said yourself that we needed them to make an error so that we could trap them! This could be that error!"

He held up a calming hand, "Hold your hand! We have absolutely no proof that Blake's death is connected in any way with Mary Smith! It could all have been a tragic accident!"

"Do you believe it was?" She retorted disdainfully. Underwood gave her a rather more careful answer than was his wont. "What I believe does not matter. I cannot prove it!"

Verity looked into his eyes, but his glance dropped away and began scanning the breakfast tray, as though searching for a tempting morsel. She rose to her feet. "You know who committed both murders, don't you?"

"No." His answer was short, but he would not meet her gaze. Anger made the blood drain from her face, "You coward!" She hissed, "It has grown too dangerous for you, so you are going to give up! I thought I had met a man with a little more backbone than that!"

That made him look up, and though his voice was even when he responded, she knew he was furious. "If you think it is because I have been shot at, you are wrong! I am not afraid of injury or death! But I am afraid of the hurt I can cause to the innocent! Blake is dead! How many more lives will be ruined if we pursue this matter?"

"You didn't feel that way when you began this! I suppose it is your precious Charlotte who has changed your mind! Did she throw a tantrum because you upset her darling papa?"

Underwood had never expected to hear such vitriol pouring from her puritanical little body and he was shocked and distressed by it.

"Verity . . . ." He began to plead with her, but she had gone beyond being placated. For a whole year now she had had to bear criticism, abuse, bullying, unkindness and condescension. Underwood had inadvertently opened the floodgate of repressed emotions, and now he would have to bear the consequences.

"Be damned to you! Don't make your excuses to me! I don't want to hear them! You go and play the lover with your pretty little mistress! I shall find Mary's murderer alone!"

With that she stormed out of the room and slammed the door behind her. Underwood was left with even less appetite for his meal than he had wakened with, and with even more to think about when he returned to the vicarage.

***

A procession of visitors followed, effectively preventing him from getting out of bed and getting dressed, which was all he really wanted to do.

Charlotte was accompanied by Dr. Herbert, who declared him fit enough to return home, but then his mother and brother arrived. Gil looked suitably grave, in the light of the tragic death of Blake. Mrs. Underwood was bravely tearful, immensely relieved that her boy had not been the fatality, but trying hard not to show it, since such a display of emotion was bound to embarrass her elder son.

Sir Henry waited for the departure of his family before he came to enquire after his guest's health and to ask several searching questions about the incidents of the previous night.

Underwood bore this interrogation with fortitude until Sir Henry asked a question which aroused his irritation to a dangerous level.

"Tell me Underwood, do you possess a gun?"

"I beg your pardon?"

"I think you heard the question."

"Indeed I did!" Underwood managed to retain an evenness in his tone, "May I ask why you ask it?"

"Why not simply answer? Have you something to hide?"

Underwood's eyes narrowed slightly, but he gave no other indication of his annoyance, "No. I do not possess a gun."

"Do you have anyone who could vouch for that?"

"Yes. My brother. I assume the word of a clergyman is satisfactory?"

"Brothers have been known to lie for brothers!"

"That may well be so, but I would like to remind you that you are not dealing with Cain and Abel!"

"I don't think you realize the seriousness of your situation, Underwood! The woods have been searched and there is no evidence that there was ever anyone else in there last night! That leads to only one conclusion!"

"Are you trying to suggest that I killed Blake?"

Sir Henry's colour seemed a little higher than usual, Underwood noticed. Was it his imagination, or did the man appear to be somewhat harried?

"I am not suggesting anything—yet!"

"I should like to remind you that I was injured by the same bullet that killed Blake!"

"We only have your word for that! Self-inflicted injuries are not uncommon in situations like these."

"That is ridiculous! and so is the suggestion that I might have killed Blake! What reason would I have? I met the man for the first time yesterday!"

"Again we have only your word for that! And fifty guineas is a great deal of money!"

"Are you suggesting I committed a murder so that I would not have to pay the man fifty guineas?" Underwood was incredulous, and growing more heated with every passing moment.

Sir Henry rose, "You are free to go back to the vicarage, Underwood, but as local magistrate, I must ask you not to attempt to leave Bracken Tor!"

Underwood was so shocked by these latest developments, he found it almost impossible to leave his bed, let alone the district. It was a very subdued man who climbed into the gig beside a silent Abney, and allowed himself to be returned to the home of his brother.

***

During the next few days time hung heavily upon Underwood's hands. His mother was insistent that he rest and recover from his wound, and Charlotte had apparently been banned from visiting him—unless of course she simply did not want to visit, which was a thought which gave him no cause for merriment.

Blake was buried in a grave next to Mary Smith, just in case he should have been telling the truth and she was indeed his wife. It rained on the day of the funeral, which created an aura of depression and misery with which Underwood could barely

182

contend. He had felt morally obliged to pay the funeral expenses, and for Blake's stay at the inn, since his pockets proved to hold not enough money to cover them, but he could not help but feel that this generosity did nothing to convince the village gossips that he was not responsible for the young man's death. In their eyes his actions pointed to a guilty conscience. Conversely, had he refused to pay, he knew he should have been condemned as tight-fisted and insensitive, after all, had the man not come all the way to Bracken Tor to see him? In a no-win situation Underwood generally disappeared off the scene until the event had passed from memory, but on this occasion he had no choice but stay and face the silent recriminations.

The reaction of the villagers and his mother's solicitude convinced Underwood that a few days indoors would be, by far, the best course to follow, but how to occupy his mind?

The sudden notion of examining the church records proved to be a happy one. Gil, seeing no harm in this particular pastime, was delighted to hand over several heavy and dusty tomes, and his brother filled many happy hours tracing the lives and deaths of generations of villagers.

It was thus that he came across a piece of information which he found puzzling. At first he was inclined to thrust the memory of it to the back of his mind, having decided that his investigation must cease, but again and again he heard Verity's contemptuous voice telling him of his cowardice. It occurred to him to wonder why her opinion mattered so much to him, but that was another unpalatable thought which was thrust determinedly aside.

Still, the troublesome snippet refused to lie dormant. At odd moments when he was resting or reading, it would drift across his brain, taunting, coaxing, a will-o-the-wisp tempting him to tread on the unsteady, bog-like terrain of other men's secrets.

When Verity arrived to see him, shame-faced and repentant, he found himself telling her all about it almost before he knew what he was about.

"Are you going to see him and confront him with his lie?" She asked, almost breathlessly.

"I don't know." He replied quietly, "After all, it is the man's own business! I had no right to demand he tell me the truth about his family's affairs."

"But why should he lie at all? Why did he simply not tell you not to meddle in his life? There is a reason he lied, but I can't imagine what it is."

"Can't you?"

They exchanged a look. Verity did not know what he meant, but something in his eyes told her that whatever it was he thought he knew, it was murky, unpleasant and very probably dangerous. She shivered slightly.

183

"Do you want me to come with you?"

"How did you know I intended to go?"

"Because I know you—better than you imagine." She met his eyes again and for the first time Underwood knew that everyone had spoken the truth to him, Verity was in love with him. The knowledge gave him no pleasure, it simply confused him. In order to cover that confusion, he responded to her original question, "I don't think it would be a good idea for you to become publicly involved. There may be serious consequences and I don't wish to bring trouble upon you."

"You know I am not afraid of trouble." She said seriously.

He smiled softly at her. "Cowardice is not an insult I should ever be able to throw at you." She blushed deeply, almost painfully.

"I should not have said that to you. I ought to beg your pardon."

"Please don't! It was your anger which made me decide to carry on. Without it, I should have taken the easy road and known for the rest of my life that I had let poor little Mary Smith down."

At that moment they were disturbed by Gil, who looked around the door and informed them both that tea was waiting in the parlour.

The conversation was postponed until a later date.

CHAPTER TWENTY-TWO

("Justum Et Tenacum Propositi Virium."—
A man upright and firm in purpose.)

A terse missive requiring his presence at Wynter Court in order to reconstruct the events of the murder was delivered into Mr. Underwood's hands by an uncomfortable Abney. He shifted from one foot to the other at though itching to be away, his lined face creased by a worried frown. Underwood took pity on him and asked. "Is there anything wrong, Abney?"

The groom took a deep breath, as though making a momentous decision, "Well, Sir, it's like this, I'm not happy about any of this! Not happy at all! It seems to me Sir Henry is asking you all these questions, and all the time the young rapscallion who did the killing is getting clean away!"

"But Sir Henry thinks I may be the culprit." Pointed out Underwood with a gentle smile. This remark seemed to cause uncommon annoyance in the normally phlegmatic Abney, "That's just nonsense, sir! You wouldn't kill anybody! Why, you're the vicar's brother!"

Underwood's smile spread into a full grin, "My dear fellow! If only life was as simple as that! But thank you for your faith! It is nice to have someone who believes me innocent. That will be a great comfort to me as I climb the steps to the gallows!"

Abney shuddered and raised his hand as though to ward off ill-omen, "Don't joke about it, sir! It's no laughing matter!"

"No, I'm sorry Abney." He forced himself to hide his smile and retain a suitably solemn expression. "I'm sure Sir Henry is simply being thorough! In no time at all, I shall be crossed off his list of suspects and the search will continue."

"I certainly hope you are right, sir. It gives a village a bad name, does this sort of thing! Two murders in a twelve month, and one suspected!"

"Suspected? Oh, you mean Hazelhurst! Tell me, Abney, what do you think of that?

"I don't hold with gossip." Said Abney, sanctimoniously,

which, as Underwood knew full well, was always the prelude to an outpouring of other people's business.

"Nor do I." He responded gravely. "But if one is to find the truth one must, unfortunately, ask a great many searching questions."

"That's true enough." Abney quickly overcame any qualms he might have about discussing another man's business. "Well, it was no secret that it weren't a love match—Hazelhurst and his wife, I mean. Her father owned a piece of land that Hazelhurst's father was eager to get his hands on. The parents arranged the wedding and the two youngsters went along with it, but it's my opinion they were never happy together. She couldn't get along with his mother or his sister, and when Harriet got in the family way, it gave her the perfect excuse to throw her out. I don't think Hazelhurst ever forgave his wife for that, or himself either, for letting her do it. Any one of the reasons given for Mrs. Hazelhurst's death could be the true one. She could have killed herself because the misery of her marriage finally got too much for her, but equally, Hazelhurst could have pushed her because he had had enough of her whining, nagging and complaining."

"And could it simply have been an accident? Could she have wandered too near the edge and fallen over?

"Have you ever been up there?" Asked Abney, Underwood shook his head, and the other man continued. "Then I suggest you go, and judge for yourself whether or not it is a pleasant place for a stroll. I think that will answer your question."

Underwood agreed to do just that, then hoisted himself into the gig beside Abney.

Sir Henry and a couple of other men were waiting on the drive, at the spot where Blake had breathed his last, so Abney drew the pony to a halt and both he and Underwood jumped lightly to the ground.

Underwood bade them all a polite good morning, which Sir Henry returned, but which obviously made his companions extremely uncomfortable, since they merely shuffled their feet, exchanged glances and muttered unintelligible replies.

"Now Underwood," Said the magistrate, without further ado, "Can you tell us exactly what happened?"

Mr. Underwood walked slowly to the spot where he thought he had been when the shot was fired, "As I recall we had reached about here. Blake had been complaining how tired he was, and had begun to flag a little, he must have been about two paces behind me when we reached this point." Underwood stopped and narrowed his eyes as he peered into the trees ahead and to the right of the path as he faced it. "Blake was on my left, and as I said, slightly behind me." Sir Henry indicated that one of his men stand in the position which had been Blake's, "If the bullet winged me then hit Blake, the shot must have come from over there." Underwood raised his arm and pointed to a clump of willow which grew along the banks of the stream which ran through the estate, and under a small bridge almost at the gates.

"From Tam Brook, you mean?" Asked Sir Henry, he seemed surprised.

"Tam Brook? Is that the stream that feeds Tambrook falls, then?" Inquired Underwood, with sudden interest, "Do you know, I had no idea that river had its origin here."

"Yes, it does!" Said his companion impatiently, "What the devil has that to do with anything?"

"Nothing at all." Was the mild reply, "I was just interested."

"Confine your interest to the matter in hand!"

"Very well." There was a pause, during which Sir Henry stared in the direction Underwood had indicated, and which finally prompted the younger man to comment, "Do you have any conclusion to draw?"

"No!" Snapped Sir Henry, "I'm just wondering why any poacher should be on that particular spot. It is too marshy for rabbits and not enough woodland to hide a man shooting deer."

"It does, however, give a very clear view of the drive." Added Underwood quietly.

"Are you still trying to suggest that someone was trying to kill you or Blake?"

"I have absolutely no idea! I only know Blake is dead, and it might very well have been me!"

Sir Henry appeared to ignore this remark. He began to walk towards the trees and the rest of the party silently fell into line behind him.

Underwood was intensely irritated when Sir Henry ordered his men to begin searching the area for evidence of recent occupation. As far as he was concerned, this was a week too late! It should have been done on the morning after the killing; the notion that anything would be left when a sennight had passed, giving the ground time to expunge footprints and any other evidence, was ludicrous.

He was wrong though. Abney called them all to witness a broken branch on a bush, and the dottle from a pipe on the ground nearby. Sir Henry was inclined to dismiss these pieces of evidence, but Abney insisted that there could be no other conclusion that Mr. Underwood had been correct; someone had waited here amidst the trees, and was probably the person who had fired the shot. Therefore Mr. Underwood did not fire the shot, had not murdered Blake and had not injured himself to cover the crime. All the men stood gathered about Sir Henry and seemed to be waiting for him to speak. He knew exactly what they wanted, and with a very bad-tempered look on his face he snarled,

"Very well, Underwood! I was wrong about you and I apologize! Is that satisfactory to all?" He glared round at his assembled men, who were now looking a great deal happier.

"All right! You can go!" They drifted slowly away, having shaken Mr. Underwood warmly by the hand. Sir Henry escorted Underwood back to the gig, followed by a ridiculously grinning Abney. He rather reminded Underwood of a great, lumbering hound, suddenly and unexpectly forgiven for some misdemeanour and unable to stop wagging its tail.

"Now that my name is cleared, do you think I might be allowed to see Charlotte?"

Sir Henry looked shifty, "She isn't at home. I sent her to stay with Maria for a few days."

Underwood correctly assumed that Charlotte had caused her father considerable inconvenience, when she had been refused permission to see her fiancee. He smiled slightly, God bless the child! It did his heart good to know she had fought for him. Well, he would simply follow her to Maria's, it was the least he could do, in the circumstances. Perhaps he ought to take her a gift? But what did one buy for a young lady? He had not bought a present for a woman for years. He always gave his mother handkerchiefs—she must have drawers full of the things by now! Especially since he had discovered that Gil gave exactly the same thing!

It was whilst he was pondering this problem that Sir Henry spoke again. "Dashed fine looking woman, your mother, Underwood! How old did you say she was?"

Underwood eyed his future father-in-law with an expression bordering upon abhorrence, "I didn't—and she is engaged to be married!" Underwood never thought he would have reason to be grateful to General Milner!

Abney told him where Maria lived on the way back to the vicarage, and since it was only about ten miles away, he went at once, hired a hack from Tom Briggs, and left Bracken Tor within the hour.

***

Edwin would have liked to deny Underwood access to his sister-in-law, but he did not quite have the courage. The best he could manage was to leave his guest kicking his heels in the hall while he sent the butler to ask Miss Charlotte if she was at home to a Mr. Underwood.

Charlotte flew down the stairs, straight into Underwood's arms, leaving Edwin in no doubt that she was indeed home! He turned away from the lovers with a sneer of extreme distaste

188

upon his weak-chinned visage.

He went to report to Maria that her sister had a visitor, and was stunned when she too hurried to greet Mr. Underwood. What did the fellow have, that all the ladies gathered about him, like flies around a dead horse! He smiled grimly to himself, rather pleased with this very uncomplimentary metaphor.

Underwood immediately released Charlotte when he saw Maria approach. She looked paler than ever, her eyes more troubled than he had ever seen them. When she gently asked Charlotte leave them alone so that she could have private speech with him, he quickly stemmed all Charlotte's protests, and followed his hostess into her drawing room.

"Please be seated Mr. Underwood." He obeyed, though he had no desire to remain in this house for any longer than it would take him to persuade Charlotte to leave with him.

"I know you have come to fetch Charlotte, but I beg you not to take her from my care." Her voice trembled as she spoke, and he could barely discern her words, so quiet was her tone. It suddenly occurred to him how much trouble he would cause her if he took Charlotte now and so he replied, "For your sake, Maria, I will wait until she returns to Bracken Tor."

She leaned forward, as though to impress her sense of urgency upon him, "Please believe me, Mr. Underwood, I do not ask this for my own sake! You do not understand what has happened in the past, and I could not begin to tell you, but you will find out and when you do, everything will change!"

He was beginning to think that she was losing her mind! Scarcely surprising, of course, married against her will to that cad Edwin!

"I don't know what you mean, Mrs. Wynter." He said softly. His very kindness seemed to distress her. "Oh God!" She groaned, "Why did it have to be you!" She covered her face with her hands and began to sob harshly. He was astounded and more than a little distraught. He had never known how to deal with tears, and to hear her cry was extremely painful. There could be no doubt that she was broken-hearted about something—but what?

"Is there anything I can do for you?" He asked gently. She raised her ravaged features and looked into his eyes. "There is only one thing! Take Charlotte away from Braken Tor and never bring her back! Forget everything that has happened, and never ever mention it again."

His face grew severe, "I have something to do in Bracken Tor. I cannot leave until it is done!"

"If you love Charlotte, do not go back!" She pleaded with him. "It is because I love her that I must finish what I have begun—or have her think I am a coward who was frightened away from discovering the truth by the threat of death!"

She rose wearily, as though too tried to argue further, "What will happen will be worse than death."

He looked at her strangely, wondering if she was indeed on the verge of a mental collapse, but she seemed not to notice, "I shall send Charlotte into you. You may stay with her an hour, no more. She will be back home at Wynter Court before the week is out. I shall travel with her."

Underwood spent his hour with Charlotte, talking of their future, making plans, discussing where they would live and what each would do. He seemed not to notice her distinct lack of enthusiasm when he told her of the plays and concerts they would attend, and the books he would have her read. Charlotte felt she had been educated to her limits and she had no intention of returning to the schoolroom! He was happy in that hour, happier than he had been for many years, so why did that familiar cloud of melancholy begin to descend over him as soon as he rode away?

He knew the answer. He had known for days, possibly even weeks. He had been trying to convince himself that he was wrong in his suspicions, that everything was going to be resolved happily, but he now knew with dreadful certainty that he had been right all along—and the cost to him was going to be the greatest he could ever have to pay.

CHAPTER TWENTY-THREE

("Magna Est Veritas, Et Praevalebit."—
The truth is great and shall prevail.)

Hazelhurst was in the farmyard when Underwood arrived. He glanced up with very little interest until he recognized his visitor, then his expression became both belligerent and fearful. "What the devil do you want?"

"I want to speak to your sister."

For several seconds the two men stared at each other, Underwood noting the vague familiarity of the other's features which had troubled him on his first visit. At last Hazelhurst seemed to make a decision and he jerked his head in the direction of the house. "She'll be in the kitchen."

She was. And she too looked startled when she saw Underwood.

"Well, I knew you would come back, but I wasn't expecting you quite so soon."

"I hope my presence is not inconvenient?"

"I've got a feeling that your presence is going to prove very inconvenient indeed, but come in anyway!" She answered wryly.

She had been scrubbing the surface of the table, but now laid down her brush and began to dry her hands on the coarse, and grubby, apron she wore. She gestured him to take a seat and offered him tea in the same breath, and neither spoke until she had accomplished the task and joined him on the settle.

She sipped her tea, then glanced covertly at him, "I trust you've recovered from your injury?"

"Yes, thank-you."

"You were a lucky man."

"So I've been told."

"What do you want with me?"

"I want you to tell me the truth."

She laughed, "Who knows the truth about anything?"

"I think you do."

"Allright, Mr. Underwood! Ask away!"

191

"What was the sex of the child you had by Sir Henry Wynter?"

Was he mistaken, or did she react with subdued violence to that question?

"You are very forthright, Mr. Underwood! You realize that I should throw you out of my brother's house for that insult?"

"Why bother? You know I will only come back again—and again, until you answer me!"

"Very well. It was a girl—and she is dead! Are you satisfied now?"

"Not really. You see, I happen to know that your child was a boy—and he is very much alive."

She grew a little white, but kept her serenity admirably. "Now what makes you think that? Surely a woman knows the gender of her own child?"

"I looked it up in the church register. Your child was a boy."

"I have a very bad memory. It was all such a long time ago!"

Mr. Underwood took a sip of his tea, and when he began to speak again, he seemed to have changed the subject, "Sir Henry's son Harry made a remarkable recovery, didn't he? From such a sickly child, to such a strapping boy—one could easily believe that he is a year, or even more, older than he actually is, according to his registration of birth in the Church's books!"

"I suppose so." She said sulkily. "I really have very little interest in Sir Henry, or any of his family."

"But he came up here to visit you, didn't he? You are not one of his tenants, so why should he put himself to the trouble of bringing Harry up here?"

"I have no idea. You will have to ask Sir Henry that question."

"I fully intend to do so."

"He'll kill you, if you do!" She spoke suddenly, in a harsh voice, quite unlike her previously quiet tone.

"Perhaps he has already tried." He murmured, and rose to leave.

"Wait!"

He turned back to confront her. Her face was deathly white now, and her hand trembled so violently that her cup of tea was spattered on the flags beneath her. "He'll pay you! Is that what you want? He will pay you anything you ask, just go away and never come back!"

"I don't want his money, Harriet. I want him to pay for the crime he committed—and if you have any sense, you'll tell me now everything you know. What you did was wrong, but it was understandable. I don't suppose you ever thought it would end with murder."

Suddenly she dropped to her knees, her arm was thrown

192

across the settle and her head dropped onto it. He left her to sob for a few seconds, then he returned to her side and placing his hand under her arm, he helped her to her feet, turned her to face him, and put his arms about her. She held onto him as she wept, her face buried in his shoulder, and he patted her back, and whispered words of comfort as though she were a child.

Then she told him everything.

Sir Henry thought it odd that the Underwood brothers should write and ask they be allowed a private interview with himself and his daughter Maria, but he acquiesced, there seemed no reason not to.

The brothers were prompt and were shown immediately to the library, where the master of the house and his eldest daughter were waiting for them. Sir Henry had already drained his glass, Maria held a brandy glass in her hand, but had never raised it to her white-edged lips. Sir Henry was worried that she looked so ghastly, "Pull yourself together, girl! For God's sake!" She looked at him with utter loathing, "Shut up! When this is all over, I never want to see your face again!" He was rather stunned by the vitriol in her voice. She had never spoken thus to him before, and it made him at once conciliatory. "Now, now, Maria. There is no need for this! We have only to keep our heads and nothing will come of it!"

At that moment the door opened to admit the Underwoods, and Sir Henry never glanced in his daughter's direction again.

"Well, gentlemen, what can we do for you?"

The brothers took the proffered seats, Underwood seemed perfectly calm, though a little pale; the Reverend Underwood was also pale, but he demonstrated none of his brother's calm. He was extremely agitated, and he showed it.

Underwood spoke first, "Sir Henry, I believe I have solved the mystery of the death of the young woman found in your wood last year."

Sir Henry gave every indication of being delighted to hear this news. He smiled broadly, "Congratulations, young man! You have done what all my men were unable to do! Perhaps you would like to enlighten us further?"

"Certainly. The girl was your youngest daughter. I believe she would have been named Adela had your wife lived to name her."

The smile slid from the older man's face, "What nonsense is this? Everyone knows my youngest child is my son!"

"That is not the story Miss Hazelhurst tells, sir." Responded Underwood calmly.

"Bitch!" Sir Henry spat the word, and seemed ready to rise from his seat, then just as quickly regained his composure and fell back into his chair, "The woman is mad! There can be no other explanation! The loss of her child all those years ago has clearly robbed her of her senses!"

"That of course is a possibility, but I own I find myself believing her. You see, her brother bears quite a remarkable resemblance to your son."

"What story has she been telling?"

"Miss Hazelhurst?" Asked Underwood, the magistrate nodded curtly.

"Her tale was quite simple. She says she bore you a son, and that you persuaded her to take the child to London. Your wife had just told you that she was to have another child and you decided that this should be the last attempt. You were desperate for a son, a legitimate son! Should your wife fail on this occasion, you were going to take the child immediately to London, and substitute Harriet's son for your daughter."

Sir Henry interrupted harshly. "This is all fantastic nonsense! How could I possibly prevent anyone from knowing the sex of the child as it was born? My wife would have been the first to ask!"

Underwood was unmoved by the passionate interjection, he continued with his story. "The only other person present at the birth was the local midwife—Harriet Hazelhurst's mother. I don't know if you were merely fortunate in your wife's death—I suspect you may have been, for she must have been totally exhausted by repeated pregnancies and births—but there is the definite possibility that she was your first victim."

Sir Henry was ashen-faced and speechless. His mouth opened and closed as though to protest, but no sound issued from him.

"Once she was dead, it was easy enough for you to act the grief-stricken widower, unable to bear spending another night beneath the roof which sheltered your dead wife. And there was the child—born sickly and near death, and needing the immediate attention of the best doctors—doctors only to be found in London. No one would be surprised that you should make such efforts to save the life of your only son."

Underwood paused, as though hoping Sir Henry would have some sweeping explanation to cover all these accusations, but he said nothing.

"Your error was to leave Harriet short of money. She would have raised the girl as her own if you had given her enough money to live comfortably, but London seemed a long way away, didn't it, Sir Henry? Harriet had a hard time of it and by the time Adela was thirteen, they had both drifted into prostitution. Then Harriet was beaten by a dissatisfied customer, and she suddenly decided that she had had enough. She told Adela the whole story—and Adela came here to find you, and to demand that she be reinstated as your child. She went to the Hazelhurst farm first, and he persuaded her to let him act as go-between. You agreed to see her, but only if she came at night, and

194

ensured complete secrecy—foolishly she agreed to your terms. She came here that night—and she did not leave alive. When you dumped her body in the wood, satisfied that she would simply be dismissed as an unknown vagrant, you realized your fatal error. She was a red-head, just like your other daughters, who all inherited their red hair from their mother. Possibly she bore more than a passing resemblance to one of them."

A strangled sob came from Maria and Sir Henry licked his dry lips before saying, "She looked just like Charlotte."

It was Underwood's turn to be shocked, of all possibilities strangely enough, that one had never occurred to him. It made him feel quite ill to imagine Charlotte leading such a life, and ending with such a death. For weeks he had fought to avenge a faceless girl, now he knew what her face looked like, and he found the knowledge horrifying.

"What did you do with her head, Sir Henry?" Asked Underwood, as calmly as he could.

Maria rose slowly to her feet, "My father knows nothing about it, Mr. Underwood. You see, you have almost everything right, except for that. It was not my father who killed the girl. He was quite happy to give her money and send her away. She wanted to take it. She didn't want to come back here and live as his daughter. She hated him for what he had done. She told him as much, here in this very room. It was I who could not risk her returning and telling what she knew."

"You killed her?" Asked Underwood incredulously, his throat dry.

"Yes, I killed her. I struck her on the head with a heavy brass candlestick."

"But why? What possible reason could you have?"

Maria began to twist the wedding ring upon her finger. "You can have no idea how much I hate my husband. I hated him before I married him, but I have learned to hate him much, much more since. If Harry fails to reach his majority, or is proved to be an impostor, Edwin will inherit this house, the estate, everything! Do you think I will allow that despicable little toad-eater to walk over the threshold of this house as Master? I'll see him dead first!"

"Then what did you do with her head?"

"I put it into my saddle bag and the next morning I rode up onto the moors and cast it as far as I could into the peat bog up there!"

Gil closed his eyes as though in pain, and briefly rested his head upon his hand.

"C.H., does this mean that Mrs. Hazelhurst's death was not an accident either?" He asked, unable to disguise the despair in his voice. Underwood shook his head sadly, "I'm sorry, Gil, but I very much doubt it. She must have spotted the girl and suddenly everything became clear to her. To preserve the secret, Hazelhurst must have pushed her over the cliff."

There was a knock at the door, and Brownsword entered. "I beg your pardon, Sir Henry. Mr. and Miss Hazelhurst are outside. They are quite insistent that they see you and Mr. Underwood now."

Sir Henry glanced at Underwood, who nodded swiftly.

"Show them in, Brownsword. The more the merrier."

Hazelhurst scarcely waited for the door to close behind the now mystified butler before he launched into his previously prepared speech, his words tumbling over themselves in his effort to get them out before being interrupted. "My sister has told me what she said to you, Mr. Underwood, and we are here to deny every word!"

"It is too late for that Hazelhurst!" Intercepted Maria wearily, but firmly.

"You try and take us into a Courtroom and you'll find yourself with two completely silent witnesses!"

Sir Henry grinned maliciously, "Well, Underwood, there go your two best witnesses, what are you going to do now?"

"Be quiet, both of you!" Maria cried harshly, and strangely they both obeyed her, "There is only one thing left to do, and that is ask Mr. Underwood what he intends to do."

Underwood saw that he was not the only one of the company who was stunned by the sudden change in Maria's character. She was decisive, even aggressive, and Underwood could not help but regret that the alteration had come so late. Had she learnt to control her husband as she was now controlling her father and Hazelhurst, there was a possibility that at least two lives might have been spared.

Gil spoke, unconsciously sparing his brother the necessity of answering Maria's question—for the truth was, he did not know quite what he did intend to do.

"But who killed Blake—and why?"

There was a stark silence, and since it was obvious no one was actually going to admit to the crime, Underwood answered his brother himself. "Sir Henry—you were not quite as drunk on that occasion as you would have had me believe, were you Sir Henry?"

Sir Henry said nothing, so Underwood continued. "He was trying to kill me, of course, having decided that it was too dangerous to let me live. Having missed, he would have been quite happy to try me himself for the murder of Blake—and to ensure that I was hanged for it. Unfortunately you reckoned without Abney, didn't you, Sir Henry?"

"Blast his eyes! Was it Abney?"

"It was. He displayed an extremely touching belief in my innocence and saw no harm in providing a little proof that my story of a hidden assailant was true. He broke a branch and dropped the ash from his pipe. It was then that you gave yourself away, Sir Henry. There was never a more surprised man than you, when Abney found some clues where you knew no clues ought to be!"

"Damn him! I'll have him off the estate faster than . . ." Began Sir Henry furiously, then realizing the gravity of the situation, he trailed off.

"What are you going to do, Mr. Underwood?" Asked Maria again, quietly and with great dignity.

"He can't do a thing, you fool! He has no proof! If Harriet and Hazelhurst refuse to testify, there's nothing he can do!" Sir Henry was more confident now, gloating over Underwood's helplessness.

"Is that true, Mr. Underwood?"

He looked at Maria for a long time before he replied, "Yes, I'm afraid it is. You have all managed to live with your consciences thus far, so I see no reason why any of you should now feel the need to confess."

"I told you! He is completely powerless!" Sir Henry crossed the room and poured himself another brandy.

"However, it is my duty to inform the authorities of all I know. I think you will find that Edwin is hardly likely to sit back and allow himself to be usurped by your father's illegitimate son."

All his attention was on Maria, so it came as something of a shock when he suddenly heard hysterical laughter behind him. He turned and found that Harriet had sunk into a chair and was rocking backwards and forwards, laughing until the tears rolled down her face.

All eyes were upon her, startled and confused, and it was left to Gil to step forward and slap her sharply on the face. She gasped and lifted her hand to cradle her crimson cheek.

"What was that for?"

"I apologize. It was necessary to bring you to your senses."

"I'm not out of my senses! I'm amused! I've never known anything so funny in the whole of my life before!"

No one said a word. The feeling that she was running mad was general, but if she knew it, she did not care, "Oh Henry!" She shifted her gaze from Gil to the magistrate, who stood with his glass in his hand, frozen by the sound of her laughter. There was something about it that frightened him, though he could not imagine why. What was she? Nothing but a simple little peasant, whom he had used and cast aside with less thought than he would shoot an injured hound.

"You thought you were so clever, didn't you, Henry? You fathered a son, then you managed to palm him off as your wife's child! And all along you were the one who was being hoaxed!"

"What do you mean?" There was quiet menace in his voice, and Underwood found all his muscles tensing, just in case he should need to leap to Harriet's rescue.

"Only this, my dearest Henry, Harry is not your son! Do you hear me? Your boy, your precious little boy, is none of your making!"

He did not attempt to reach her, but shrank from her as though he had seen something loathsome and disgusting, "You harlot! You liar!"

"I'm no liar! You've lived with lies for so long, you simply don't recognize the truth! Harry is not your son!"

Underwood thought the older man would collapse, but no one went to him to support him, and he was forced to stagger to his chair and drop into it, gasping for breath. Underwood almost found it in his heart to pity the man. Everything he had done had been for the sake of his son, for the sake of the boy he believed to be his son. For a man to look down the years and see his sins laid before him, and to know that he had perjured his soul for nought, must be a severe trial.

At length the magistrate recovered himself sufficiently to say, "Who is it? Who is Harry's real father?" He was still hoping that she would take it back, that she would shrug and say, "Of course he is yours. I only said it to hurt you!" but she did not. She glanced at her brother, who looked steadfastly at his feet and refused to raise his eyes to hers.

"He is." She nodded in the direction of her brother, who threw her one look of pleading before dropping his eyes again. "That was why he killed his wife! That was what she had provoked him into yelling at her one night when he was too drunk to control his tongue. She knew nothing about Harry or the girl! She had threatened to publish his shame throughout the district—he couldn't bear the world to know that he had fathered a child on his own sister!"

"May God forgive you all!" Gil's voice was loud and harsh, and it hurt Underwood more than anything else he had heard that night. He knew his brother's faith had been severely shaken by all that he had heard. And for the first time he was glad that he had no religion which could be tested by his fellow man.

He glanced around at the faces of the group. Sir Henry's lined, broken-veined and bloated with his years of self-indulgence and debauchery; Maria, self-pitying and bitter, always the victim, even now refusing to acknowledge her own part in her downfall; Hazelhurst haunted by his youthful folly and hag-ridden by his wife, mother and sister; and Harriet, used and abused by the men who had known her and never quite able to take control of her life.

Underwood felt suddenly sick and tired of them all.

"Get out of my house!" Sir Henry found sudden strength and

addressed his remark to the Hazelhursts. "And take your little bastard with you!"

Maria was stirred to action, "Father, you can't do that to poor Harry! He is the innocent victim of all this! And if you throw him out, it will give credence to Underwood's story!"

Sir Henry gave a roar and swept his arm across his desk, sending the contents flying across the room. "Do you think I give a damn what that witch's get feels? Throw them all out, now!"

Maria hustled the brother and sister out of the room. Sir Henry slumped once more into his chair, his eyes fixed on some point at the far side of the room. When he spoke it was almost conversational.

"You understand that Charlotte will never marry you, Underwood?"

"I knew I was saying goodbye to Charlotte when I left her at Maria's home."

"If you had loved her as you said, you could not have done this to her."

Underwood stiffened visibly at these words, but was able to control himself. "I would have been a poor husband, despising myself for my cowardice."

"I think you would have been a braver man to have kept all this from her."

"Wondering whether I was right or wrong will be the cross I shall have to bear for the rest of my life, Sir Henry."

He felt his brother's hand upon his shoulder and for a moment knew a sense of comfort before the crushing misery descended once again, like a cold, wet earth being shovelled into a grave.

"Let us go home, C. H." Said Gil softly, and without replying his brother followed him out of the room.

He managed as far as the hall, when he staggered and almost fell, Gil was forced to reach out and grip his arm.

"I'm sorry, Gil. I'm afraid I am unwell."

Abney stood by the door and Gil spoke to him, "Do you think we could have the carriage, Abney?"

"It is waiting outside for you, sir."

As Abney handed Underwood into the carriage, the latter grasped him firmly by the hand. "Thank you for everything, Abney."

"The pleasure was all mine, sir."

CHAPTER TWENTY-FOUR

("Nemo Repente Fuit Turpissimus."—
No one ever turned villain all at once.)

There were tears in his mother's eyes as she kissed the vicar goodbye.

"You will take care of yourself and him, won't you Gil?"

"I will, mother. Don't worry. You will see us both when you marry the General."

"And you will perform the ceremony?"

"I will—with a grateful heart." He smiled and she touched his cheek softly before climbing into the stage.

He waited until the last vestige of dust had disappeared from view before wending his melancholy way back to Bracken Tor. The village was shrouded in a preternatural silence which was chilling and he found, for the first time, that he had no real desire to call the place home.

His spirits lifted a little when he found his brother out of bed and downstairs for the first time in a week. Underwood still looked pale and somewhat shaken, but at least he was up, albeit in a comfortable chair with a rug solicitously wrapped about his legs by the fretful Mrs. Selby.

"Feeling better, Chuffy?"

"A little, Gil, thank you. I presume you saw mother safely on her way?"

"Yes. She is looking forward to our joining her presently."

"The sooner the better."

Gil made no answer to this, but settled himself in a chair beside his brother and said quietly, "I have received a reply to my letter. Rev. Blackwell says he would be delighted to have you to stay for a few days, and he has also agreed to take my place in performing the funeral ceremony."

"When do I leave?"

"Tomorrow, if you feel well enough to undertake the journey."

"I do. Has there been any word from Charlotte?"

200

The vicar sadly shook his head.

"I did not really expect it."

Gil was given no opportunity to speak further, for Mrs. Selby knocked on the door and announced the arrival of Miss Chapell.

"Show her in, Mrs. Selby." Said Underwood swiftly, before Gil could direct her to dismiss their visitor. It was fortunate that Gil had not been allowed to send her away, for it was a distraught young woman who entered the room. No sooner had the door closed behind the housekeeper than Verity abandoned all attempts to control her feelings and began to sob helplessly.

Gil was on his feet and holding out comforting arms to her immediately and Underwood was surprised to find himself extremely hurt at the ease with which she flew into his brother's arms and buried her face against his chest. It was not a sight to which he had ever had the chance to grow accustomed, his clerical brother tenderly cradling a female in his arms, so perhaps it was for that reason he found the vision so very disturbing.

When she had finally calmed herself enough to explain her extraordinary behaviour, Verity had a story to tell which infuriated both men.

"I'm so sorry." She blew her nose and sank into the proffered seat, "You must think me terrible rude."

Neither man knew what to think, so both shook their heads in disagreement, then waited for her to elucidate.

"I could not think where else to run—and I had to get away." She closed her eyes and shuddered, as though at an appalling memory, "How I hate that man!"

"Which man?" Asked Underwood, only to be frowned at by his brother, who felt Miss Chapell ought to tell her story at her own pace, without any prompting.

"Edwin Wynter! After all that has happened . . . how could he?"

"H . . ." Underwood began to ask, but his brother quelled him with a look.

Verity had been carefully avoiding Underwood's eye, and even now she could not bring herself to speak directly to him. She addressed herself to the vicar, "I'm making a very poor show of explaining, I'm sorry. It is just that I have never had this happen to me before, and I think I am still a little too shocked to think clearly." By this time Underwood was almost out of his mind, wondering just what exactly had happened to her, but he kept silent in the face of his brother's determination.

"He arrived this morning, to take over at the Court, and when he called me to the library, I expected that it would be to hear my dismissal. I was quaking in my shoes, for I have not been in the library since Sir Henry . . ." She trailed off, wiped away another tear then determinedly began again. "They have cleaned up all the blood from the carpet, but they had to burn the curtains."

Neither brother wished to hear these details, but they understood her need to speak of it. Death by gun was ever a messy affair, especially when wielded by one's own hand, and she could have no knowledge of their own involvement in this particular death. No one other than themselves and certain members of the Wynter family knew why Sir Henry had suddenly disowned his son, re-instated Edwin as his heir, then shut himself in the library and taken his own life.

"I thought he would dismiss me there and then, for all the girls are to go to their great-aunt and Maria . . ." Once more words failed her, for how did one describe the horror of seeing a young woman lose her mind so completely that she was turned into a demented animal. Maria had been dragged, screaming, away from the body of her father, which she had discovered, only to be found an hour later trying desperately to set fire to the house and herself, muttering that she would see it all burn before she allowed her husband to enter into his inheritance. She was destined to spend the rest of her life shut away in a sanatorium—at least she was to be spared the indignity of Bedlam, even if she was not aware of it.

Underwood covered his eyes with his hand. Gil saw his gesture of despair and gently encouraged Verity to continue with her story. It was useless and painful to dwell upon these incidents.

"What did Edwin do, Miss Chapell?"

"That odious little man! He asked me to stay on at Wynter Court. At first I thought he must have decided to bring the girls home again and he wanted me to continue as before, but I have never been so wrong! He wanted me to be his mistress! As I stood before the desk, too stunned to answer him, he grabbed me and tried to kiss me! I have never been more revolted! I kicked him in the shins and ran out of the house! I didn't stop running until I reached here!"

Underwood could bear no more, he leapt to his feet and started towards the door.

"Where are you going?" Asked the vicar swiftly.

"To teach Edwin Wynter some manners!" Snarled the furious Underwood.

"Oh no, pray do not!" Gasped Verity, "You have been ill! He might hurt you!"

Underwood had never been more humiliated; to have a woman refuse his chivalry on the chance that he might be hurt was an occurrence he would not soon forget.

"It would take a better man than Edwin Wynter to injure me!" He snapped bad-temperedly. Gil rose and took his arm, "Come and sit down, Chuffy. There is nothing you can do in

202

defence of Miss Chapell. You cannot possibly be seen in the vicinity of Wynter Court anyway. It would be more than tasteless, don't you agree?"

Underwood was forced to concede, but when he returned to his chair, it was obvious from his glowering expression that he had not completely set aside the possibility of confronting Edwin.

"Do you have anywhere to go, Miss Chapell?"

She shook her head, "I suppose I should have considered what my next move would be, but it has all happened so suddenly. I know Helen Herbert would welcome me, but with the baby on the way, I do not like to ask."

The news of a Herbert baby was a surprise to both brothers, but this did not seem an appropriate moment to comment upon it.

"Do you have any particular desire to stay for Sir Henry's funeral?"

She shuddered and shook her head emphatically.

"Then you shall take the stage tomorrow to my mother's home. You can stay there until you find new employment."

"Oh, but I could not impose . . ."

"Nonsense. She would be delighted to have your companionship."

Verity did not have much choice but to accept this offer of hospitality, and if the truth were told, she had no desire to reject it. She had grown fond of Mrs. Underwood and could think of nowhere she would rather be.

Gil rose, "I shall go and tell Mrs. Selby to prepare a room for you."

Verity wasted no time, as soon as the door closed behind him, she turned her attention to Mr. Underwood.

"I have assumed that the events of the past week have something to do with Mary Smith, Mr. Underwood. Am I right?"

He nodded, and told her the full story. When he came to the end, tears had formed themselves in her eyes once more.

"Oh God! You wanted to stop and I would not let you! What have I done?"

Underwood had been tormenting himself with the same question for a week, but he could not let her suffer as he had, "Verity, forget any idea you might have had about taking responsibility for any of this. I knew what I was doing. I knew at the end there was going to be a culprit, and I imagined that he or she was going to die on the gallows!"

"But Maria, Sir Henry, poor Harry! And you have lost Charlotte! I can't bear it!"

"Do you think I don't feel for them all? For Blake and the Hazelhursts too! But a young life was taken in violence and she did not deserve that! I wish as heartily as you that no one who was innocent would have to suffer, but that is always a consequence of wrong-doing! The guiltless are always dragged in, and they are always left to make the reparations."

"What will happen to Harry now, and to the Hazelhursts?"

"I think Harriet has always wanted her son back and with a little luck they can rebuild their relationship. Harry is young and resilient enough to cope. As for Hazelhurst, he has only his conscience to contend with. He was tried for his wife's murder and found not guilty—and no man can be tried for the same crime twice."

She looked at him, her heart never more clearly on her sleeve than in this moment, "And you? What will you do? Surely you will go to Charlotte? You cannot lose her over this."

"I have lost her, and there is nothing to be done about it," He smiled softly, "Pray don't look so tragic! I will survive. I have my work. I recovered before. I shall recover again."

"I don't think I have ever felt such pain as this, Cadmus." Her voice was so quiet as to be only vaguely discernible, and he could not be sure he had heard her correctly, "What did you call me?"

"I'm sorry, it was impertinent of me."

"Did my mother tell you?"

Verity looked shocked that he could suggest any such thing. "Certainly not! She gave you her word that she would not!"

"Then how . . .?"

"Charlotte told me of the clues you had given her. She asked me to help her find your name."

"And did you?" He asked coldly. She did not raise her eyes to his face, indeed she had scarcely looked at him since entering the room, feeling that a glimpse into the hell reflected in his eyes would cause her tears to flow once again.

"No." She whispered, "I did not need to look it up. I knew it at once, but I did not tell her—I wanted it to be mine alone."

He stared at her, his brow creased, as though trying to see into her mind, "I don't understand." He said at last.

"No, you would not. It doesn't matter. Can we discuss something else? You need have no fear, your secret is safe with me—and I shall not use the name again."

He gave a short, mirthless laugh. "After all the years of hating it, I found it sounded quite pleasant on your lips—but please only use it when we are alone!"

She experienced the strangest sensation, as though the sun had suddenly come out from behind storm-blackened clouds and flooded her with light and warmth. She gave a tremulous smile, "Thank you, but I fear after today we shall never be alone together again."

"Very probably." He agreed thoughtfully.

She drew in a deep breath and, determined to not ruin the tenuous friendship she had managed to re-forge with him, she changed the topic of conversation. "Do you mind telling me how you reached your conclusion about Mary Smith's killing? You had seemed so sure that Mr. Renshaw was the culprit, then suddenly you knew the fault lay with the Wynters. What changed your mind?"

Mr. Underwood seemed relieved to turn away from the personal and discuss the machinations of the murderous mind.

"It was a silly little thing really, but the night Blake was shot I noticed several things happening that did not quite add up."

"What do you mean?" She asked, suddenly forgetting her own misery in the fascination of learning how his mind worked.

"Well, to me that night was as perfect a reflection of the morning the body was discovered as I was ever going to witness. Luckily you had given me a picture of the events of that occasion and I was able to mentally compare them. For example, you told me that Brownsword had insisted on getting dressed before coming downstairs, but when I hammered at the door, he came down almost immediately, with only his coat thrown on over his night shirt. He had learnt a lesson a year ago, namely that when the door is hammered upon in the dead of night, it is likely to herald an emergency, therefore when it happened again, he did not wait to get dressed. However, several other members of the household behaved in the same way as they had the year before. Sir Henry being the prime example. He pretended not to be woken by the knocking on the front door, for the same reason as he had last year because he knew what had occurred and did not want to arouse suspicion by being too quickly on the scene and thereby showing that he had never been undressed, had never been to bed, and was certainly not asleep at the important times."

"Yes. I see what you mean. The innocent parties altered their behaviour because they had been shocked by the events of last year, the guilty did exactly the same as they had before because it had helped cover their crimes then."

"Precisely."

"How did you guess about Harry being Harriet Hazelhurst's son?"

"There were several reasons for that, though I did not recognize some of them at first. The major thing was his size. I know there are some strapping fifteen-year-olds, but the way Harry handled that monster of a horse made me wonder. He is also remarkably like Hazelhurst, though the resemblance eluded me for quite a while. The final conviction came when Hazelhurst told me Harriet's child had been a girl, but the church records disagreed. There could only be one reason for such a lie and that was had I checked with people who had known Harriet in Manchester and London, they would all have told me that she had lived with a daughter and not a son."

"I wonder why Harriet let Sir Henry have her son."

"Probably because she thought Sir Henry could give the boy a better life than she could—and to her credit, she never abandoned the girl, despite the drain she must have been on her resources. She would have fared better without a child to worry about, and there are orphanages, poor-house and baby farmers aplenty in London where she could have deserted her. The sad fact is that many women with unwanted children simply leave them on the street to die of hunger and cold."

"Harriet is really quite a remarkable woman when you consider it in that light, isn't she?" Verity asked differently. Mr. Underwood raised a faintly quizzical brow before nodding rather reluctantly. "I suppose she is, though one can scarcely condone her passing off her brother's son as Sir Henry's."

"No, but she had to do something, didn't she? As you have said, there is nothing easy about the life of a girl with a baby and no husband."

Mr. Underwood, who tended to have a rather black and white view of wrong-doing, despite his reluctance to stand in judgment of his fellow man, and Verity's words gave him something to think about.

"Do you intend to see her again?" Verity's quietly spoken question took him rather by surprise, for the truth was that he had been considering a trip to Hill Farm before he left Bracken Tor for good. It did not occur to him that he had been rather attracted to Harriet, but instead he had convinced himself that he ought to see if Harry was coping with his new life. He thought he might offer to pay for the boy to go to University. It was the only salve to his conscience he could consider worthwhile.

When Verity asked the question, however, he knew that he would not go to Hill Farm, that he would not offer Harry anything, and that Harriet Hazelhurst must hate him quite as much as Charlotte did. It was a sobering thought, and one which did nothing to remove the mantle of melancholy which had draped itself about his shoulders and which was growing heavier by the day.

"No. I won't see her again. I think I have meddled enough, don't you?"

"I don't consider what you have done to be meddling, I think you did what Mary Smith deserved and I know what it cost you to do the right thing. I have nothing but admiration for you."

"Bless you for that, Verity, but I cannot forget that two men have died since I set myself the task of finding Mary's murderer, and that numerous other lives have been shattered beyond repair—I have even managed to lose your place of employment for you!"

She smiled gently, "That was no loss, believe me! But for

Isobel, I should have left Sir Henry's employ within a week of arriving to take up the position."

"You were fond of Isobel, weren't you?"

"Very. She has a very sweet disposition."

"I wouldn't know. I never managed to reach beyond her shyness. Strange to think I might have been her brother-in-law."

"Perhaps you still could be. Charlotte was very much in love with you. Edwin is determined that all this should be kept quiet. Sir Henry's death is to be an unfortunate accident—he was cleaning his gun when it went off. Harry being disowned is to be the result of a violent quarrel which caused his father to change his will in a fit of pique, and to unfortunately die before being able to change back. He has no intention of admitting that Maria's illness is mental and not physical, for he intends to divorce her and that would not be allowed if it was known she is insane. He has friends in Parliament who have assured him of their support."

Mr. Underwood's disgust at Edwin Wynter's self-interest was clearly reflected in his expression, "Has that man no soul? I find it incredible that he should be able to think so clearly to protect himself when all around him is crumbling."

"Don't you think it is about time you started to do a little self-protecting, Mr. Underwood? If Edwin is to get everything he wants out of this situation, why should you not get Charlotte?"

He slowly shook his head, "I doubt she would even agree to see me. Why should she? I have ruined her life!"

"You have done no such thing! She has lost a father who cared little for her, and a home which she would have left when she married anyway!"

"I had not considered the matter to be as simple as you seem to make it!"

Gil made his presence known at that moment, though in truth he had heard most of Verity's impassioned pleas to his brother to go after Charlotte. When Underwood presently left the room, the vicar turned to his guest and without thought of the proprieties he took her hand in his. "My dear girl, forgive me, but I know how you feel about my brother and I can only be stunned by a spirit such as yours which can encourage him to go to Charlotte, when you long to have him yourself."

There were tears in her eyes and her fingers clutched convulsively at his, "I cannot bear him to be so unhappy. If he loves Charlotte and not me, then I have no right to keep him from her."

He raised her hand to his lips and kissed her fingers, "Verity, if Underwood succeeds with his Charlotte, would you do me the honour of becoming my wife?"

The tears spilled onto her cheeks, but she managed to laugh

unsteadily, "Why wait, Gil? He does not know I exist! Thank you for asking me. May I have time to think about it?"

"Of course."

CHAPTER TWENTY-FIVE

**("Suaviter In Modo, Fortiter In Re."—
Gentle in manner, firm in action.)**

For the first time in weeks Underwood felt relaxed and comfortable. The Rev. Josiah Blackwell had a talent for making his guest feel at home, and despite his mounting misery, Mr Underwood was not impervious to the man's innate charm. They had long discussions, sitting late into the night, and Mr. Underwood found himself telling Blackwell things he had never disclosed to another human being.

It was for this reason that Rev. Blackwell took the unprecedented step of interfering unforgivably in Mr. Underwood's affairs. When he returned from performing the funeral of Sir Henry Wynter in Bracken Tor, he brought Charlotte and Isobel with him.

He had found it no easy task to persuade Charlotte to accompany him, but Isobel had provided the final lever, telling her sister that it was she who had pursued Mr. Underwood and she therefore owed him the courtesy of telling him to his face that she no longer wished to marry him.

Charlotte had grown up a great deal in the weeks which followed her father's death and her sister's breakdown, and it was a very poised, though pale, young lady who faced Underwood across the expanse of Rev. Blackwell's parlour.

She was dressed in unrelieved black, and Underwood feared she would swoon, so white did she appear to him. The longing to cross the room and sweep her into his arms was almost overpowering, and he was forced to make what he considered to be the most fatuous remark of his life.

"How are you, Charlotte?" Her green eyes looked huge in her pale face, and at this they glittered dangerously. Without replying, she moved swiftly towards him, raised her hand and dealt him a stinging slap upon his cheek. He accepted the blow without flinching, though a muscle in his jaw tightened perceptibly. For a moment they looked at each other, then

Charlotte cast herself against him and burst into violent sobs. She beat her fists against his chest, crying. "How could you do it! I hate you! Why did you have to find out? Why couldn't you leave the girl dead and unknown? We could have been happy!"

"She was your sister, Charlotte. It could have easily been Isobel or even yourself whom your father cheated!"

She raised her head, tears still flowing freely, "Do you think I forgive my father any more than I forgive you? I hate him too! I did not want to attend his funeral, but Edwin forced me, saying that it would cause comment! He still wants me to marry you, so concerned is he that nothing should throw suspicion upon the circumstances surrounding my father's death!"

"Edwin is mistaken. Marriage is impossible for us. You will always see what I have done as a betrayal of your love. You and I both know that had I loved you enough, I would not have disclosed your father's secret. I do not see my actions in that light, but it is something that would ever be between us."

Charlotte looked at him, aghast, "You have said everything I have been thinking, but was unable to put into words. I have tortured myself with my thoughts for days, not able to understand why I could hate you, yet long for you with all my heart. Now I know. You could, and should, have kept what you learned to yourself, for me! If you did not love me enough to protect me, then you do not love me enough to make me happy!"

He silenced her by lowering his head and pressing his lips to hers, and though she responded, they both knew that it was a farewell and not a new beginning.

When he led her into the hall he found Isobel sitting on a chair, waiting for her sister. Charlotte took her leave of him very formally, offering him her hand which he held for a moment, then kissed before releasing her. As she went out to the waiting carriage, Isobel stood and much to Mr. Underwood's surprise, she approached him and stood on her tip-toes in order to reach him. Instinctively he bent slightly so that she could attain her goal. She kissed him softly on the cheek—the same cheek which Charlotte had slapped, and which still bore traces of her reddened fingermarks, "I like you very much, Mr. Underwood." She whispered shyly, "And I'm very glad you killed my papa! He was a hateful man."

He was appalled, "But, I didn't kill . . ." He trailed off, suddenly aware that in Isobel's and probably Charlotte's opinions, kill their father was precisely what he had done. "Goodbye, Isobel." He said sadly.

"May I write to you?" She asked diffidently. He knew that he should refuse the request, that all connection with the Wynters should be cut, swift and painless, but he could not bring himself to do it.

"I should be happy to hear how you are."

"And will you give my love to Miss Chapell?"

"Yes. Yes. I will."

"You should marry her, Mr. Underwood. She is really much nicer than Charlotte."

He smiled, "I don't think Miss Chapell would want to marry me, Isobel."

"Oh yes, she would! Goodbye Mr. Underwood." She went swiftly to rejoin her sister, and Underwood closed the front door upon the retreating vehicle.

Rev. Blackwell was walking down the stairs as his guest turned from the door, and Mr. Underwood raised his eyes to look at him.

"I have an apology to make, Underwood. Obviously I should not have brought Charlotte here?" There was a question in his tone which caused a smile to light briefly upon Underwood's sombre features, "No, Blackwell, as usual you did precisely the right thing. Charlotte and I both needed to see each other and finish the thing properly. Loose ends have a habit of tripping one up!"

Blackwell smiled with relief, "You have a succinct way of putting things, Underwood! Now you can put this incident, and others, behind you, and pick up the threads of your life!"

Mr. Underwood smiled rather humourlessly, "Strangely enough, despite everything, I think I can! Thank you for your hospitality, Blackwell, and your counsel, but I think I am ready to go home now."

"Pleasure has been entirely mine, my dear fellow. There is a stage leaving tomorrow, and I took the liberty of booking your seat for you! Your mother has been appraised of your imminent arrival, and your brother Gil has been granted a short holiday, leaving Bracken Tor in Mr. Pollock's very capable hands!"

"Are you ever wrong about anything, Blackwell?" Mr. Blackwell grinned, "Not often, Underwood. Not often!"

***

A summer spent at his childhood home did much to repair Mr. Underwood's battered reserves of strength. He began to write a very erudite, and extremely boring, book. He walked for miles with his mother and Miss Chapell, who had very quickly been convinced that she was not suited to a life of servitude as a governess, and persuaded to stay on as Mrs. Underwood's paid companion. Verity knew this was a kindly civility, and that Mrs. Underwood had managed for years alone, but she could not help but grant herself these last few, precious months in Mr. Underwood's company. She knew that when he went back to

211

Cambridge, it would be for good, and that she would never see him again. When that happened she would decide whether to accept Gil's offer of marriage, or to find other employment.

Gil returned to Bracken Tor, but only briefly, to fill the breach until the Bishop could arrange a new Parish for him. He was fortunate that he did not have long to wait, for his relationship with Edwin Wynter was uncomfortable to say the least, and Harry, though quite happy as a farmer, still blamed him bitterly for the reverse in his fortunes, and the death of the father whom he, at least, had always held in the greatest affection—until the last bitter meeting when his rejection had shocked and wounded the boy.

With the first fall of leaves, the early morning chill, the remnants of mist which lingered until mid-morning in the hollows, Mr. Underwood knew that the time had come to make his decision. Cambridge beckoned strongly, and he found he had missed his room, dark-panelled and musty, that he had even missed his boys—but only a little. He looked forward to a winter closeted within the thick stone walls which shut out the fiercest winds and held the world at bay.

Mrs. Underwood, upon being told that he intended to leave home, sent for Miss Chapell. She wasted no time upon pointless pleasantries, but came straight to the point. "He is going back to Cambridge, Verity. What are you going to do about it?"

Verity was shocked and showed it, "What can I do? It is not my business. I cannot intervene!"

"But you must! We both know that if he goes back to Cambridge now he might just as well enter a monastery!"

"Mrs. Underwood . . ." Began Verity in protest, but the older woman brushed aside her interruption with a wave of her hand. "Verity, I want grandchildren! If I don't take a hand now, I might never have them!

Verity blushed at such forthright expressiveness, "Well, Gil has proposed marriage to me." She admitted shyly.

"But you are in love with Underwood! Now, do not misunderstand me, I adore both my sons, and Chuffy is not one whit better than Gil, in fact, in many ways, he's much more of a worry to me, but on this occasion Gil must shift for himself! At least he is out and about in the world, and there is always the slim chance that he might meet a girl—but how is Underwood to fall in love if he never sees a woman from one year's end to the next? No, I am quite determined! It would be much better for Chuffy to marry a woman who loves him, rather than one whom he loves, for he has notoriously poor taste and always chooses the wrong types!"

"But I can't force myself upon him! I can't order him to marry me!" Verity said hotly, feeling that it was most unfair of Mrs. Underwood to show so little concern for her emotions in all the mess. Of course, there was nothing she desired more than to marry Underwood, but why should she settle for being second best to a man who was in love with another? She said as much to Mrs. Underwood, who was at once contrite, "Poor Verity. I did not mean to be so bombastic! It just distresses me so, to see both you and Chuffy throwing away what may be your only chance of happiness! Don't you think I know my son well enough to understand that once married to you, he could not help but fall in love with you? It is only because the idea has not presented itself that he has not done so already! If I recall, it was Charlotte and not he, who initiated their romance! Why should you not do the same?"

Verity had to admit that this was true, but it would take perhaps more courage than she possessed to risk a rebuff from the man she adored! Would it not be better to lose Underwood and retain her dignity? It was something she would have to consider very carefully.

***

By the following Saturday Miss Chapell had made no decision, and when she woke early, stricken with a painfully sore throat, and pounding headache, she was scarcely surprised. Mrs. Underwood was solicitous in the extreme, sending for the doctor and insisting that her companion keep to her bed. The doctor diagnosed a bad cold and suggested Miss Chapell should take the tonic he made himself. A more foul liquid she had never tasted, and it was while she was pulling the ugliest of wry faces that Mr. Underwood entered the room to ask how she did. His laughter alerted his mother to his presence and instead of chiding him for entering a lady's bedroom, she hastily removed herself and the doctor and left the couple alone.

Mr. Underwood, who as inordinately fond of comfits as he was of snuff, just happened to have some in his pocket and he offered Miss Chapell one to take away the nasty taste in her mouth. She took one gratefully, then bade him draw up a chair and sit with her for a few minutes.

She waited for him to do so before speaking again.

"I have been wanting to talk to you, Mr. Underwood." She said hesitantly, her voice made gruff and throaty by her affliction. He smiled, and helped himself to a comfit, "What about?"

"I should like your advice."

He gave a self-depreciatory laugh, "I'm hardly the person to offer advice, Verity, but ask away! I shall do my utmost to assist you."

213

She gazed thoughtfully at his profile—for his attention seemed to centre upon the hands which lay in his lap and not upon her—before continuing, "Your brother arrives next week to perform the wedding service for your mother and General Milner, and that means I shall no longer be needed as a companion."

"I'm sure my mother is in no hurry to send you away, my dear, she has grown very fond of you."

"I know that, but I shall have to go sooner or later."

"You need not fear that we shall be unhelpful. On the contrary, I am sure my mother will do her best to find you employment and provide you with a sparkling reference!"

"Mrs. Underwood has always been so kind, I shall miss her very much."

He looked at her and she was surprised to see concern for her in his eyes, "You know, Verity, you would do well not to allow yourself to grow so attached to your charges, or it will always be painful for you to change employment."

She smiled gently, "When my heart prompts, I wish I could but ignore it, Mr. Underwood."

"You worry me, my dear. I fear you are too vulnerable to be let loose in the world alone."

"Perhaps I should accept Gilbert's offer then!" She said swiftly, irritated that he should think her weak.

Suddenly he was all attention, "Gilbert has offered for you?" He asked sharply.

"Yes."

He recovered his equanimity very quickly, but not before Verity saw that the news had taken him unawares, "Congratulations, Miss Chapell, you have succeeded where many another woman has failed! I have never known my brother offer marriage before."

"But should I accept, Mr. Underwood? Am I the sort of woman who would make a good vicar's wife?"

"Good God! Why do you ask me? Do you love Gil? I suppose that is all that matters!"

"I am fond of him." She admitted carefully, "But I own I feel more towards him as I should feel to a brother, had I ever possessed one."

Was it her imagination, or did this seem to relieve his mind of some faint worry?

"Does Gil know how you feel?"

"Oh yes."

"Then if he does not mind, I see no reason why you should be troubled."

"And you would not object if I married him?"

He did not answer this question, but he looked into her eyes. Verity felt her resolve begin to crumble and it took every ounce of determination she possessed to stop herself confessing the whole to him. He looked as though he despised her dispassionate appraisal of the situation. "Is marriage truly what you want, Miss Chapell?"

She swallowed deeply before nodded briefly her assent, "Then it would be better if you married me. I would not have Gil marry a woman who did not value him as she should." With that he rose and went away leaving Verity feeling shamed and trying hard to hold back her tears.

***

Gilbert was delighted to be told that he had two weddings at which he must officiate. He found a moment alone with Verity to congratulate her upon her betrothal, but was puzzled to find her quite distraught.

"What ails you, Verity. I should have thought you would be delighted to have at last attained your heart's desire!"

Verity was mortified to have to admit the truth, "Oh Gil, he is only marrying me to save you from my evil machinations!"

"What!"

She explained the whole and to her utter misery he laughed long and hearty, "Good God, Verity! What on earth possessed you!"

"I thought I might make him jealous." She said, with a melancholy little sniff. He hugged her briefly, "Believe me, my dear, you have done so, with great success! My brother is suffering the greatest torments—and I intend that he shall suffer a little more, before I put him out of his misery!"

He sought out his brother and when he found him, he castigated him with as much fervour as he could arouse.

"Chuffy, you are a brute!"

Mr. Underwood was very much on his dignity and glanced superciliously at his brother before responding. "I trust you have some reason for that extremely undignified outburst, Gilbert!"

"I certainly have! Not only have you stolen the finest woman that ever breathed from me, but you have had the audacity to inform her that you have only done so for my own good!"

Mr. Underwood was at once contrite, his expression betrayed how appalled he was to think he had taken the woman he loved away from his brother, "Good God! Gil, I had no idea you felt so strongly for her!"

"I most certainly do!"

"Then why the devil has she agreed to marry me? Heaven only knows that I should never have come between you had I known how you felt—can you ever forgive me? . . . you showed not the slightest partiality . . ."

"For God's sake, Chuffy, be quiet! Are you completely blind? Verity is in love with you! I only offered her marriage because I thought you were intent upon the folly of marrying the Wynter chit! I am no more fond of Verity than I would be of a sister, but that does not stop me from seeing what you obviously do not! That she is the perfect wife for you!"

Mr. Underwood seemed a little stunned, "That is what Verity said about you—that she loved you like a brother!"

"Very fortunate—since that is precisely what I shall be tomorrow! Now I suggest you go to her and beg pardon for your boorish behaviour. In twenty-four hours she is prepared to give up her freedom, indeed her entire life, to you. Don't you think she deserves to know that she is not giving it up in vain?"

Underwood could not help but agree with this sage advice. He went to find his betrothed.

The apprehensive look in her eyes gave him cause to feel ashamed of his behaviour towards her. It hurt him to think she should be even slightly afraid of him.

"Verity." He said softly. She smiled in return, "Hello. Your hair is all awry, what have you been doing?" He did not tell her that he had disordered it by running his fingers through it, in his agitation at wondering what he could say to her to atone for his unkindness. He lifted a self-conscious hand and attempted to flatten it, very unsuccessfully. She laughed and held out her hand to him, "Come here, I have a comb, let me do it." He obediently sat on the footstool at her feet and allowed her to run the comb through his blond locks.

"My dear, I want to say how sorry I am . . ."

"Hush! It doesn't matter. I know you were going to tell kind-hearted lies, to pretend that you feel for me, when I know you do not, but please don't. I would rather our marriage was based on truth and honesty than on silly, romantic platitudes. I know when I marry you tomorrow, I shall be second best, but I shall do my utmost to be a good wife to you . . ."

He turned swiftly, anger blazing in his eyes, "Second best! Verity, don't ever again let me hear you use those words in reference to yourself! There is no woman in the world who means as much to me as you do in this moment! I shall be proud to make you my wife tomorrow. The past is gone. We shall not ever refer to it again, except to say that I have been privileged to be loved by three very fine women, and even more privileged to marry the finest of them all."

There were tears in her eyes as she leaned forward to kiss him. "Cadmus, I can't tell you how happy you have made me."

"I trust I shall be allowed to make you much happier, my dear."

About the Author

Suzanne Sullivan was born the youngest of ten children, in Manchester, but has lived all her life in the old cotton-producing town of Stockport, except for two years spent in Australia. She presently lives with her second husband and three children in a charming converted mill cottage at the base of the Pennines. She was educated at an all-girl Convent High School in Stockport and made her first attempt at writing a novel whilst still in school. Apart from writing, she enjoys reading, tapestry, furniture restoration, listening to all kinds of music, but particularly British and Irish traditional folk music, and spending time with her husband and children.